Rising to Eminence

Rising to Eminence

The Incredible Adventures
of Jeffrey Shenero, Scientist

by
Mark R. Sneller

Published by Fresh Air Press

Visit Mark's website at
markrsneller.com

This edition was prepared for publication by
Ghost River Images
5350 East Fourth Street
Tucson, Arizona 85711
www.ghostriverimages.com

Cruise ship cover image from
Wikimedia Commons by permission
from Moonik

ISBN 978-1-7368917-4-2

Library of Congress Control Number: 2022906628

Printed in the United States of America
April, 2022

Other books Mark R. Sneller:

A Breath of Fresh Air

Greener Cleaner Indoor Air

Greener Cleaner Indoor Air – 2nd Edition

Toxic Exposure

Dying to Read

The Mars Virus Trilogy

> *The Mars Virus*

> *The City Beneath the Earth*

> *Treasures*

Strange Adventures

Author's Note:

The adventures of Jeffrey Shenero are continued on the heels of his other life experiences described by this author in the novels *Toxic Exposure* and *Dying to Read* and in several short stories found in *Strange Adventures*.

Elements of the adventures described herein involve the structure, operation, and dismantling of a cruise ship, with which the author finds fascination and is anxious to share this fascination with the readers. The hierarchy of officers, staff, and crew aboard these vessels is complex. The author has taken the liberty of simplifying this hierarchy in order to make the story more readable without too many chain-of-command issues complicating the presentation. Other embellishments have also been made to create the narrative.

The author's previous home in India can testify to accuracies on that account.

Within this story, a number of references are made to Jeffrey Shenero uncovering the plot of terrorists bent on destroying the country with the use of fungal toxins used in cosmetics and by other means. The interested reader is invited to read that episode in its entirety in the novel *Dying to Read*.

Chapter 1

CHOLERA

ONE

After their ninety-year occupation of India, the British left behind several important contributions: a system of government, the English language, a postal service, and the railroad which had been completely converted to diesel and electric powered. Although virtually all of the 28 states had their own language with its own script, English was commonly spoken among the middle and upper classes, and commonly taught in schools. In fact, students spent a significant amount of time, not only learning English, but also the language of their state and the adjoining state(s), as well as Hindi, in many cases. This limited the time spent on other subjects, yet the country managed to turn out a high percentage of intellectuals and top-level scientists.

In the heat of a summer's day, Jeff Shenero landed at Indira Gandhi International Airport in Delhi, India. The sights, sounds, smells, and smog of the capital city never ceased to saturate his senses. These were the scents of unfettered life. Red double-decker diesel-powered buses towered over sweaty rickshaw peddlers and pedestrians, as scooters wove through crowded intersections that had no signal lights. Civilization at its most raw form made one question the devil-may-care approach to life versus the values of higher civilization, bringing one's life into perspective. The concentration of over a billion people in a land mass only 40% that of the continental United States computed to five times the population density of the U.S.

Jeff had been intended to visit his former graduate student, Richard Smith, who now taught full-time and did research at the University of New Delhi. Rick lived in a three bedroom home in an upscale portion of the city with neighbors from many international communities. He and his wife enjoyed a maid, cook, car, and driver, along with full medical care and good neighbors from a surprising number of nations. Not a bad life at all, for those willing to take the leap, Jeff thought. He had contemplated doing so himself on many occasions. He tried to call Richard to let him know he would be in town, only to find out he had taken his family to Bangkok for two weeks.

This time Jeff was on the trail of a cholera outbreak in a fishing village on the east coast of the country, half-way between Kolkota (formerly Calcutta) to the north, and Chennai (formerly Madras) to the south. If Jeff wanted to track the disease as a profession, he could have spent a lifetime doing so, as many had done and still do, from Haiti, to Africa, to Europe, to Southeast Asia. The occasional pinpoint flare-up of the scourge in this isolated portion of the world caught his attention and pulled him like a magnet to find out why it hadn't spread. The communicable disease was caused by an intestinal bacterium associated with drinking contaminated water or eating contaminated food. It led to severe diarrhea and terrible dehydration, followed by death and was generally associated with poverty and/or catastrophic events. But why such a small scope to the problem, when typically, hundreds to thousands could be affected during a single outbreak?

Although Jeff enjoyed fame as a renowned mold expert, his first love was microbiology. From the earliest years in high school, he had been fascinated by the field of epidemiology. He had always heard that the black plague was transmitted by the rat flea and scores of books had been written on the subject, tracing the disease from its earliest beginnings and its spread via sailing vessels. That is, until a recent discovery debunked that history of transmission when the human body louse the size of a sesame seed, was implicated as the causative agent for the plague. It feeds on blood. It was and is prevalent in areas where depraved conditions prevail. People back in 14th Century didn't bathe that often, which provided a perfect environment for hair and body lice to become prolific.

Now he was on the trail of a mysterious cholera outbreak, a disease that also had a worldwide reputation as a killer.

The trip to Delhi had not been an easy one. Instead of the 24 hour travel time, this time it took Jeff much longer. The trip went smoothly from Oklahoma City to New York and then to London. When the next flight to Athens touched down in the early morning, the pilot informed the passengers that a cabby strike was in progress, but buses would take the passengers to their respective hotels. So far so good.

Jeff toured Athens and absorbed the rich history of Greece, taking a tour bus and enjoying the rich history of the country that played such a critical role in the development of intellect and civilization. Finally, Jeff asked the location of the bus station two hours prior to boarding. The clerk said he was new, but he thought it might be located down the street. Jeff went to the old building that housed but a single man who sat at a dirty desk. After an hour Jeff became anxious and asked the man if the bus was going to come. "No English," the man said, but nodded upward, apparently understanding the words bus and airport. Jeff waited another 20 minutes. Desperate, the asked again. The man nodded again. At last another employee entered the building. Jeff explained to the second man that he wanted to get a bus to the airport, to which the reply was, "This is the old bus station. The new one is about a kilometer from here. Oh, in Greece and in Turkey, an upward motion of the head means no."

Jeff returned to his hotel and rescheduled his flight for the next morning. He was not unaccustomed to delays and minor mishaps during his worldly excursions. In fact, misadventures occurred with such frequency that if something didn't go wrong, he'd wonder what went wrong.

After two days of rest in Delhi and anxious to get on with his quest, Jeff caught another flight southward to the Hyderabad airport in the southern Indian state of Andhra Pradesh. The progressive westernized city offered temptations for those who had limited cash, yet could live lavishly with the exchange rate of 20:1 rupees per dollar, while enjoying all the amenities Richard Smith and family had in Delhi.

Upon arrival at the Hyderabad airport, Jeff inquired as to the location of the train station. He needed to get to the relatively small seaport city of Visakhapatnam, or Visak. From there he could take a bus to the fishing village associated in some manner with the outbreak, at least, according to the World Health Organization.

An employee told him, "Just over there," pointing. Jeff should have remembered the old admonition: When in India, if you want directions to someplace, you ask three people. When two agree, you take the odd man out. Instead, he took one man's word and began walking "just over there." As an add on, the airport employee announced, "Oh, sir, in case you haven't heard, the railroad workers across the country are going on strike and the last train out will be leaving shortly."

First a cab strike in Athens, now a nationwide railroad workers' strike. No worries, Jeff considered, shrugging off the news. Comes with the territory. He thought, *How complicated can it be to get to a train station?*

Jeff had traveled the Indian trains before, from First Class Reserved to Third Class Unreserved. He was fully aware that Indian time was different than everybody else's time, but punctual habits are hard to break and he needed to hurry. He would have preferred to fly to Visak, but reportedly, a torrential monsoon rain had temporarily closed the airport, which meant he could pay a fortune to take a taxi, versus a very inexpensive train, which would get him there about the same time.

He pulled out his collapsible sun hat and, preparing for the worst, began a fast walk. An electronic sign flashed outside a clothing store:

Temperature: 102 degrees Fahrenheit
Humidity, 90 percent.

Thirty minutes later, rolling a single suitcase behind him and carrying a full backpack, sweat dripping, clothing soaking from the inside out, Jeff checked his watch while dodging emaciated cattle, cars, buses, wandering dogs, bullock carts, scooters, countless people, and rickshaw drivers.

A piece had broken off one the wheels on the roll-along and it clunked several times a second. It had been constructed to roll smoothly over the flooring in airport terminals, not tortured while traversing concrete, asphalt, gravel and rocks.

Another time, he might lean back in a chair and people-watch. At the moment, seeing no end to his efforts, he flagged down a rickshaw-walla peddling his bike and finally reached the station, with five minutes to spare, only to find the train packed with humans, hanging onto the railing outside the car doors. Untold numbers rode on top of the cars, willing to brave the miles to be traveled. How many times had he seen pictures of this on television only to find himself a part of it?

Jeff had read that the Indian rail system covered some 72,000 miles with over 7200 stops. Thankfully, coal burning engines had been upgraded to diesel and electric locomotives that now dominated the rail system. He'd ridden the old coal burners in years past and didn't enjoy having to wipe coal dust from his clothing or his face.

Looking at the poor souls desperate to reach their destination, he couldn't imagine subjecting himself to such torture, yet here were men who, from all appearances, were accustomed to such travel. The temperature would reach well over 100 degrees and with the train traveling at freeway speeds in this humidity, a wind-heat index could approach 130 degrees or above, yet here they were. Looking at them, he couldn't help appreciating what he had, and yet, he could also appreciate how to live with much less than what he had. Unfortunately, his life calling had taken a different direction.

Jeff walked the length of the concourse dodging people, with the train to his right, looking for a place to get on. Finding none he felt as though he were a meaningless dust mote among a million others wondering if he would end up on top of the train with the others. He thought, *If you want to experience life, then do it, right? Good luck finding a spot.*

At last, he found a nondescript uniformed conductor standing on the platform outside one of the cars. Upon entry to the car, the man asked him for a ticket, which Jeff had neglected to purchase in his haste. With sweat dripping from every pore, his shirt and underwear soaked, he considered walking back to the station to buy the ticket, but he had no choice. He couldn't take a chance with departure time nearing. He didn't want to argue with the man about whether those on top of the train had a ticket. He had to go with the flow. He handed the conductor a ten dollar bill. The man took the money and remained in place, smiling, until Jeff handed him another ten and still another. The conductor smiled politely, then aggressively pushed others aside to enable Jeff to enter with his suitcase in his one hand and the bulky pack on his back. Both served as weapons to push others out of the way to permit his entry.

The train stayed in place for six hours. When it did begin to move, the ten-hour ride afterward became a nightmare, with only a single bathroom per car. Occasional braless women dressed in cheap washed-out saris would shove through the packed mass of sweating and overheated humanity while smoking a fat stubby cigar. No shiny silken gold-and-silver-brocade saris here.

Upon reaching the door to the bath, the women would take the cigar from their mouth, reverse it, enter the closeted space, and, after coming out, would reposition the cigar with the lit end outward again. Jeff later learned that the people who did this had the highest rate of oral cancer in the world. No surprise there.

Jeff had experience enough to carry a stash of water and nutritional food with him on such occasions. He had also learned, the hard way, to keep his credit cards and IDs in his left front pocket and his cash and cell phone in his right front pocket to eliminate the possibility of a rising entrepreneur razor-cutting his back pocket to extract the wallet of a Westerner. He also learned to use a wide, comfortable, elastic bandage to connect his right wrist to his suitcase. On this lengthy journey, he brought his backpack to his chest to protect its contents. He considered himself to be a weapon, if it became necessary for self-defense purposes.

Over the hours, the train made a number of stops. When it did pull into a station, passengers on the top of the train, and within it, found a way to readjust or depart. On one such occasion, Jeff worked his way into a newly vacated seat, his suitcase jamming the area between his seat and the one in front of him and his backpack clutched to his front. Around his neck, he wore a man-purse in which he carried his passport, secondary IDs, chargers, and a loaded electronic book. He'd never touch one at home, but on the road it served as a wonderful tool for limitless games and books to read, access to Google's data base of the world's knowledge and weighed only ounces. The best part: One never ran out of books to read and knowledge to explore.

At one stop, he chanced to look out the window to see a thermometer reading 104 degrees. His sports watch read 1:27 am.

Over time, the journey brought Jeff to Visak in the middle of another exceedingly hot and humid day. Hiring a taxi to take him to his hotel, Jeff showered, changed clothes, ate a good dinner, drank a quart of beer-the smallest quantity available-got totally shit-faced, and watched a soap opera on TV. Beyond tired, he had no difficulty sleeping in the bed housed beneath mosquito netting with a noisy fan overhead.

In the morning, his several days of travel from home neared its end, with only a short bus ride left to the village. Jeff looked out the window of his fourth floor suite, newly rebuilt after a devastating hurricane had struck the port city only a few years before.

Out of a little over two million people, many thousands lost their lives.

Finally winding down, feeling relaxed, and finding that the hotel lacked a gym, Jeff worked in a full-hour of calisthenics in his room, dressed, ate a light breakfast of eggs, whole wheat toast and guava juice. Escaping the confines of the hotel, he took a short time to explore the various stores, having no idea where he would stay in the village of his destination. His online research had borne no fruit. He thought he might take a bus to the village to make initial inquiries about the disease and return to the hotel the same day. Depending on what he found out, he could go from there.

The hotel was situated in the middle of a long

thoroughfare. Along both sides of the wide dirt boulevard, Jeff passed fruit and vegetable stores. He passed cigarette stands selling single cigarettes for those in immediate need. He passed clothing and hardware stores, most with awnings to keep out heat and rain. In some strange regard, Jeff felt totally comfortable in these surroundings. Call it eugenics, call it racial memory, call it what it you will, Jeff felt at home, yet always wary in any new environment.

Within several minutes, he found a small book store not much larger than a bedroom with the heavily bearded proprietor seated and reading at a small front desk. The man stood at Jeff's entrance. "Welcome, my name is Raj Singh, you can call me Raj. Please let me know if I can help you with anything," offered the turbaned Sikh in perfectly accented British English. Immediately, Jeff thought the man's family probably originated in the northern state of Punjab, a state that bragged noteworthy politicians, businessmen and fighters. Now the man operated a small book store. India was indeed a land of curiosities.

TWO

Jeff turned to the man at the entry and replied, "Yes, thank you, I'm sure I will. My name is Jeff."

"Ah, an American. Please look around and ask if you have any questions," said Raj, obviously astute as to the nuances between the languages.

Not surprised at Raj's response, Jeff stood for a moment looking at three walls of mostly hard-cover books. Enveloped by a cloak of knowledge, he became immediately attracted to a massive tome of some 1200 pages on the oceans of the world, pictures included, located on a shelf labeled Earth Sciences. Pulling out the book, he found the pages extremely thin, almost like onion skin, but extremely well printed with readable font. He walked it over to Raj to ask him about the printing. He had never seen anything like it before.

"Yes, a large number of our books are all copied and reprinted in China and sold to us for pennies on the dollar. The price is $12.50 for you instead of $150 you would pay for it in the States."

Surprised at the answer, Jeff returned the book to the shelf and browsed through the philosophy section, keeping a wary eye on the time. He did not travel all this way to browse in bookstores. Randomly scanning the books he found himself dumbfounded reading titles of such outliers as *The Neurophysiological Basis of Mind* by Eccles, *The Philosophy of Time*, *The Physics of Throwing a Baseball*, and Huxley's *Brave New World*.

He picked up another titled *Pictorial Guide to the Seashells of Southern India* by Grace Chatfield, impressed by the detailed descriptions and the colored photographs. Turning to the Microbiology section, he saw his own book *Medical Aspects of the Fungi,* by Jeffrey Shenero, PhD. In a strange way, he felt honored that the Chinese would chose to steal his copyrighted book. He decided to purchase it for the rupee equivalent of an even $14.75 when his students paid many times that amount.

Totally delighted with his finds, he placed his purchases in his virtually empty backpack and returned to browse the shelves. To him, there was absolutely nothing better than finding an unexplored bookstore in an out of the way place. Say what you will, the feeling lasted a whole longer than did sex. When in these situations, Jeff felt himself to be inside of a warm and protective cocoon.

A short while later, another man with a British accent walked into the store. He heard Raj say that an American was in the store. Dressed in summer white and wearing a broad- brimmed sun hat, the man greeted Jeff, "Hallo, chap, my name is Henry James. You are the American?"

Jeff turned to see the inquisitor in his sixties, clean cut, three inches shorter than himself with a slight paunch, gray beard, jovial eyes and honest smile.

"No, not that Henry James," admitted the Brit, before Jeff could respond, pointing to one of books from the 19th Century author.

Jeff found the man to be compelling, open,

and obviously willing to chat. The men engaged in small talk for some time, feeling out one another, when the Brit announced, "Say, old boy, are you ready for lunch. I'm feeling like Chinese food at the wharf."

Accustomed to receiving direct approaches in foreign countries when compared with an avoidance of strangers in his country, Jeff wondered if Henry was all he seemed with his offer of lunch, or whether the man was a simple con artist who preyed on foreigners. Jeff checked his watch, then glanced at the man, wondering. Henry stood placid, same cheerful countenance, waiting patiently.

"Going someplace?" Henry asked.

Jeff shrugged it off. "At some point I need to get to Bhiminipatnam."

Not expecting any response, Henry brought Jeff out of his thoughts. "Bimli? Why, I live there," declared the Englishman, jovially. Jeff half-expected a slap on the back. "I'll drive you there after lunch, if you like. My treat."

Now a free ride to the village. He supposed another day wouldn't matter. Jeff made the decision to go all in and accepted Henry's invitation for lunch. "That sounds like an offer I can't refuse," he contributed. "Lead the way."

"Splendid," Henry replied.

About to leave the store's open front, Raj looked up from his book and said, "Henry; and Jeff, is it? Why don't you both come to my house this evening and have dinner with us, if you're up to another visit, Henry."

Henry looked at Jeff, who appeared confused for a moment, and nodded. He got it. Nothing complicated. It was called basic human hospitality.

Henry saw the acceptance in Jeff's eyes and told Raj, "Absolutely, we'll see you at 9:00."

In an instant, Raj said to Jeff, "Say, you look familiar. Have we met before?"

Jeff's mind had stabilized after the onslaught of unfolding events and replied, simply, "Not unless you go to Norman, Oklahoma."

Raj cocked his head slightly, apparently processing information. Watching the two men walk away, he saw them wave down a couple of rickshaw drivers in a sea of traffic. Pulling out his cell, he made a call.

At Henry's direction, the rickshaw drivers pedaled the men to the restaurant designated by Henry. It stood on the wharf overlooking the Bay of Bengal where numerous ships lay at anchor. Seagulls floated, or landed on posts, while cormorants dive-bombed for fish. The air was breezeless, heavy with moisture, the sky ominously dark gray overhead and black on the horizon. The pair found a table for two with merchant seamen occupying the larger tables, some speaking Japanese, others Greek, and others Italian. Plates and bowls of Chinese foods of every ilk were passed around.

Henry ordered beer and food for them both and explained, "I've known Raj for a number of years. He's one of six sons. His father is a federal judge. One brother is a scientist, another a lawyer, another a doctor, another an inventor, another a pilot, and Raj doubles as district supervisor. Twice a month he and his driver take the 4-wheel-drive Jeep Cherokee into the jungle to visit the different tribes to see if they need anything. He'll have the vehicle loaded with goodies, mostly foodstuffs and medical supplies. I've gone with him. You should too. It's quite an interesting ride. He told me to always be prepared for the unexpected out there."

A surge of excitement swept through Jeff. There it was, without him having to search around for a way to get into the jungles, the second reason for his coming to India—to explore the unexplored.

In the distance, reverberations sounded like a drum roll. Both men looked off to the southeast where lighting flashed to announce the storm cell moving toward them. The wind increased.

Returning to his conversation, Jeff felt comfortable enough with Henry to ask, "I'm curious about you. I mean, why do you live in a fishing village? What are you doing here?" He waved his hand around.

Henry laughed, pulled out a handkerchief from somewhere and took off his hat to wipe his forehead and temples beneath a mop of gray hair. "Me? I made my money by buying a single motel and developing a nationwide chain both in the States and in Britain. A number of years ago, a good friend of mine named Chatfield came to know Raj's father, the judge, on a business trip here and said he was looking for place off the beaten path to retire. The judge introduced Chatfield to Raj, who found him a decent house in Bimli, so he recommended it to me and my wife. She passed a few years ago.

"Bye the bye, if you've heard of Chatfield pharmaceuticals, well, that's him. As for me, when at home, I play tennis and cards with retired businessmen, mostly Indians, and occasionally fish. Every two or three weeks I come here into the big city to eat well and go to the theater. Are you looking to retire here, as well?"

The moment of truth. "Not at all, I'm going there to follow the cholera crisis," Jeff announced.

Henry narrowed his eyes and looked at Jeff somewhat askance, placing his hand on his head to keep his hat from flying off in a sudden gust of wind. Thunder rumbled in the distance. "What crisis?"

Jeff examined Henry's face for a hint of a jest behind the statement. He could be telling the truth, or perhaps he had run to Visak to escape a terrible scourge in his home village. The ultimate conspiracy theorist, Jeff believed that the latter must be it. Henry masked his concerns well.

Jeff played it straight up. "The WHO reported it. I'm a scientist and an investigator of sorts. How can you not know about an epidemic in your own village, or maybe one close to yours? WHO didn't exactly specify, only that it may have stemmed from the Bimli area."

The food and beer arrived, along with two glasses of water.

Henry advised, "Don't drink the water."

Using chopsticks, the men ate in silence for some time, until Henry said, "Look, old boy, tell me where you're staying and I'll pick you up around 8:30 this evening. After Raj's party, I'll bring you back and I'll go to my own hotel. In the morning I'll drive you to my little village and you can see for yourself that all is well. In fact, I'll introduce you to some friends and to the local chieftain. No doubt, he'll welcome you as an honored guest and use your visit as an excuse to have a party, drinks included. Rumor has it a new shipment of Johnny Walker came in."

Jeff looked out at the boiling water of the sea. A hard gust of hot wind had sprung up, blowing away the paper napkins on the table as though it had a mind of its own with malice aforethought. Heavy drops of rain began to smack onto the table while the smaller boats in the harbor bobbed. Henry called over the waiter, paid him and stood to leave.

Henry suggested, "Look chap, the big weather will be in shortly. This one should be a short blow. Tell you what, I'll treat you to the seaman's club only a kilometer away from here. We can relax there for a drink and a chat, then I'll get you back to your hotel.

THREE

The storm cell had passed when Henry pickup up Jeff, who awaited his arrival beneath the portico of the hotel. Henry drove his black Tata Motor's sedan through an industrial portion of the city area into a residential area with large expensive homes set far apart separated by a score of tree species. Shortly, Henry entered a lengthy gravel driveway flanked on either side by two huge Banyan trees with their expensive aboveground root system and seconds later arrived at the home.

At first glance, Raj's colorless two-story appeared to be built of concrete and stucco. A number of other similar cars were parked in front, along with a two convertibles and a Cadillac Escalade. Henry found a place to pull in between two BMWs and the men walked over gravel to reach a lighted portico. A bench stood against a wall along with numerous pairs of shoes and sandals lining the wall. Following Henry's lead, Jeff sat on the bench, removed his shoes, and replaced them with booties conveniently provided in a box next to the bench.

"Looks like we lucked out, Henry. We got invited to a big party. No cheap dates here," Jeff said. He hadn't yet recovered from the drinks he'd had at the seaman's club, despite the nap he'd taken afterward in his room. Not normally a hard-liquor drinker he had worked on beer only, still drinking more than his usual amount. Henry seemed content with several rum and Cokes, yet still seemed to function perfectly.

Henry smiled. Jeff didn't get the point of the party. "Yes, Raj does know a lot of people. Don't worry, old chap, I'm certain you'll be another face in the wilderness."

After Henry's knock, a servant met the pair at the door and led them into a sitting room where a good dozen men awaited their arrival, including Raj and his father, a tall handsome man. He was also bearded and turbaned, which gave him even greater height.

The women remained in the kitchen and dining area, completing preparations for the feast and setting the large dinner table. They would eat later. A large jar of mentholated cream stood on a small table beneath a mirror outside the door. Henry stopped at the jar, unscrewed the cap, took a sniff and passed it to Jeff. "Clears the sinuses," he said, in answer to Jeff's unasked question.

Jeff felt emotional warmth within the home well decorated with expensive furnishings and paintings, similar to homes of the wealthy around the globe, a complete turnaround from the sterile appearing exterior. The colorful and exacting art consisted of paintings and hand-woven wall hangings that depicted religious motifs and mythological animals.

The seated men all wore either dress slacks or designer jeans along with a variety of shirts, either of plain tan or white with few multi-color. Apparently, the women wore the color with their infinitely varied saris, a literal world of difference between in the sexes here. Raj introduced the pair, although Henry was already known to several. Raj mentioned simply that Jeff was a visiting American. Then he gave the names of the guests and their line of work.

During the ensuing discussions, one of the men innocently asked Jeff what he did for a living. Before Jeff could answer, one of the brothers—the scientist—announced, "Yes, you're the one who stopped the terrorist threat in the States not long ago. You even received The Presidential Medal of Freedom award for it."

The other guests, already advised by Raj as to Jeff's identity, began to recall what they had heard, some of it exaggerated and not all of it true. Embarrassed, Jeff soon found himself fawned over, forced to tell the story in some detail. In his naiveté, Jeff finally realized the truth. Raj had set up the party for him.

Saved at last, a senior staff woman announced to Raj's father that dinner was served.

Half of those at the table ate the various dishes with their right hand only, others used utensils. Jeff sat at the proffered seat to the right of the judge at a large oval table, with Raj to the judge's left. Before Jeff stood dishes of beef and vegetable curries with lentils, rice, tandoori chicken, lamb, and Nan. He soon found that several of the dishes were hot enough to equal the spiciest on the planet, if not to take top honors. Within minutes, Jeff's head and armpits began to sweat freely.

Little conversation occurred during the meal, each person devoted to his own palate. When a guest inquired as to Jeff's present profession, he also politely asked about the deep scar above his left eyebrow, beneath his bald pate. Jeff explained that he had been mushroom hunting in an underground tunnel system in one of the islands belonging to the Palau archipelago, got trapped, and had been cut by a stalactite while trying to escape. His reputation among the guests increased. They had a true adventurer in their midst—an adventurer who wanted to take the opportunity to inquire about his mission to the country, especially with all the knowledgeable minds in the room, but was compelled to follow protocol.

Once the judge had ensured that Jeff had consumed enough refills to prevent starvation, he requested deserts to be served. These consisted of gulab jamun, along with a variety of sweet cakes. At last the judge leaned over to Jeff, who suffered from a severe case of bloating and overeating, saying, quietly, "They're waiting for you to burp."

"Thank you," Jeff whispered in return, letting go over an hour's worth of pent up energy, at which time everyone sighed in relief knowing their guest had enjoyed the meal. Jeff looked over at Henry, leaning back in his chair with his hands over his stomach.

"Shall we adjourn?" the judge declared, making a move to stand. Jeff noted with some interest that half the buttons on the man's shirt were broken, a sure indication someone laundered his clothing by rubbing it with bar soap and beating it against rocks or a concrete basin to loosen the dirt, the standard cleaning practice.

Everyone arose at once and moved to the smoking room where a few drinks were poured and smokers lit up either cigars or cigarettes.

After only short minutes, Henry announced "Jeff came here from America because he heard there is a cholera outbreak in Bimli. Isn't that right, Jeff?"

At last. "Correct," Jeff admitted. "I try to track these things and sometimes they're linked to odd events, such as volcanic explosions and odd weather patterns. It is also well known to be associated with algal and phytoplankton bloom here and in South America. What can anyone tell me about this outbreak? Henry claims ignorance of the problem."

The large group of men looked at one another, a clear sign no one had knowledge of the issue. The doctor said, "I do see occasional incidences of cholera associated with hurricanes, even as recently as four years ago when we were devastated. Sanitation became poor—well, poorer than it is now—but none have occurred in the local region to match what you describe."

Raj felt almost like a personal attack had been made against him when he said, "Jeff, that's the district I supervise. I certainly would have heard about a cholera outbreak. We don't ignore something like that."

Jeff looked around the room. All eyes were on him. He was confused. Had he traveled half way around the world on a wild goose chase? Was it all for nothing? But the WHO reported it. No, they did not present any details; only that it had occurred. Willing to accept their word at face value, he felt compelled to pursue the issue further when he got the chance.

"I believe you," he said, ready to let the subject go for the moment thinking he must look the fool in their eyes.

Henry made an effort to save his new friend when he deflected by saying, "Jeff also told me he wanted to explore the jungles while he's here. Isn't that right?"

Jeff picked up the cue and opened a short discussion about exotic life forms having curative effects, a topic most Indians are conversant with.

Despite his nap, Jeff became drowsy and felt a sense of relief when the long get-together ended and Henry drove him back to his hotel.

Unlike the previous evening's sleep when he had passed out from fatigue, this night he slept poorly, suffering from gastric upset combined with a fan hangover. He had defined the latter clinical condition years before during his travels when a fan blew onto his head throughout the night to drive the mosquitoes away, and, exceeding the decibel level of white noise, the screech of its motor kept him awake. After he turned it off and returned to bed, he soon heard mosquitoes cavorting outside the net, some with high pitch whines and some with lower pitched whines, sometimes one immediately following the other, as though racing past the net near his face trying to sneak a peek at their prey before mating.

Following Henry's forecast, the big storm did hit in the early morning and when he drove in to pick up Jeff for the ride to Bimli, he parked beneath the covered roof of the hotel's exterior to prevent Jeff from getting soaked. On the drive to the village, he asked Henry to contact Raj to find out when he planned to make his next trip into the jungle and could Jeff come along. Jeff already had the permits, mini-freeze packs to keep samples cold for 36 hours, a small, but complete, medical kit, and he had researched the vipers, cobras, banded kraits, and poisonous plant species he might encounter.

The 20 miles ride from Visak to Bimli took a good 45 minutes. Although the paved road had a single lane in each direction, Henry had to slow or swerve frequently to avoid bullock carts, oncoming buses, and pedestrians.

The rain had stopped when Henry finally pulled in front of his home overlooking the beach some 100 yards to the east where numerous fishing boats could be seen. Dark-skin natives, four-to-six per boat had been working their nets since sunup.

By late afternoon the boats would bring in a haul of grouper, snapper, tuna, and an occasional smaller shark to be gutted, cleaned, and sold on the market the next day. Bimli's single, but large, ice machine, located in the post office, served to provide enough cubes each day to preserve the catch, with the postal workers getting their fair share of returns in exchange.

To Jeff, the village appeared as it should. Granted several weeks had passed since he had read the report and could make travel arrangements, but it takes a while for a community devastated by a terrible disease to redefine itself. For the first time he began to question himself.

A few crabs had left the sanctity of the sand to find the concrete flooring of the home an interesting surface upon which they might scuttle.

The home had been constructed almost a century earlier by the British and occupied some 3000 square of feet of cement flooring with two great rooms, a small kitchen and dining area, and a single room large enough to sleep ten. The commode and shower were located in a separate building to the north. Showers could be obtained by ladling cold well-water from a large bucket to be poured over one's body, unless one chose to place a heating coil into a bucket of water for a special treat of warm water.

Henry made the requested call and to Jeff's pleasant surprise, Raj said he would be leaving in two mornings for the entire day and part of the evening and he would be honored to have Jeff along for the ride.

"You'll like the people, natives and otherwise. They're quite welcoming," Henry offered.

Jeff nodded, "That's been my experience wherever I travel. It's the nature of people, as long as the government stays out of their lives."

"Here, here," Henry assented. "Are you ready for a little walk down the beach? I want to introduce you to the local chief. He's elderly, but enjoys a good laugh. He doesn't speak English, but I speak Telugu and Hindi. I'll introduce you."

Henry led Jeff down a path past an old 17th Century walled-in Dutch graveyard from the age when the Dutch East India Company had visited the subcontinent in the early 1600s; then to the shoreline itself, less than 100 yards further east. The men turned south to walk perhaps a half-mile where they encountered several loin-clothed natives debarking their small fishing boat, hauling it onto the land with a pile of fish in the boat. One thin young man ten years of age stood atop a huge sea turtle that had crawled onto the sand to lay its eggs.

Henry greeted the men, one of whom asked whether Jeff would trade his camera for the man's loincloth. Jeff politely declined the offer but handed the man a five rupee note for his kind offer, and the westerners walked on for another few minutes until turning abruptly westward into the foliage. Within seconds, they found themselves amidst a number of huts, mostly vacated by men at the moment, who spent their days in their boats.

Huts stood some distance from the water amidst palm trees and local vegetation. Numerous animals walked about at random including pigs, chickens, cattle, goats, water buffaloes, an occasional peacock, as well as domestic animals. Fighting cocks cackled beneath large overturned baskets made of woven palm fronds.

Jeff saw an elderly man on a rocking chair on the packed earth in what appeared to be a broad circle of huts surrounding the one the men headed toward. The tribal chieftain grinned when he saw Henry, who came over to introduce Jeff as his American friend. The chief stood, looked

Jeff over up and down. Touching his skin and bald head, he said something to Henry in Telugu, who laughed.

"He said 'A real American. "Now he's seen it all,'" Henry remarked

Jeff said, "Tell him I'm from Hollywood."

"Are you?"

Jeff replied, "No, I'm from Oklahoma, but we might get some perks, if you tell him a stretch. I did go through there once."

Henry laughed and did as Jeff requested.

Obviously impressed, the chief asked if he had been in any movies, Jeff considered this. Movies were huge in India, a country that probably produced more per year than almost any other country, including the United States and China. Its term for the industry was Bollywood. Because the chieftain hadn't specified the type of movie, Jeff told him he had been in several. He failed to mention they were home videos, of which the man would likely have no knowledge, anyway.

The chief slapped his leg and told Henry, "We will have a celebration tonight. A shipment came in," and pointed to a closely guarded crate next to his chair.

Henry had already heard about it the day before from one of the fishermen, but said nothing to spoil the chief's announcement.

The two men returned to Henry's home, ate a very late lunch of soup and bread at Henry's house and walked the single main street of Bimli to receive greetings from the natives, some of whom wanted to touch the American. Pictures of President John Kennedy adorned the walls of many of the small stores.

Well after dark, they returned to the chief's domain at which time the party began. A bonfire greeted them with men sitting in a circle around it drinking rice beer served by braless women wearing loose saris. The case of liquor remained unopened.

Upon the arrival of the guests of honor, the chief asked everyone to stand and applaud, went to the case, opened it, pulled out a bottle, took a drink, and set it next to his chair to denote that it belonged solely to him. He took another, passed it to Jeff, who took a swallow, and passed it to Henry. Not normally a drinker of hard liquor, Jeff's sense of duty overrode his personal preferences. The chief took out more bottles to make the rounds. Curiously, the men only drank about half of each bottle as the evening wore on, at which point one of them returned it to the case.

A cauldron of hot soup stood over on a fire pit. Women ladled out the thick fish and vegetable soup into wooden bowls for each man who drank from the bowl directly or used a wooden spoon. Marveling at the flavor, albeit spicy, Jeff asked Henry about the unrecognizable pieces in the soup.

"Sea turtle," Henry replied.

After each man had downed several bowls of soup and had consumed a sufficient amount of whiskey to satisfy the chief, the dancing and singing began which lasted well into the night. The affair ended abruptly when the chief declared it so, curiously at the same time the liquor ran out. In any case, the sun would rise soon and the boats must go out at dawn.

The two men fairly staggered along the beach back to the house, using the flashlights on their cells to help them avoid occasional rocks. On an impulse, Jeff desired to play music from one of his phone apps. Within seconds, The Rolling Stones began one of their great performances.

"What the hell is that," Henry mumbled, mush-mouthed.

Jeff paused, staggered a beat and read from his phone, "It's from Radio Moscow. I swear they play more Elvis music than Voice of America ever did."

Making their way along the beachfront, not caring whether the tide washed onto them, Jeff's cell phone vibrated in his hand. He didn't expect any calls down here in Bimli, and certainly didn't expect any robo-calls at 2:00 am, although in today's world, anything might be possible. Any cells in Bimli were well within the range of the towers in Visak.

Ignoring the call, he asked a question that had been burning his tongue all evening. "Where did they get the booze from?"

"Come on, old chap, there's a seaport only twenty miles up the coast, the one where we met. Like Raj said, this is his district and when he can, he likes to keep his people happy."

"But why do they only drink only half the bottle?" Jeff inquired, completely stumped by the practice.

"Ah, yes. Well, they fill the other half with USDA pesticide, then send it up the coast to another village. When the others get sick, our chief claims his people took a little out of each bottle and had no trouble at all and can't understand why anybody would get ill. It's not Raj's concern, because the other village is out of his district. Not knowing what happened, the other chief is up against it with his own people and has to tell his own district supervisor that cholera hit many of his people. Once in a while he'll report it as smallpox. By national law, the supervisor must report both diseases to the World Health Organization. No big deal. No smallpox reported for a number of years. It's politics between tribes, as usual. When you first inquired, I thought you meant a real epidemic and I didn't think of this until now."

"Wait a minute. Why didn't our guys drink all the booze and be done with it?" Jeff slurred, trying to wrap his head around what he had learned.

Henry shrugged. "Our chief likes to maintain good relations with his neighbors. Besides, he doesn't believe what he added to the whiskey will hurt anyone. Okay, it tastes bad by itself, but when blended with alcohol, hell, it wouldn't hurt a fly."

Jeff struggled with trying to apply his intellect to the thought process of a fishing village chief and couldn't make it work.

At least the issue of cholera outbreak had been resolved, even if it cost him a couple of thousand dollars for a trip at the other end of the world for two nights of partying.

He decided against lamenting about time and money spent on this investigation and focused on flopping onto his bed, turning on the mosquito fan, and was on the verge of passing out when his phone vibrated again. He would return the call when he damn well felt like it.

Chapter 2

PIGEONS AND THE ORANGE MOLD

Before noon the same day, Jeff sat by the open doorway of Henry's house within the screened-in front porch measuring some six-feet by thirty-feet. With electronic book in hand, he looked out at the turbulent waters of the bay through another downpour. According the Henry, the landscape of the bay would completely rearrange with the appearance and disappearance of sand bars and rip tides.

A standing fan served to blow the heavy moist air from his skin, his head hurting from the recent debauchery only hours before. He also felt chagrined by Henry's disclosure about the cholera issue as well as his public announcement about it at Raj's party. Whatever reputation he might have had before must certainly lay in ruins at this time.

Henry had been out somewhere when he

suddenly appeared with a man and woman in tow, all three wearing sandals and holding large black umbrellas. "Jeffrey, old chap, I'd like you to meet two friends of mine I was telling you about, Steven and Grace Chatfield. They're also from across the pond," Henry announced.

The man was lean, clean shaven, and stood over six feet in height with gray hair sparse over the ears and bald on top. He appeared to be comfortable with himself and in his mid-to-late sixties. The woman was short, well kept, with a cheerful countenance wearing a sun hat with no makeup. Both were dressed in loose shirts and shorts, befitting the season. Steven identified himself as a retired pharmaceutical executive who had traveled the world with his wife, had been to the States on a number of occasions, and had certainly heard of the famous Dr. Shenero. Out of modesty, he failed to mention that his father had founded Chatfield Pharmaceuticals a century ago, a multi-billion dollar corporation, and had turned over the company to his son, Steven, who had retired in turn, because his own son had become CEO.

Jeff remembered the book on seashells he had purchased and mentioned it to Grace. "Yes, it's my book. It took me some time to put it together. I'm not certain I've earned back my money. It's not exactly flying off the shelves," she cheerily announced.

Henry led the trio inside where he ordered

his servant to prepare tea and cookies while the four sat at the dining room table. A very large screened-in window looked out over a hand-smoothed clay tennis court in the backyard where the water ran off in different directions.

Several minutes of polite discussion passed when Steven asked, "Jeffrey, I'm wondering if you can help us with something. We need fresh ideas."

"Of course, if I can," Jeff replied.

Grace said, "We have something running around in our attic, mostly at night. We can't figure out how it gets up there or goes in and out. Sometimes, it sounds like its fighting with another creature. We haven't been able to get a good night's sleep in a long time. It's making us crazy. When it gets too bad, we have to go into Visak for a good night's sleep at a good hotel."

Jeff frowned. "Do you have any exterior holes to the attic?"

"Only bird holes for ventilation," Grace contributed.

"I'll take a look at it, but no guarantees," Jeff offered, puzzled about how he could possibly help the couple.

Steven looked at Grace a moment, thought, and said, "Tell you what. If you fix the problem for us . . . how are you getting home?"

"What? Oh, flying," Jeff replied, confused by the question.

"Good. You fix this thing, then give me your

tickets, and we'll change them all to First Class. Our treat."

Jeff laughed out loud, definitely not taking the offer seriously. "Okay, but only if I can fix the problem. How about today, if the rain ever lets up?"

"Good, and I'll show you my shell collection," Grace announced, enthusiastically, looking forward to sharing knowledge about her hobby.

Three hours later, Henry led Jeff to the Chatfield residence only a quarter-mile up the hill. They crossed the main thoroughfare of the village with a population of perhaps 8,000, although only a few hundred might be seen at once at the various stands lining both sides of a single dirt road. A bus stop was situated at the end of the street next to a hotel, or *hottle*, a name reserved for a small café.

The single story home appeared as any other with a heavy red clay shingle roof and a concrete porch resembling the one in front of Henry's house. Jeff asked Steven about the purpose of ledge beneath the bird holes.

Steven replied, "It's decorative."

"Makes no sense," Jeff said.

"Have you ever been to a country where everything makes sense?" Steven asked.

"Got me there," Jeff replied, honestly. "Not where humans are involved."

"Pigeons roost there and even make nests. It's quite a mess," Grace inserted.

Jeff said, "No big deal. You can get somebody to clean the ledge. I see the bird holes are screened over so your critter can't be going in through them."

Steven pointed, "The portion you're looking at got repaired a couple of months ago during the dry season after we had leakage problems. It stayed open for a couple of weeks."

Jeff rubbed his chin. "Hmmm, I have an idea. Do you have a ladder?"

Steven left and soon returned with a stepladder. Jeff climbed up and noted the piles of pigeon droppings on the entire length of the ledge. He pushed on the screen of one of the bird holes and it held. He did so on a second with the same result. The third one easily folded inward, hinged by wire on the inside at the top.

Jeff climbed down the latter to face the others and said to the three waiting at the bottom of the ladder, "Here's my theory. Your friend doesn't go in and out because he can't go out. He lives in there and probably got in during construction.

"Any pigeon pushing against the screen goes right into the attic space, but can't get out again because the wire only goes one way. Your little attic friend is happy to have the company and the food after it wins the fights you're hearing. You can set up vertical spikes around the ledge or a roll of wire, if you don't care what it looks like to keep off the pigeons and your friend won't last long without food."

The husband and wife looked at each other and smiled. Grace said, "We'll make sure to reinforce the screen and check the security of the others so more two or four legged creatures can't get in there."

About to reply, Jeff's phone vibrated once more. This time, almost automatically, he pulled it out of his pocket and checked the screen. The call came from Carmen, his sweetheart. That must have been her on the previous occasions. He'd forgotten to return her calls. Something was going on.

He held up a finger to the others and walked away several yards to answer the call.

The three watched Jeff and all thought the same thing. The man was everything they had read about: eccentric, adventurous, intelligent, self-confident but not cocky, kind, and helpful. The man was a living vortex of activity that could easily suck others into that vortex. So far, no ill had come from it. What else could they expect to see from him?

For Grace, the few minutes she had spent with Jeff gave her feelings she hadn't felt in a long time. She'd had her years of adventure with her husband traveling the world and she loved him dearly; yet, with Jeff, simply being near the man made her tingle and her breath quickened. There was something else about him, something untamed, primitive and feral that a coating of civilization couldn't completely mask.

Once clear of ear shot, Jeff said into the phone, "Hi, babe. It's great to hear from you."

"Why didn't you call me back?" Carmen asked, sounding somewhat piqued.

"Sorry, it was 2:00 in the morning here and we were coming back from . . . a get together." *Damn, it was her calling.*

"I'm happy for you," Carmen said.

Jeff couldn't tell whether she was being sincere or sarcastic, until she added, "Well, our lives have been threatened and I'm scared, but I guess you were too busy to call me back," she added.

A wash of guilt swept over Jeff, quickly recalling the pleasant dinner with Raj's family, getting hammered at the seaman's club, and at the party with the fishermen, followed by an episode of chasing a rat, or whatever, in somebody's attic.

"Threatened. How so?" Jeff inquired, back on track.

"Threatening calls on our home and business lines that say we're both going to pay for what you've done," Carmen rejoined. "They're also lighting up my cell phone with similar calls."

"Both of us? Done what?"

"They don't say," Carmen summarized.

Jeff massaged the back of his head with his off-hand, and said, "Oh, boy. Honey, I'll wrap things up here and get right come home. I'll let you know my schedule when I can."

It hurt him to see her flustered like this. Why would anybody threaten him or her? On the other hand, why wouldn't they? He had plenty of enemies. Painfully, Jeff would have to decline Raj's offer to go on a jungle ride. He had to return to his new friends to ask a big favor.

Taking the short walk back to the house, he noticed a pile of rubble to one side comprised of roofing tiles, tar paper, and a few pieces of lumber. Patches of orange on the tar paper caught his attention. Most of them measured inches in diameter, some much smaller at a quarter inch across. He saw none of them on the lumber or tiles. Moving in for a closer look he took out his cell phone, opened the magnifier app and zoomed in for a 30x magnification. The orange patches were growths of some kind. Although the patches were nearly flat with the paper, there was a certain fuzziness about them. Jeff counted eight of the larger ones, some circular, others oval. Walking around, he noticed more on other areas of the paper on the distant side of the mound. A tingle of excitement ran through him. After taking several more photos, he turned to his friends, asking about the pile.

Grace said, "Leftovers from the roof repair. They were supposed to take it away a long time ago."

"Mind if I take a sample of this with me?" Jeff inquired.

Steven laughed. "Jeffrey, you can take the whole damn pile, if you want."

Jeff tore off a piece of the tar paper with the orange growth on it and held it up to his eyes. *How strange*, he thought. *How can this be? It's a life form, all right, but I've never seen anything like it. It's an orange fuzzy mat.* He placed the piece in a Ziploc baggie, which he put into another bag that held one of his cold packs. He cracked the pack to allow the chemicals to mix, thus refrigerating the sample collection; although sitting out here in the hot sun and rain didn't seem to have affected it much. He tore off another sample and put it into another bag without refrigeration, just to ensure he had enough.

"Come on in and I'll show you what I promised. Everybody around here has already seen them," Grace told Jeff, pleased to spend some one-on-one time with him.

The group entered the home and Jeff immediately saw a glass case with hundreds of sea shells, all labeled. Grace pulled out a large conch that had the tip broken off. Smiling, she put it to her lips and blew into it. A long piercing sound like a French horn came forth. She tooted it several times and handed it to Jeff. Grinning, he gave it a try and succeeded in producing a tone, not to Grace's level of skill, but a tone nonetheless.

With everyone pleased at Jeff's success as a musician, he figured the time had come to ask for that favor—the First Class ticket home the Chatfield's had promised.

Everything was all right until it went all wrong. There didn't seem to be much in between. Not counting travel time, he'd been in country for only two days, not much time to accomplish a lot.

Chapter 3

POISON IN THE MAIL

ONE

Jeff not only flew First Class, but flew head of the class, getting bumped in seating and in flights ahead of others. After telling his friends what Carmen had said, in exchange for the travel offer, he promised to let them know about events happening at home, as soon as he found out himself.

The long journey home gave Jeff a chance to catch up on sleep with a lot of time to think. He needed more information from Carmen, of course, but he felt confident the threat had nothing to do with his research institute. A lot of big people got sent to prison because of the terrorist plot he had unraveled, which opened up endless possibilities. The president, his senator, and the FBI would likely become involved. On the other hand, his gut told him it might be tied to one of the countless in-home jobs he had conducted. Would he have to go through all of his years of job notes?

Some 30 hours later, Carmen picked him up at Will Rogers International Airport in OKC and drove down to their home in Norman, a short 45 minute drive. On the way she explained about the calls to his medical institute and at home, a single male voice making the simple statement. Both of them are going to be destroyed for what he had done and they need to start looking over their shoulders. The calls could be traced to a burner phone. The caller had the slightest of foreign accents and it wasn't Spanish. With the trace of a rolled "R" in his pronunciations, the caller could be from almost anywhere outside the U.S.

At home, Jeff copied the recording onto his phone's memory, then they drove to his institute where he did the same thing. Before leaving, the couple found some carton boxes and loaded into them the past five years of his record books, those records after his involvement in the terrorist plot and his subsequent startup of the research center.

Unless tied to the plot, a strong possibility, Jeff wondered why anybody would wait years to come after him. For the next several hours, the couple paged through his house-call jobs where he had inspected for mold, took air samples to check for general air quality, collected surface and wall cavity samples, came back to the lab to check them under the microscope, write the report, and email or snail-mail the bill along with it.

After sending out for pizza, the evening turned out to be surprisingly interesting, as each recounted a particular case that drew their interest, occasionally causing laughter.

Carmen remembered the case where Jeff had monitored a single-wide mobile home. The wife sold real estate and the husband worked construction. Upon marriage years before, the husband had ordered her never to enter the second bathroom. He declared the bath to be his alone. When Jeff had entered, he found it so disgusting that he almost vomited and decided against telling the wife what he had discovered to save their marriage.

Jeff began to chuckle while he reviewed the Doug Johnson notes, remembering the case. He had been called to inspect a better home where the wife suspected mold might be present due to an under-sink water leak. He found the husband at home with the wife at work. During the course of his testing, Doug said, "Say, Jeff, do you drink?"

"Not much," Jeff answered. "As a matter of fact, I'm thinking of quitting all together."

"Oh, too bad," Doug said.

"Why too bad?" Jeff asked, curiously.

"Well, last night my wife and I threw a big

blowout party, the last hurrah. We had promised each other we would never drink again and would support each other though our efforts as we went through life."

"I'm impressed with your strength of resolve," Jeff told him with sincerity.

Doug continued, "We also said we'd give any liquor we had left over to the first person who came along, which would be you."

This stopped Jeff in his tracks, and, like a good politician, quickly back tracked.

"Well, I said I was thinking about quitting. I mean, it wouldn't be all at once, anyway. It would be a phased approach. Why, what do you have left over?"

"This way," Doug said with enthusiasm, and led Jeff to the garage where shelves were lined with bottles, like a liquor store. Some bottles were small, others large, some half empty, others unopened.

"You can have them all if you want," offered Doug.

Fifteen minutes later, at 11:00 am, Jeff drove off with four large boxes fill with liquor bottles and a check in his pocket. Carmen took two bottles white wine, he took a bottle of Patron Tequila, his drink at the time, and gave the rest to friends.

Finally, pay dirt. This had to be it. When Jeff read his notes about a retired policeman who had hired him, his internal alarm bells rang. The job occurred years before and involved a situation he soon forgot after it had closed. Real life intervened and his mind had turned elsewhere.

The simple four-page report had turned into 10,000 pages issued by in insurance company on the man's background. A policeman in Alabama had been fired by the department for numerous instances of abusive behavior and he found another job as a repairman in Seattle, before moving to Oklahoma City.

"Right," Jeff said, leaning back in his chair, remembering, thinking about the threatening calls. "A couple of months later, this guy, Abbot, a renter, filed a million dollar suit against me, the management company, and the home owners. He complained both he and his wife and their two year old son had of a variety of symptoms. Many of the symptoms were remarkably ingenious."

Carmen completed the picture. "Abbot got sent to prison for five years, not for filing a bogus claim, but because you found him engaged in illicit arms trading and he needed money to pay off a debt."

"Let me make a call to the attorney who represented us," Jeff offered. "The first step is to locate this guy."

Some twenty minutes later, he found out that Abbot had been released from prison only four weeks prior to the threatening calls. The attorney could offer that he had received a memo regarding Abbot's release and the name of his parole officer, and the name of the half-way house where he was staying.

"What are we going to do?" Carmen asked, clearly frightened.

Jeff said, almost too casually, "I'm not worried about the house. Between the security system and the Rottweilers, we should be all right there. Keep in mind, bad guys are looking for Abbot, too, because he still owes them. I'm sure he has problems of this own."

Jeff then called the parole officer's number he had been given. A recorded message stated that the parole officer would be gone for two weeks but gave an alternate number for his partner. When Jeff called the partner's number, a recorded message informed Jeff that he was ill and to call the courthouse. The courthouse referred Jeff back to the parole officer. The half-way house would not honor his call without prior clearance.

Carmen didn't like the lack of obvious concern on Jeff's part. It was though he were going through the motions without paying attention to her. She was frightened to the core, while Jeff always went around almost impossible to read. She had seen him laugh a lot. She had never seen him cry or pound his fist on the table in anger. Was her lover a human being or a robot? Did he even know?

Carmen began to lose sleep. They were at a standstill. When another threatening call came in late one evening when they were preparing for bed, she turned on him. "For God's sake, Jeff, do *something*. We have an abusive former police officer who got fired, is running guns, went to prison, got out, filed suit against you, and is looking for payback."

Reflecting on the situation, Jeff had a disconcerting thought. Focusing his attention on the obvious might be the wrong approach. He might be missing the real problem.

TWO

The time-delay factor served to be a major issue: Typically, a person isn't threatened for something wrong they'd done years before. The accuser generally recants, changes lifestyles, dies, or moves away. Rarely does a person seek revenge after spending time in prison.

Jeff and Carmen had no choice but to continue to work the next day, although they kept a wary eye taking care to vet any person wishing to come to the research center for any manner of business.

Jeff maintained a full-time staff of eight with another three graduate students, thanks to a generous government grant. After uncovering the plot by the terrorists to poison the ink of newspapers and add the toxin to cosmetics, the government believed Jeff to be the best man to analyze and clear hundreds of products in the consumer marketplace. Now, with his own laboratory paid for by the feds, Jeff retired from his professorship at the University of Oklahoma and occasionally traveled the world looking for new species of fungi possessing antimicrobial properties such as cephalosporin, penicillin, amoxicillin, griseofulvin and many others.

His problems at work revolved around disgruntled workers. They were top of the line researchers recruited from around the world relegated to performing menial tasks college graduate students could do. Self-satisfaction doesn't come from receiving a lot of money for a job you're not happy with.

Jeff didn't know who to call first, Henry, or the Chatfields. They must be wondering what had happened to him. Accounting for the time difference, he thought about texting both parties, but he had too much to say and texting was a coldly impersonal way to reenter their lives. He solved the problem when he called Henry, but received no answer and no chance to leave a message. So he called Steven and Grace, turning on the video. Carmen sat by his side. Steven picked up.

"Jeffrey, how nice to hear from you," he announced. Jeff saw Grace leaning over Steven's shoulder.

Jeff introduced Carmen, who waved and Steven said, "Jeffrey, how in the world did you land such a beauty?"

This was a normal response when one compared Carmen's flawless skin and dark beauty to Jeff's shaved head, high cheekbones, Asian-like eyes, and the scar in his forehead.

"I could ask you the same thing, Steven," Jeff offered. Everyone laughed. Grace looked pleased.

Jeff explained the latest developments to the pair, or rather, all that had not developed. He told of his search through the records, the third threat, and their suspicion of Abbot.

Steven remained silent, thinking it over, and said, "Jeffrey, old boy, listen. Why don't you tell me more about this Abbot character and exactly where he is staying? I'll see what I can find out for you. And let me know if you get any more calls, exact date and time."

Jeff agreed to the request and the conversation changed to more comfortable talk about international relations and parties with the fishermen. The lengthy chat finally ended with Steven's promise to relay Jeff's story to Henry. Grace sent her love.

Two weeks later Jeff received another threat. There was no change to the recorded message. He found it texted on his cell and on his message phone at the office. Both occurred at approximately 11:00 pm. Jeff texted the information to Steven who called him at work six days later. "Jeff, Abbot is not your man. Sorry."

Amazed that Steven was connected enough

to make such a claim, Jeff could only say, "How do you know for certain?"

Steven chuckled and began his tale. "A number of years ago, I accidentally ran into a toughened retired police detective who'd worked the south side of Los Angeles for most of his career and was looking for another job. He turned out to be just the man I needed for my company to handle certain internal matters, so I hired him at a good salary. After he retired, we stayed in touch.

"I called him about your problem and we arranged for him to get thrown into the half-way house in Oklahoma City and even share a room with Abbot. The two bonded like superglue and traded war stories about their days with their respective police departments. My man says Abbot never used the phone a single time and didn't want revenge against anybody, but he did fear for his life as soon as he left the half-way house, because he owed a lot of money. Apparently, he sold small arms to minority groups in Oklahoma City and Tulsa, many of which were used to shoot and even kill police. The man was unpopular all the way around.

"At the time you said your call came in, the men were in bed telling stories. The day after I told my man about your call, he said Abbot didn't make it. The following day he walked out the front door, entered a waiting car, and drove away, never to be seen again. Right now he's probably back at home watching the telly. He did ask me to thank you for the little adventure. And no, Abbot did not have an accent, unless you want to call Alabama a foreign country."

Neither was pleased to hear the news. Both were at a complete loss as to how to proceed.

Shortly after Jeff left the front office to report the news to Carmen, he was intercepted in the hallway. Emily Harrison stood before him. Diminutive, wearing her white lab coat, with spiked black hair and glasses, she was one of Jeff's brainiac doctoral candidates who played first chair violin for the Oklahoma Symphony Orchestra, when she could get away. She specialized in using fungal toxins as antibiotics in combination with other antibiotics, the same as Jeff's specialty. She was one of those people who are easy to dislike because they don't have any evident faults and are successful in everything they attempt.

"Yes, Emily," Jeff said, his mind spinning from Steven's phone call and Carmen's near collapse after hearing the news. He feared going home tonight.

"Doctor, the orange sample you gave me won't grow in culture unless I add a little mineral oil. I can't figure out where the heck it might grow in nature. After I added the oil, I grew a batch of it in liquid culture in only three days instead of the normal two to three weeks. It's a nice orange flat mat with no spores. On Petri plates it creates a clear zone of inhibition around it. Nothing can get close. So it's excreting a powerful toxin."

She handed Jeff a number of photomicrographs and led her into her office. He paged Carmen to join them. When she came in, the three looked closely at the pictures. "Where are you now on this?" he asked.

"I should have some pure crystals in a couple of days for structural analysis, then we can run toxicity tests with it."

"I like exciting new, Emily, thanks, I needed that," Jeff replied.

Emily turned to leave Jeff to ponder his next move. For the moment, he decided to give up who was making the threats and joined Emily in the lab. He wanted hands-on experience researching the new orange fungus that refused to produce spores, yet somehow managed get from one place to another. Did it fragment under dry conditions to be carried on the wind? Preliminary experiments suggested the new mold possessed extremely high toxicity. He wanted to run more experiments to study the phenomena.

"I stayed up late last night and searched the literature online. I can tell you it hasn't been described," Emily said, as Jeff walked in her lab.

Jeff took a flask of tiny brine shrimp commonly used to test toxicities and prepared a sample with a known number of shrimp in it.

Holding his breath, he weighed a couple of the almost weightless orange crystals and added them to the solution. A quarter hour later he tried to count the number of shrimp again to find none were alive.

"That's crazy," he mumbled.

"What, doctor?" Emily asked, coming over to see what he was talking about.

Jeff shook his head in disbelief. "It's far more toxic than aflatoxin B1, the most potent mycotoxin known and we've only started playing with this. You do it." he requested.

Emily repeated the experiment and came up with same result.

This time they tried it again using their stock of aflatoxin B1 and confirmed his suspicions.

The next step would be to find out how this toxin worked. Did it destroy the cell membrane or bind to DNA? Steven couldn't wait for Jeff's latest reports, but knew better than to suggest Jeff turn over the project to his people. He did offer to have one of his most experienced scientists come down to assist in the investigation, to which Jeff acceded.

Jeff did not have an ego problem, per se. He did, however, have a problem with giving a newborn child to someone else to care for and raise. A nanny in the house would be allowed.

Several days later, a suited simple-appearing pale skin gray-haired man of average height in his mid-to-late fifties, appeared at the door of the institute. With a slight German accent, Arnold Kaufman displayed credentials and a letter from the senior vice president of Chatfield pharmaceuticals.

Jeff interviewed Kaufman, to whom he immediately took a liking. The man had an honest smile and offered a wealth of ideas on how to move most efficiently on the project. "As you can imagine, it frequently takes years to develop a good pharmaceutical, even one with promise. Other times, political circumstances and public emergencies force us to do drag our feet or make it available almost overnight, as the case might be," Kaufman offered, smiling slightly.

Kaufman down-turned his mouth in surprise at the amount of information Jeff told him about the life form and its toxicity and asked to see the lab where Jeff conducted the research. Jeff gave his guest a tour of his facility and a walk-through of the lab earmarked for the study of their new orange friend. He introduced the man to Emily and the two began chatting. Within seconds, they had bonded. Jeff liked what he saw in terms of a potentially strong working relationship and could see why Steven had recommended Kaufman.

In the following weeks, Kaufman worked with Emily creating elegant experimental designs while allowing them to study six variables simultaneously. Jeff found himself having mixed feelings. Although this aspect of research might speed things along, it freed him to tend to necessary, but loathsome administrative duties.

At one point in their work, Kaufman asked Emily, "So, I understand you play music?"

"Yes, I dabble a little," she replied, surprised that a stranger knew about her private life. Carmen probably told him.

"Ah, like I dabble in science," replied Kaufman, grinning. "Who do you enjoy playing most?"

"Mozart and Bach, of course, although I am particularly intrigued by Paginini," she responded, rapidly becoming pleased to find someone who had an interest in music as a working partner.

Kaufman's hand went to his mouth in a gentle touch of surprise, in quite the European gesture. "We must speak more of this some time. I once knew someone with similar tastes."

"They don't have them anymore?" Emily queried.

"No, she died in a car accident some 30 years ago," he responded, wistfully. Recovering quickly, he abruptly added, "Sorry to be so morose. Let us get back to work, shall we?"

One month after their conversation, Emily announced that, even though she always found time to practice, she needed to take three days off to prepare for a concert in OKC. Kaufman inquired about the event and asked if he could attend.

"I know you can afford it and I feel a little embarrassed by doing this, but when I get a chance, I'll get you a ticket," she informed him, to his great delight. When she did, it turned out to be front row center in the packed 800 seat auditorium. The final piece played in the concert featured one of the most difficult violin concertos written, double-stringed with plucking, Paginini's *God Save the King,* featuring Emily Harrison. She stood to take a bow to a standing ovation, Kaufman among the first to rise.

Duly impressed and delighted beyond words, Kaufman went backstage to congratulate Emily, who accepted his invitation for desert at an all-night diner back in Norman. Tomorrow would be Sunday and with nothing pressing in the lab the following day, they spoke of the different composers who wrote violin concertos until Emily left for home and Kaufman drove to his nearby hotel.

THREE

Jeff left the day-to-day operations to Carmen and returned to work with Emily and Kaufman in order to speed their rate of discovery. Like true professionals, all partners operated smoothly and efficiently, keeping intimate records of their successes and failures.

Within short months, broken by the same occasional threat, the team received information about the unusual chemical structure of the toxin from an independent agency. Jeff had begun writing a number of scientific papers about the mold, which, by nomenclature standards would bear his name as the discoverer. To make certain of this, he had assigned one of his researchers to find if such a mold had been discovered before and verify Emily's statement that it had not. Certainly, many microbial life forms grew on petroleum-derived products, including glue-down mastic beneath water-damaged flooring tiles, but none proliferated on tar paper outdoors with a bright orange color after being washed by monsoon rains and subjected to scorching heat.

The next steps would be the most difficult: To see exactly how the toxin acted on living cells. The three scientists published several papers in peer-reviewed journals. Immediately upon their release and for the next several weeks, the institute began to receive calls and emails from other scientists who also noted the same orange-colored mold growing on a variety of structural materials, but had not investigated this proposed *Jeffrus shenerii* to the extent they had. Not all were pleased at the name given to the life form, insisting it was merely a simple mutant of another species, which one they couldn't be sure, but they'd find out. Being protective and possessive creatures, scientists are reluctant to give credit to another. However, the thoroughness of the institute's research spoke for itself.

Jeff pondered the larger problem with Carmen, his resident medical doctor and business partner. The couple sat on their home porch on a fine Oklahoma evening. Jeff's two dogs lay by their side as they looked out at their fenced in yard with forest on three sides and Lake Thunderbird only a few miles to the east.

"New life forms show up on occasion, even globally," Carmen offered. "Look how fast the Covid-19 pandemic spread. And don't tell me this is any different because it's a mold."

"I'm totally fine with what you're saying. But diseases like Covid tend to have a point source of origin. It spread so fast, in part, because it traveled inside people's lungs. People flew everywhere, so we helped spread it outward. This could be our case, except that I can't fathom a point source for this."

"Unless there are several," Carmen contributed.

This gave Jeff pause to think. "Good point. I've had some 47 inquiries since our publication." He pulled out a piece of paper from his pocket and unfolded it. He read, "Some 75% are from the farther northern and southern polar regions such as Alaska, Russia and Siberia, Greenland, Australia, and even South Africa and southern Argentina. Is it luck of the draw or do the locations mean anything?"

"Not enough data points to reach a conclusion," Carmen opined.

Jeff scratched his head. "On the other hand, maybe it's a clue. What's different about those areas from the rest of the planet?" Answering his own question, he said, "Some are lot colder than others, and some, like South Africa have every climate extreme. Nope, I'm stuck in a rut."

"Honey, why is it so important to you. It's not like this thing is causing diseases," Carmen offered.

"None we know of. That's what bothers me," Jeff replied, with a note of concern.

"Don't be so droll," she frowned. "Maybe it started growing on oil slicks in the ocean and the wind is spreading it."

"Where would it come from to start with?" Jeff inquired.

"I don't know. Maybe it came from a volcanic explosion," she suggested.

"That's not a bad idea," Jeff admitted. "I could tell you a lot about volcanic explosions."

"I'll bet you could," Carmen agreed, all too readily. The man had an endless number of stored factoids.

Jeff took her statement as an invitation to continue. "Did you know that virtually all major climate changes on Earth over the past hundreds of years to hundreds of millions of years can be traced to those eruptions? A single explosion releases more greenhouse gases into the world's atmosphere than everything man has ever emitted with his pollutants? Remind me to check on the number of oil spills in the various oceans in recent years," he concluded.

Well accustomed to Jeff's eccentric ramblings, Carmen said, softly, "I'll keep that in mind. Here's another brilliant idea. How about if you focus on taking care of me?" she teased, running her fingernails lightly over the nape of his neck. She had relegated her concerns about the threats to the back burner, reminding herself of one of Jeff's sayings: "Always laugh in the face of danger. There will be plenty of time to cry later."

FOUR

Jeff gave up trying to figure out the origin of the new life form until he had more information. Meanwhile, Emily and Kaufman were a regular feature in the lunchroom and weekly deliveries of cosmetics and personal care products still came in from around the country for analysis. These samples consisted of toothpaste, eye shadow, skin toner, face cream, sun screen, aftershave, blush, deodorant, foot powder, shampoo, conditioner, and literally any skin-care product. These were representative of batches slated for public usage, which meant nobody in the country could use a damn thing until Jeff gave his okay.

When he accepted the task assigned to him by a representative of the Consumer Product Safety Commission, he didn't think that kind of responsibility would be his alone. Overnight, someone had named him Mr. Clearinghouse, a title he loathed. He wasn't afraid of responsibility, per se, and didn't shy away from the money the government sunk into the program. He did want to spend more time in pure research, not in business management. So did his staff, of which some members were talking about preparing letters of resignation.

Once cleared of mycotoxin presence, the samples were discarded in a designated dumpster. The staff maintained meticulous records in duplicate, which required an add-on room for their storage and the hiring of a records manager.

Of the hundreds of samples thus far analyzed, none had been found to contain mycotoxin, until one day several did.

Two of his lab-coated scientists approached Jeff in his office with the news. One of them, Howard, held a tube of toothpaste, and another man, David, held a number of machine printouts. Howard said, "It's positive for Roridin A, doctor. We triple checked."

Jeff swiveled his chair from his desk to face Howard and held out his hand to receive the tube. Turning it back to front he saw it had standard labeling: large brand name on a blue oval background with the added words: SPECIAL INGREDIENTS FOR TEETH WHITENING. In small print on the reverse were words: Active

Ingredients: baking soda, peroxide. The inactive ingredients included the usual preservatives and anti-microbial agents. Below it all in small print were printed three words: Made in Mexico.

Jeff handed back the tube and took the print-outs from Dave depicting a graph with a large spike. On the papers someone had written his name, date, time, batch number, and the words Roridin A. Jeff knew that the mold *Fusarium,* a contaminant of grains, such as wheat, oats, and maize, produced the toxin. It had no business being in toothpaste unless somebody put it there. The toxin was in the same class as the one produced by numerous mold species including *Stachybotrys,* the much maligned black mold. The fact that it came from another country opened up a can of worms, not for Jeff, but for the nation. It meant that other products made by the same company had to be screened, as did other imported products. It also meant more bad guys needed to be tracked down.

Jeff said, "I'm surprised they couldn't come up with something more original. What's the concentration of the toxin?"

"It's low," answered Dave.

Jeff nodded slowly in understanding. "Slow burn, won't be immediately yanked from the shelves or discovered for some time."

What a mess. Jeff returned to the lab with the two men who took him through the standardized series of tests they conducted numerous times daily. At least this time he didn't have to personally get involved, wind up in jail, get into fist fights, have a shotgun pointed at him, or have his dogs chew up somebody trying to burn down his house.

"When did this come in?" asked Jeff.

"Sometime over the weekend, I guess," Howard replied.

"I thought we got our shipments on Wednesday," Jeff said.

"The boxes were stacked beneath the rear porch, as usual," Dave answered.

"Where are the other boxes?" Jeff asked.

"Everybody's working on them," answered Howard.

Another worker appeared at the doorway and announced, "Doctor, I was looking for you. We've got a positive for Roridin A in this eye shadow."

Jeff's hackles rose. He quickly picked up the phone and told Carmen to sound the signals for an emergency meeting. He wanted all staff members in the conference room. This meant everyone had five minutes to quit what they were doing, even if it meant getting off the pot or shutting down a machine.

Jeff went directly to the conference room and took a seat at the head of the table as a collection of lab-coated men and women took their seats. Aside from old Arnie, their gofer, Carmen was the only one without the lab coat, notepad in hand, her long black tresses trailing behind her Indian print blouse, turquoise skirt and blue sneakers like a flower at the end of an oval of white surrounding an oval of brown.

Jeff addressed Arnie first. "Arnie, how many cases did you find this morning?"

"Twelve, sir," he answered. "I dropped two off outside each of the labs and slit them open."

"Howard, Dave, you reported first. How many tubes were in your box," Jeff inquired.

"Twenty four," Howard answered.

Others reported in turn, "We got the eye shadow."

"We got the blush."

"We got the aftershave."

Jeff held up his hand. Eight more cases of different personal care products awaited analysis. Obviously, these would take precedence over the standard fare they had been receiving. Did this chance discovery justify all their efforts? Again, less talented people could have come up with the same result.

"Somebody's playing games with us," Jeff said. "I suspect the entire new batch is contaminated. Only touch the samples you're working with and report to me your findings in detail—printouts, everything. Then sample two others from your batch. Three total. Don't touch any of the others. By the end of the day, we're probably going to need the feds."

Jeff concluded, "They'll need fingerprint

samples from the untested jars and tubes, so, other than the three you use, keep your hands off them. Now, let's get back to work."

Jeff reviewed the video feed of the drop-off. He saw a man in a hoodie driving a white panel van with no license plate take out boxes from the back at 2:45 a.m. Nothing solid there, but he'd pass it on.

Jeff returned to his office and tried to think it through. It appeared as though the threat were tied to the shipment. After all, the male voice said he was going to destroy Jeff, not kill him. What was the point of sending him *all* the bad stuff? Were they sending him a message saying they could do what they wanted when they wanted? Everything in the marketplace had to go through Jeff's institute anyway before it got approved. Granted there was a backlog . . . unless distribution might be occurring without Jeff's approval. Might they be seeing more name brands with poison in them? Or, perhaps manufacturers were buying generic ingredients, unbeknownst to them, were laced with poison to bypass Jeff's inspection in order to avoid a lag in sales.

He decided against trying to figure out all the intricacies of the scheme. Two things he did feel certain about. Somebody put a lot of money into this venture and he had a target on his back with national disgrace as a reward for his efforts. Once the poisons took hold, millions of people could be affected and Mr. Clearinghouse would be blamed. Goodbye institute. Hello lawsuits.

After Jeff turned over the bad samples to the authorities, lab work returned to the screening of regular shipments. Enthusiasm had returned to the researchers, which would help buy him time while he returned to the business of working with Emily and Kaufman on the orange fungus.

They soon found by diluting the concentration of the crystals 1000-fold over what he had used the growth rate of bacteria was slowed without killing them. They found the rate of reproduction of rapidly growing bacteria was slowed more than that of slower growing bacteria. In fact, the faster the cells reproduced, the slower the rate of reproduction. Kaufman said they already had drugs like that against tumors, but those tended to cause side effects in humans and weren't nearly as effective as the one in their possession. He also surmised it might be used where other cells proliferated abnormally, such as in leukemia.

But, as in all experiments of this kind, what happens in a test tube doesn't always translate into what happens in biological systems. What dosage of a medication can be used without harming the patient? If harm is to be expected, what is the nature of that harm and will it be affected by additional medications? Well-paid volunteers would be needed for clinical trials.

Meanwhile, more reports about the new fungus were received from Polar Regions than from equatorial regions. A concentration of anything is highest nearest the source, whether it be a point source of radioactivity, following the size of gold nuggets in a stream to find the mother lode, or tracking a strange orange mold that appears out of nowhere.

To Kaufman, it didn't matter where it came from. It is what it is. He wanted to turn the project over to his people who could put a score of scientists to work on it immediately. Jeff wasn't ready for that. After discussing the matter with Emily and Kaufman one day, he brought up the subject of its origin once again.

Emily offered, "We have to tie in what is happening in the Polar Regions today with that hasn't happened before, right? We already know our orange friend loves petroleum and hydrocarbons. I say it might be tied to oil spills in the ocean in some way."

Jeff said, "Carmen thought the same thing."

"Maybe a combination of oil and colder water helps it reproduce," Kaufman offered.

"We already tried growing it in the lab under various temperatures with and without oil, and its growth slows at lower temperatures," Jeff said. He began to pace and added, "We're thinking inside the box. Let's try the opposite. Maybe it lived someplace all along and something changed to expose it to the air, like removing centuries of dirt to find a buried city."

The three almost said the word at the same instant, as realization struck them. *Permafrost.* Jeff felt a chill and saw it in the others. He began to expound, "The warming of the Polar Regions is exposing trillions of tons of early vegetation and organic material. Ages of frozen ice are melting."

"And seeping up from beneath the permafrost is layers of oil with pockets of methane gas created by bacteria that, along with our orange friend, are digesting the organic material," Emily threw in, excitedly, reaching up to push her eyeglasses back in place. "Want to see global warming? Wait until all the methane hits the atmosphere."

Kaufman got into it the conversation and said, "Which means we may have untold riches awaiting us in terms of new life forms and cures for diseases."

Jeff philosophized, "Everything that makes sense isn't always true. It's an interesting theory we might want to present. We need more data, then I'll consider letting you, Arnold, have *Jeffrus shenerii* to take back to your company. Meanwhile, I'm going to talk to some friends in India."

When he did, he called Henry first, who said Raj wanted him to come for another dinner and take a ride into the jungle with him to look for new species to discover. And the village chief would throw another party in honor of their Hollywood friend. At the mention of both offers, Jeff's stomach began to rumble.

FIVE

Standing at the kitchen counter, facing Carmen, Jeff wanted to say, "A word of advice …" Picking up the package, he took the gentle approach. "My dear, maybe it's best not to look a gift horse in the mouth. Don't always take things at face value."

"What does that mean?" Carmen retorted, inhaling, eyebrows raised, nostrils flaring waiting for the other shoe to fall.

"When somebody gives you something, don't examine it too closely because you might be disappointed." Jeff set down the box. It was wrapped securely in expensive paper from a well-known seller of high-end women's personal care products. The return listed an address in Philadelphia with Carmen's name and address machine printed.

"It just arrived. I haven't even opened it yet and you're after me," she retorted. "Jeff, I know this company."

Jeff stepped back pushing his palms downward. "Look, honey, with everything going on with the threats and the toxins delivered to us and the FBI involved, I mean with the whole thing blowing up, we need to think about your safety."

"Jeff, don't be stupid. You're never here when this comes, or if you are, you don't pay any attention to it. Now you do. Look, it's an auto-ship that arrives every two months. It's just cleansing cream and eye shadow." She picked up the box and shook it. "See, it's not a bomb."

"And it's been two months since your last shipment?" he inquired.

"About, I guess, why?"

"Can you do me a favor and check your records, please?" he implored.

"No, I'm not going to check anything. You're being paranoid and it's starting to bother me," Carmen stated, emphatically, ignoring the rare note of pleading in his voice.

Jeff picked up the package, then said, "Sorry, baby, I'll make it up to you." He departed the house, listening to the voice behind him come out with such a stream of invective in Spanish that he lost track of what she said after the first three words, none of which were polite.

Great, just great. Nice way to spend a Saturday afternoon, Jeff thought.

After he had turned over the box to a local OKC independent laboratory for analysis on a rush order, he drove back down to Norman and speed-shifted through the gears of his supercharged Mustang on the way out to the lake. He needed to get away. In a few minutes he could take off his shoes, sit on the shore, watch the ducks, and think. He wanted to analyze the contents of the box on his own, but he knew Carmen would say he rigged the results to make things go his way, his paranoia expressing itself in physical terms.

Hell, he didn't even know what could be in the box, despite Carmen's claims. It would never have passed through the U.S. mail if it were a pressurized canister or explosives. Maybe he overreacted, but damn, he loved her so much he would rather put up with her wrath than to see harm befall her. But harm *was* befalling her. And she was wrathful. His own house was crumbling and he blamed himself for not solving the problem.

By Thursday of the following week, and after putting up with Carmen's distance, he was on the verge of calling the analytical company when he finally received an email at work that read:

Dr. Shenero: We apologize for the delay in processing your rush order, but our initial analysis required further confirmation from a second laboratory. Within the box we found three quality products for women, all of which contained Roridin A, the mycotoxin you asked us to look for. It's in an extremely high concentration. I'm sure you are aware that once used, these products will result in permanent scarring and pitting of the face along with blindness. Please find the attachments for the reports for each of the three products from each of two laboratories. We retained the samples and the cover wrap for your pickup, as per your request. I am available to discuss this project at your convenience.

Please verify your receipt of this email. Your billing statement is enclosed in the attachment.

FYI, within the box, we also found an embossed card with a generic statement that read: We hope our products meet your expectations.

Signed,
Chris Matthews
Chief Technician
Biochemical Analytics

Jeff downloaded the reports and printed everything. He immediately drove up to the city to pick up the box of samples and the original reports. He followed that by driving to the local FBI office to give them a copy of all written documents pertaining to the case. They would add this to the data from the original poisoned samples along with video of the van dropping off the parcels in order to build their case.

During the drive he tried to formulate a plan. In a few minutes he would have to tell Carmen the bad news. Somebody knew where they lived. They were trying to cause great angst for him with her serving as the moving target. Perhaps he could save a little of the cream to apply to the face of his adversary, if he ever got the chance.

When Jeff arrived home, he saw Carmen's

Toyota in the drive. He found her in the kitchen preparing dinner, her back to him. Another package stood on the counter identical to the first.

"Hi, what's this?" he asked simply. Start with something light.

"They made a mistake and sent me another shipment," she replied, without turning around. "You can take that one too, if you want."

Enough is enough. Jeff threw down the copy of the email and lab printouts on the counter. "Read these." It was not a request.

Sighing, Carmen turned around and picked up the papers without looking at him. She went from one to the other and back again until her shoulders slumped. She finally looked at him with sadness in her eyes. She threw down the papers and wrapped her arms around him. "Oh, baby, I'm so sorry I didn't believe you," she sobbed, with a release of pent-up energy, honest tears flowing freely. Pulling away, she said, "But what's this other one, I mean . . . "

"Most likely, it's your regular shipment. If it's all right with you, I'll have this one tested, as well."

Backing off and looking at her closely, he asked, "Where do you order these from, office or home?"

Carmen took a tissue, wiped her tears away, and gently blew her nose, trying to recover. "Well, I haven't placed an order, for a long time because it's all auto-shipped," she replied.

Jeff nodded, "Which suggests our computer has been hacked." He added, "Come on, it's over. Forget dinner. I'm ready for some Mississippi gumbo."

Jeff did not consider himself a well-balanced person. Neither did anyone else. He was obsessive about his work, protective, vindictive, vengeful, and relentless. If at all possible, he personally would figure out who was behind this and hurt them. One line of reasoning said there may not be mass poisonings, after all. First, the deliveries were made so he could find the poison. It might be in the marketplace, but no recalls had been reported. He saw it as an expensive and sick prank with no consequences to the public at large.

The products sent to Carmen at home were of the same vein, except the perpetrators believed she would use them. In fact, they wanted her to use them. That pissed him off. The fire inside him flared.

To his ear and his experience, the guy on the recording with the slight accent was likely from the Middle East. He'd heard enough of their languages to hazard a fair guess the caller might be from that region, or he had spent a lot of early years there. He was definitely not a good ole' boy from Arkansas or the Louisiana Bayou. Therefore, if the Middle East were his place of origin and he wanted to play the mycotoxin game, he could have been affiliated with the Ma-

Hood's who engineered the poisoned newspaper ink fiasco—perhaps a stray man who slipped through the cracks of Interpol, CIA, FBI, Homeland Security, and bounty hunters. The data base of each of the agencies is so large it would be foolish of them not to share information and work together to catch the really bad ones.

What to do? There were too many moving parts for one person to be involved. If his home computer were hacked, then an expert might be able to find a clue as to who did it. If that were the case, the bad guys must have thought they hit the jackpot when they discovered Carmen's standing order for the cosmetics. So they purchased their own items, added the poisons, and shipped them earlier than she would expect in the same box they came in. When she got the regular shipment a week or ten days later, she would either keep it or return it. In any case, there was a strong likelihood Carmen would lose a good part of her face sooner or later and incur blindness when she used the eye shadow.

Thinking it through, he reasoned that if his computer were hacked, he didn't notice any of the telltale signs such as sudden slowing, pop-ups, programs not connecting properly, sluggish cursor, and another half-dozen indicators. But what did he know? He needed a game plan. Involving what, exactly? Set a trap? Surely the bad guy must be watching closely to see the fruits of his labor.

Jeff thought about it until the next day when he called Steven Chatfield in India and discussed the situation with him, because Steven had earlier declared he wanted to be all in. In fact, the retired executive's avocation was helping people through difficult times. What's the point of having money and connections if you can't use them to do good?

Steven listened attentively when Jeff went through the details of what had happened, beginning with the delivery of the box to their home. He told Jeff to give him a few days to set it up, which Jeff did. Then the pair launched the plan.

As per plan, Jeff emailed Steven from the home computer.

Dear Steven: As I told you on the phone, we haven't received any more bad products at work, but I'm afraid my reputation will be ruined if this keeps up. To make matters worse, since I last spoke with you, Carmen has somehow gotten a terrible rash on her face and her eyes burn. She refuses to leave the house and I can't blame her. The rash gets worse daily. The doctors I speak with ask endless questions, but they don't give answers. Do you have any suggestions? I'm desperate.

Thanks, Jeff.

Dear Jeff: As a matter of fact, I can recommend a terrific product. It's so new it's not yet in the pharmacies, but you can order it online. It's called Face Clear by C.K. Pharmaceuticals (www. ckpharmaceuticals.com). It's an excellent anti-inflammatory and it's selling out fast, mainly by word of mouth, so I suggest you get right on it. Expect a delay in fulfilling your order because of their backlog, so maybe you can put a rush on it.

Regards, Steven

While Jeff set the time-delay trap, Carmen thoroughly enjoyed her days off, staying out of sight, working out in the exercise room, catching up on reading, and waiting. At least they had a plan and were taking the offensive.

Only two people contacted the fake corporation to order the fake product: Jeff and one other person. In Jeff's case, he had no plans to poison the fake item.

Monitoring the situation, the FBI quickly tracked the owner of the email and arrested three men on terrorism charges, all Saudi nationals, still reeling from the collapse of their plot to destroy the infrastructure of the United States through the use of poison in their cosmetics. To Jeff's frustration, he never got the chance to punish the criminals in the way his imagination envisioned.

Dear Steven: I must say you have exceeded yourself. If you read the papers, you'd have seen the little manufacturing plant these guys had in their basement. From what I'm told, they believed I would be looking for aflatoxin like the first time, so they hired a microbiologist/chemist who went with another mycotoxin like Roridin A to throw us off. Their rented farmhouse facility wasn't close to being big enough to produce poison on a national scale, but served their purposes of making me chase my tail. The millions they had in the bank got confiscated and another half-dozen of their associates were arrested here and in Saudi Arabia. Doubtless, there's more like them out there.

As you probably know, Emily and Kaufman communicate almost daily. He's offered her a job when she graduates in a couple of months and she's accepted. We'll miss her, dearly.

The next time I find some old mold on your property, I'll name it after you. Thank you so much for your kind assistance.

Say hello to Grace and Henry.

Warmest, Jeff

Dear Jeff: You've already returned the favor in spades. We believe the orange life form you gave us has great potential to cure or assist in the curing of many diseases. (I should claim the rights to it because you found it on our property!) In addition, my people tell me it may have action on the telomeres. This would be huge. In fact, it's what we've been looking for and we've shifted another six of our scientists over to 'Orange Department' as we named it, with Kaufman at the helm. (From what I hear, he is anxiously awaiting Emily's arrival.)

Drop by next time you're passing through Bimli.

Regards from Grace and Henry.

Steven

When Jeff read the email, he thought, *Whoa! Telomeres are DNA-protein complexes at the end of each chromosome and the amino acid phenylalanine is a big part of the complex. Telomeres shorten upon aging, which means that in the tiniest trace amounts of our orange toxin, it might slow the aging process.*

What was it he used to tell his students? *Welcome to the world of the fungi and the molds. They can poison you to death. They can make you sneeze or bring down a building. They can cure whatever ails you or get you burned at the stake. They make bread and alcohol and at the same time, destroy billions of dollars of crops each year. Do not underestimate them.*

Chapter 4

SHIPBOARD

ONE

The temperature read in the low 70s, fairly average for this time of the year in San Diego, with an off-ocean breeze coming in from the south-south west at 7 mph. Jeff and Carmen stood on the bank holding hands, looking at the monster in front of them that bragged nine decks above the water line with another three below. Based on displacement, the gross weight pushed 200,000 tons. In terms of cubic feet, the figure of 24 million would be accurate. Not as big as they got, but close enough.

This particular ship bragged over 300 cooks. The couple only needed to meet up with one, the executive chef, to be honored as his designated guests for the voyage.

At 10:00 am, and personally escorted by a ship's mate, the couple stood at the head of one of the lines of some 6000 guests. The gangway was a short connection from shore to ship. In some ports, a telescopic gangway originated from the ship to stretch 50 feet or more to reach the land.

Upon entering the ship, the entrants displayed their passes and passports, were surveyed by wand, and placed their luggage on a moving belt to be screened. They passed through an x-ray device similar to those used in airports, and finally could look about them at the vast entry area that exceeded the size of those found in many large hotels. Security and other ship personnel were strategically situated.

While thousands of entering guests efficiently processed at the reception desk, the mate assigned to the couple, led them to an elevator that would take them to the very top to a large luxury cabin at the front of the ship, considered prime real estate. From there they could have an excellent view of the ocean and any upcoming ports of call. This was opposed to the least expensive interior cubicles enclosed by four walls with no views, which comprised the highest percentage of accommodations.

Each cabin had about the same interior size, but exterior suites boasted a balcony with chairs and a railing. Almost all, however, had the same amenities, including TV, vanity, shower, commode, blow-dryer, pull-out desk, and two beds, in most cases. In the unit assigned to Jeff and

Carmen, a sofa occupied one wall. On one of the beds, two swans made of towels faced each other with their heads touching. Supposedly, a dozen figures could be created with the two towels. The exception to the room size was the crews' cabins, one-third the size of theirs, with bunk beds.

At that moment, a pleasant young woman introduced herself as Jenny, the cabin steward for the floor. She would be straightening up and changing sheets daily, unless she found a "Do Not Disturb" sign on the door. She would be pleased to provide them with whatever they required. Carmen requested a bottle of Chardonnay on ice and the smiling cabin steward departed.

The couple unpacked the few belongings needed for the lengthy 16-day voyage, and, armed with maps and guides, left their suite to explore the floating city--complete in all regards; not which were all good, they would soon discover.

Pierre LaMonde served as the Executive Chef. A year earlier, his wife had called Jeff from Oklahoma City, where their relatives also lived. A pipe had broken in a bathroom and although a plumber had stopped the flow, a remediation company told her it would be some time before they got to the home because the passage of a recent bad storm was keeping all remediation companies busy. By the time anyone did arrive, the room smelled musty. The wife called Jeff to conduct his tests and to advise the remediation company on how he wanted procedures to be conducted; no ifs, ands, or buts.

While at the house, the wife was preparing guacamole in the kitchen with their eight-year-old daughter, who put the pit in her mouth to suck off the remaining avocado. The mother didn't see it and asked her a question. When the daughter tried to speak, she swallowed the pit and it lodged in her throat. The mother tried slapping her on the back, but the pit remained stuck. Jeff heard the commotion and grabbed the girl from behind beneath her arms with his fists in the sternum area and yanked upward a couple of times to dislodge the pit.

Several days later Jeff received a call from LaMonde insisting that he and another person of his choice be his guest on a cruise, all expenses paid. After months of badgering from Carmen, Jeff relented and informed LaMonde they would be happy to take him up on his offer.

They had both been to San Diego before and could not help but noticing the cruise ships. They had chatted about going aboard one, but never imagined they would be wined and dined by what was arguably—excluding the captain and the engineering staff—the second-most important person on the vessel.

The company had assigned LaMonde to work

this trip at this time, as opposed to the Caribbean tour, or even the world tour, although any cruise Jeff and Carmen chose would be fine with him. If they chose this one, he would personally meet them the morning following the boarding, once things settled down. Now the first day belonged to them alone for exploration.

On the balcony outside their room, Carmen stood at the glass enclosed patio with the railing some four feet in height. She opened out the schematic of the vessel to review. Reading the legend, she said, excitedly, "Where do we start, honey? Let's see, food 24-hours a day, theaters, magic shows, casinos, auctions, libraries, gyms, a full-size basketball court, a rock-climbing wall, 15 swimming pools, 30 places to eat, a 1000 seat auditorium, salons, jewelry stores . . . it's an entire floating city. It even has a helipad and a park. In addition to the guests, there's a crew of over 2300. I mean, how can anybody not like this?"

Jeff laughed at Carmen's enthusiasm. "You sound like a salesperson for the cruise line. I know several people who didn't enjoy their trip. Their rooms were small and cramped, the hallways narrow, the noise of all the activities was annoying, or they got seasick, and people were present in mass everywhere they went. It is not a trip for the claustrophobic."

Carmen folded the schematic and put it in her purse. Grabbing Jeff's arm, she said, "Fine.

Let them find fault and don't you start pouring cold water on our vacation before we even start. We're going to have a good time. I'm ready to play tourist."

Three hours later the ship left port and began the travel north toward Ketchikan, Alaska, traveling at a speed of approximately 22 knots or 25 mph. First stop, Seattle, over two days away. Plans called for them to disembark for sightseeing mid-morning of the third day and to return by evening to continue onward to the north. The entire journey would be unusual in that the cruise would not only take them to Alaskan ports, but would return down, bypassing San Diego with Puerto Vallarta, Mexico, and Cabo San Lucas at the tip of the Gulf of California, on the list of stops before returning to home base. The entire journey was scheduled for a full 16 days. A long journey.

The following morning at 7:30, the pair found the reserved table at a restaurant designated by LaMonde and began eating their breakfasts of fruit, yogurt and coffee, deciding to save their big appetites for later. The selections had not been easy in this one room already serving customers in an obscenely overcrowded buffet. With six servers behind the buffet bar, virtually every taste was catered to from sea foods, dairy, meat lover's paradise, starch lovers paradise, cereals of every ilk, and fruit salads.

They made an interesting-appearing couple. Jeff was well-tanned from outdoor jogging. He wore loose-fitting white pants and sneakers with a blue polo shirt, while Carmen wore similar garb with one of her Indian print blouses. Indeed, they had drawn eyes the afternoon and evening before when Jeff's face and Carmen's beauty stood out. Many recognized him because his picture had been in many newspapers and television broadcasts.

Not long before, Jeff had unmasked the great terrorist plot and the government had confiscated billions in assets. At the time, Carmen had received several requests for interviews which included requests to appear on the cover of various fashion magazines. She declined the offers. She did not like to show off her beauty, which didn't stop the publication of their pictures captured by photographers hidden behind trees.

Pierre LaMonde stood about five inches shorter than Jeff's 5'-11". He wore all white and had left his white chef's hat behind. According to his wife, she had met him shortly after she had won the Miss Lebanon contest. At that time, the French-born Pierre grew up in Lebanon and aspired to greatness as a cook, so they move to France where he excelled at culinary school. He became a 5-Star-rated head chef and after a dozen years, ran across an ad from the cruise lines. They needed executive chefs.

LaMonde sent in his résumé and got hired immediately. That was years ago. He spoke English, French, Arabic, and Spanish, and had stories galore. That is, if one were patient enough to put up with the garrulous man. Reportedly, he could regale one with the latest cruise-ship happenings and hear-say, including ribald stories about crew members.

When he appeared at their table, Jeff stood to shake his hand. LaMonde shifted his eyes to Carmen, who remained seated, appraised her instantly, and asked in Spanish if she spoke Spanish. When she replied in the affirmative, LaMonde took a seat at the table and the two conversed for several minutes with Jeff enjoying the exchange.

Jeff and Carmen frequently spoke Spanish at home and he followed the exchange when LaMonde asked her, "Do you know the difference between a shark and cruise ship passenger?"

Puzzled at the question, she smiled slightly, shaking her head no. Jeff had heard the joke, and waited in amusement for the punch line.

LaMonde said, "One constantly searches various waters for food, never satisfied, surveys the food for some time, or attacks instantly to eat beyond fullness. The other is a fish."

Jeff grinned as Carmen burst out in laughter.

The chef added, "That's why they only eat a single meal a day."

She broke out anew in laughter.

Returning to English, Carmen said, "You must have a lot of stories."

"Oh, one or two more, perhaps," laughed La-Monde. "Some people prefer a ship to a retirement home for a lot of reasons."

Jeff didn't like the glint in Carmen's eye and quickly changed the subject. "Depending on your time, could you point out the highlights for us and what to look for on the cruise?"

Jeff saw LaMonde as a treasure trove of information and wanted to probe the depths of the man's knowledge while he had the chance. He asked, "Pierre, this beautiful ship can't last forever. What will happen to it someday?"

LaMonde grinned. "Ah, yes, there is that. Hundreds of ships die each year, many are smaller older freighters, others are cruise ships of different sizes that can be retrofitted and turned into hotels. But most end up on the shores of Turkey, India, Pakistan, or Bangladesh, for salvage or to rot away offshore. It is a sad ending."

"India, huh? I know a little about that country. What coast, east or west?" Jeff asked. He wanted to know more.

"Just up the coast from Mumbai is the world's largest ship graveyard," LaMonde answered. "Dismantling ships may be the world's most dangerous job, aside from working with explosives, of course."

For some unexplained reason, Jeff found a fascination with the subject. He'd never thought about it until this point in time and now he couldn't learn enough. Perhaps he might find out more about it someday.

LaMonde started to say something else, but caught himself.

Jeff knew the charismatic chef would treat them to a memorable vacation. How memorable, he had no idea. Again, LaMonde began to speak, then caught himself a second time.

Jeff said, "All right, Pierre, out with it. What's on your mind?"

"I'm a little embarrassed to ask this, but I need your help with something," the chef said, sheepishly.

Jeff quickly glanced at Carmen, who raised her eyebrows in a "Here we go," gesture.

"Come on, we're all friends here," Jeff replied. He immediately regretted the use of that sentence. It reminded him of time share salespersons whose sole purpose was to con people into upgrading what they already owned, never to be sold by them again.

"Yes, please, Pierre. Tell us. We'll do what we can to help," Carmen added. She liked this man as a person. He gave off good honest vibes, something not often run across in today's world, as least in her view.

"It's a problem," said LaMonde.

"We all have problems," Jeff returned.

"It's a medical problem," LaMonde said.

"You have a medical staff," Carmen stated.

"It's not about me. Yes, we have two doctors and three nurses, but there are some things the cruise ship companies would rather keep quiet," LaMonde continued.

"Welcome to the real world. Pierre, do we play word games or will you please get to the point," Jeff said, glancing around to ensure no others in the crowded restaurant were within listening distance. He began to wonder if LaMonde was preparing to ask for a loan or perhaps get involved them in some unsavory scheme of his.

"Are you familiar with norovirus?" the chef asked.

Glancing at Jeff, Carmen answered, "Of course. It's a big issue on cruise ships. Diarrhea and vomiting. Spread through food and water, like cholera."

"Yes. We've had it, but what's going on now is not through normal . . . he spoke to Carmen in Spanish. She replied, "Distribution."

"Yes, distribution," LaMonde, said. "It's not a big enough problem for the media to take the story and the company isn't reporting it, but it's costing them a fortune with quiet payoffs to settle lawsuits and some people are pointing a finger at me."

Jeff shrugged. "I'm sure there are always going to be lawsuits for a variety of reasons, what with thousands of people per ship per cruise. Besides, some claims may be valid."

Carmen added, "It's no secret that norovirus hit the industry hard. I can't imagine having to scrub down an entire vessel. How many are there on the ocean these days?"

"A little over 300 of these ships, each making several trips a year serving millions," LaMonde replied. "Not all the ships were affected, but I know this particular one got hit hard. And when Covid appeared, most ships had to shut down and were forced to donate their food to keep it from wasting. We're talking some serious donations here. They gave it to countries hit by natural disasters and to other relief agencies. But, again, noro or Covid is not our problem."

"Go ahead," Jeff encouraged.

Taking a breath, LaMonde rubbed a palm over his eyes before replying, "This ship, The Princess Fairie, has five times the complaints of any of the others and almost all of the complaints are different than what the other ships are reporting."

"How do you know that?" Jeff asked,

"Come on, doctor, I've been, how do you say, around the block a few times. This ain't my first rodeo."

At that, Carmen began to laugh, followed by Jeff, and then LaMonde. The man was truly a curiosity, conversational in at least four languages and who understood many others, couldn't come up with certain words, but could come up with idioms specific to a particular sect or lifestyle.

The ice had broken. LaMonde appeared to read Jeff's mind when he said "What we have is very different from norovirus. If it were noro, we'd be in deep trouble and have to report it. And you don't lie about that kind of thing."

"How do you know it's not something in the food? Sorry, had to ask," Carmen said.

"I'm glad you asked," replied LaMonde. "Because I've been in the business some 30 years and I know food problems when I see them. We have over 30 kitchens aboard ship. My duties are basically managerial. I work 12-hour days to oversee cleanliness of the kitchens that must conform to international standards. In our case, the symptoms don't match anything caused by food issues that I know of."

"Which are?" asked Carmen

"Coughing, inflamed sinus cavities, watering eyes, intermittent difficulty in breathing," answered the chef.

"Tell you what, Pierre. We've got hours together, so why don't you give us the tour and if we have any questions, we'll ask," Jeff offered.

"Deal," LaMonde said, pleased to change the subject. He began to stand, thought for an instant, then regained his seat. "There's more," he said, obviously embarrassed again about what he wanted to say.

"Get it out, Pierre," Jeff suggested, gently, as one friend to another.

LaMonde began, "Cruise ships deal with the same problems as everybody else in the world. Drugs. They come onboard with the initial food supplies. They could be anywhere. They get distributed among the passengers and we're at a loss as to how this thing operates."

Jeff asked, "Why kind of supplies come onboard this ship when you get ready to sail?"

LaMonde pulled out a piece of paper from his pocket and unfolded it, placing it in front of the couple. Carmen picked it up and read, "6000 gallons of soda, 20,000 pounds of chicken, 140,000 eggs, one ton of coffee, 30,000 meals a day and, well, you get the idea. That's for one week. Throw in beef, fish, fruits and vegetables, desserts, alcohol, and so forth And think about all the dishes that have to get washed. When all the food gets loaded, it gets sent to different freezers and kitchens for prep work."

"And somewhere in that mess the drugs are coming in," Carmen said. "Pierre, you have a security force for that."

"True," replied the chef. "Unfortunately, I'm not sure I trust them all, but I do trust you two."

"My guess is that cocaine is the drug of choice," Jeff offered.

"Correct. That and meth and opioids. Nothing too crazy like LSD or magic mushrooms. This is a world-wide network of dealers that supply the cruise lines with both old and new staff who move product to the on-board customers. They rake in tens of millions a week world-wide. Authorities think it's tied to food, which comes back to me. The company needs a fall guy, but getting rid of me won't solve the problem."

"So we're looking at the movers, not the suppliers," Jeff summarized.

"Yes, that's the way I see it," LaMonde answered, contritely.

"If that's the case, I'll need more information from you," Jeff stated. He thought an instant and said, "Wait a minute. Doesn't the head steward get involved in food preparation? Why pick on you?"

LaMonde answered, "There's some crossover in that we're both charged with maintaining cleanliness and sanitary conditions of the kitchens, all the ship's cleanliness in general. I have to ensure that proper nutrition is presented in what we serve. In other words, I'm closest to the food preparation itself, he's closer to the ordering."

"By ship cleanliness, does that include the cabins, too?" asked Carmen.

"Yes. Those would be the cabin stewards," replied LaMonde.

Suddenly standing, LaMonde changed faces from a concerned citizen to that of a gracious host, indicating the conversation had ended. Carmen slipped her arm into his, as though they were a couple, and permitted their host to be his jovial self.

Over the remainder of the morning, LaMonde gave the couple a grand tour. On the roof he took them poolside where snacks and drinks were served ranging from cheese nachos, chicken wings, hot dogs, hamburgers and even full meals in a full service restaurant. He took them through a park that bragged thousands of plants and trees from around the world, and to a children's playground and amusement park.

From there, LaMonde took his guests to the bridge, having previously obtained permission to do so. Climbing a dozen stairs, they reached a door and were seen by one of the crew members. He allowed them to enter the spacious area at the front of the ship, aghast at its immensity. Before them on three sides were wrap-around windows spanning a full 100 feet across in a room some 30 feet in depth. Indeed, the room was wider than the ship itself. Even the sides of the ship could be seen through a glass flooring and windows looking out to the rear.

Four people were present in the room and LaMonde introduced them as Staff Captain Christine Compton, assistant to the Captain and second in command; the Quartermaster, who is capable of driving the ship when it comes into or leaves the port and is in charge of discipline along with food and water supplies and assists, and the 1st and 2nd Officers in charge of navigation.

Christine Compton was a tall woman who appeared to be about 50, stately and shapely, wearing a white dress uniform. Her brunette hair hung freely at shoulder length flipped at the bottom. Her brown eyes sparkled with intelligence and she smiled broadly upon meeting Jeff and Carmen. LaMonde had explained that she'd had over a quarter century of shipping experience.

"Dr. Shenero, I finally get you meet you," Compton said.

Jeff canted his head. "How so?" he asked.

"My husband works for the CDC and is responsible for approving several of your grant applications. Breakthrough work, I believe he called it. He mentioned your name on a number of occasions," she replied.

Turning to Carmen she said, "And this is your . . ."

"Girlfriend," Carmen said. She thought quickly, not wanting it to sound as though Jeff were taking his secretary on a little flirtatious adventure, "and longtime business partner." Keep it simple.

Jeff looked around him, ignoring the banter. "How does this thing steer?" he inquired.

"It's pretty much electronic and automated, except for when we pull into and leave port," Compton answered. "Here in the bridge, we handle lookout to avoid collisions, we have two types of radar, control the speed and direction though a variety of navigational instruments, we monitor weather, and there is an echo sounder for depth plus and communication equipment for outside and inside the ship. We have a telegraph to the engine room with a printout and

GPS for exact positioning down to 100 meters."

Compton pointed to a room at the back of the bridge. "A lot of this is duplicated in the Control Room back there where we monitor every aspect of our machinery."

Jeff looked behind him into the room where he could see wrap-around TV screens, wiring diagrams and active flow charts. Three other men were present noting readings on numerous gauges.

From what I understand, you'll meet our captain, Sven Larsson, when you have dinner tonight at his table. He works one of the shifts here, of course."

Captain's table, no less. Jeff looked over at LaMonde, who merely grinned.

The couple walked from side-to-side looking out the windows and the various navigational and weather screens.

"Shall we?" LaMonde suggested, hinting it was time to leave.

"Where to next, Pierre," Carmen chirped, putting her arm into his for the second time. He didn't seem to mind and replied, "Level 5. We'll take the inside stairs."

They bid the crew goodbye and left the room through an internal door down another dozen stairs, shallow enough to minimize missteps, to the upper deck.

On the way, Jeff asked, "Pierre, isn't it unusual for a woman to be of such a high rank as

Mrs. Compton. I should think shipping is man's domain."

"You're right. It's extremely rare," responded the chef.

Carmen asked, "Weren't women considered bad luck on a ship at one time?"

LaMonde laughed. "They still are. Times are changing, though. As far as Christine, her parents worked in the industry as cooks and maids. No officers. After she got her college degree, she joined the lines and worked her way up. She did everything from working as a cabin steward to waiting tables. When she wasn't working, she studied everything she could about the industry and took classes during shore leave. The rest is history."

Minutes later, LaMonde led the couple through the various levels, using the common stairways, finally stopping at the security office on Level 5. He knocked on the door and opened it.

At a bank of computer monitors sat a crew-cut man whom LaMonde had told them about on the walk down. John McKenzie was a former naval officer, who headed the security team. He served as Control Officer who oversaw everything from boarding, cargo and passenger safety, threats to the ship, drunks, and friendly disputes. Another man and a woman in the room ignored their entry and continued to watch wall monitors mounted one above the other.

McKenzie, nearing 60, stood tall, fit, and dressed in white with the word SECURITY emblazoned across the back, similar those present during the boarding process. His disposition was warm and friendly to off-set a craggy face. "Well, the famous Dr. Shenero, and you must be Carmen. Pierre told me about both of you," he said in greeting, extending his hand.

Carmen glared at the chef in mock disapproval. "Is that right. I never would have guessed."

LaMonde actually blushed slightly, then turned his attention back to the security chief, who said, "This ship has over 1200 ceiling-mounted cameras in virtually every hall way, and especially in the common areas. We store all the data in the cloud for 60 days in case we need to recall something. Most of our staff consists of former law enforcement personnel who are hired, nor only for their experience, but for their outgoing personalities. We like to make friends. "

Carmen began, "Your office . . . I mean we walked in."

McKenzie said, "We don't have anything to hide here and occasionally we will permit entry to the public. For example, the same afternoon when we left San Diego, a woman said she was writing a book on ship security and took photos. She had a serious camera."

"We won't keep you, John. I'm certain our tour guide has plans for us," Jeff said.

"You'll probably see me when you return from your tours," McKenzie said. The three shook hands and departed the office.

"If you think John was friendly, wait until you meet Will Bishop, our Cruise Director. This man is joviality personified. He and his crew are responsible for all the ship's activities and announcements. Although he gets a lot of complaints about the constant flow of announcements, they're useful."

From Level 5, the three took broad stairway to level 2 where LaMonde found Bishop in attendance with three others, two women and a man, making changes to a white board. A slightly overweight fleshy-faced man with short brown hair and of average height turned to them as they entered the open office. He looked to be in his late teens, but LaMonde said he was thirty-eight. With a beaming smile, Bishop walked toward them with hand outstretched. "Dr. and Mrs. Shenero. Welcome to my home," said the beaming man.

Carmen did not correct him in thinking they were married. What was the point?

The jovial Bishop showed them the charts listing the coming activities at the wide variety of venues while keeping an eye on a wall clock. Of the numerous monitors present, four of them showed the exterior of the ship in four directions, enabling Bishop or his assistants, to announce weather, or other sights worth looking at. At one point he excused himself, sat at a microphone, turned on the power, and said spoke into it: "Ladies and Gentlemen, we would like you to be aware the Cirque de Soleil will be performing in our main movie theater this evening at 8:00 pm, as explained in your show guide. You may purchase tickets online or through our various venders located in the promenades." He repeated the message and returned to his guests spreading his hands outward as if to say, "That's how it works."

LaMonde concluded the visits by taking the couple through the largest of the food preparation areas on the same level where a score of white-coated glove-wearing specialists placed food on rows of plates numbering in the scores.

Carmen appeared openly delighted at every sight, as though she had come from a village in a third world county to enter an American supermarket. Jeff also felt delight, but didn't outwardly show it, brooding over the two onboard problems LaMonde had described. He had always chastised himself for not letting go of a problem so he could actually enjoy life to its fullest. Now he had two problems to solve and they were somebody else's.

By noon, the chef excused himself to attend to his duties with the words, "Call me anytime day or night and I will be at your service."

The couple went to their room to retrieve some reading materials and returned to the roof to eat a light lunch. They found a pair of shaded lounge chairs outside the forest which served to block the breeze from the moving ship. This early in the trip, few wandered the roof area, not yet having discovered its many features. After some time reading and occasionally checking her watch, Carmen said, "Honey, on our tour I saw that one of the small theaters is showing old movies. Today's feature is *The Towering Inferno.* I've never seen it and I really want to. Let's go. It starts in a few minutes. "

Jeff had seen the movie starring Paul Newman, Steve McQueen, O.J. Simpson and many other noteworthy performers. The 1974 thriller featured a fire chief charged with the mission of putting out an upper-level fire in a skyscraper that resulted in many deaths.

Jeff believed in omens. He considered their watching this movie at this time to be one. He didn't know what the omen meant, only that it wasn't on the plus side. With him as the fire chief and the ship as the skyscraper, LaMonde had already enlisted him to, at least, assist in putting out two fires--drugs and illness, fires that had already begun. This gave him a sinking feeling. In his experience, the worst thing about a bad omen is that nothing can be done to prevent events from unfolding.

At 8:00 pm, the pair, freshly showered and changed, sat dining at the Captain's Table along with Sven Larsson, Captain/Master, enjoying their meal served on fine china and drinks in crystal glasses, eating lobster tail, filet mignon, prime rib, and drinking expensive wines.

Sven Larsson looked his name. Tall, blond, blue-eyed and Norwegian, he had been hired away from Norwegian lines and had been with the new company five years. He learned from LaMonde that Carmen had a degree in medicine, albeit trained in Mexico and within a hair's breadth of getting her U.S. certification (until she met Jeff). Combining that with Jeff's reputation, coupled with the possibility of a shipboard health-related scandal, he willingly acceded to LaMonde's request that they join his table. His background check on the man found that he had top secret security clearance with both the U.S. Government and Interpol. Not a bad man with whom to share knowledge, or to learn from.

Jeff and Carmen tried to digest all they had learned from LaMonde, but were unable to discuss it under the circumstances with several others present. Among them sat a European actress; another, a known writer of mystery novels; and a state senator with his wife.

The conversation at the table proved to be open and friendly with each person contributing equally. The discussion of politics was forbidden in order not to sour the mood. Instead, each person told of previous travel adventures along with curious people they had encountered during those travels.

At last, happy and tired after a long day, the couple retired to their cabin, each in their own bed and lay quietly for several moments until Carmen offered, "It can't be the food that's causing those symptoms. They're respiratory in nature."

"Nope. Why anybody would blame him is beyond me," Jeff replied. "I think he's a little paranoid." Her opening statement made him feel good about himself in that he wasn't alone in thinking about LaMonde's, rather, the ship's problems.

"He has a right to be. You got any ideas yet?" she asked.

"Maybe," he answered.

"I'd sure like to get my hands on the medical records," she added.

"Yep, but no can do."

"Why not?" she asked.

"Good question," Jeff said. "Maybe can do. The captain did fawn over you."

"Your reputation didn't hurt, either. Let's see what tomorrow brings," she offered.

"Sweet dreams," Jeff said, and turned off the light. In an instant he turned them on again, picked up the room phone and called a number LaMonde had given them. He spoke for a moment, listened, hung up, turned off the light, and rolled over to fall asleep.

TWO

Jeff tried to reason out what LaMonde had told him about the drug problem. The issue wasn't supply or demand. Both were present in abundance. It wasn't getting the product to the customer. How it got to the customer became the issue. He doubted if anybody did the old hand-shake switcheroo between drugs vs. bills any-more because of concerns for disease transmis-sion. To him, the basic question boiled down to this: If the customer knew coke was available, simply because it's always available just about anywhere, how does the seller let the customer know? So far, authorities had concentrated their efforts on trying to discover the source of the supply chain. Did the bad guys hide the prod-ucts in hollowed out eggs, or in chicken parts, or any one of a hundred imaginative ways to hide anything? Stop the source to stop the problem. Needle in a haystack. Keep looking.

Leaving for a late breakfast the next morn-ing, Jeff followed Carmen out the door, when the room phone rang. He picked it up and lis-tened, then replaced the receiver.

"Meeting's set with the captain at 9:00. He'll have the medical records with him," he reported. "We'll meet him in his suite."

Prior to the meeting, Jeff worked out in a kick boxing class that overlooked one of the sur-face swimming pools and the ocean beyond. As the ship cut through increasingly choppy waves, he paused in his efforts to watch the water in the pool slosh from one end to the other, shooting some 20 feet into the air before the slope of the surrounding deck drained it back into the pool, where it sloshed against the other wall. Not a good day to do laps.

One of the ship's two medical doctors stood next to the captain when Larsson greeted his guests at the knock.

Earlier, Larsson had opened the drapes to reveal an outer deck and the brightness of the day flooding the room, as the ship headed due north. In the distance, at the horizon, the sky appeared to darken denoting a squall in progress, presently pounding Seattle with a summer storm. Passengers were advised to limit their walking and take Dramamine, if necessary, and to go to the center of the ship where the rise and fall of the vessel would be less. The ship would soon be entering rougher waters. One of the seemingly endless stream of announcements advised passengers to bring along their umbrellas once they disembarked.

Before the doctor lay a stack of ten manila folders he had placed on a small table. The three took a seat while Larsson stood, looking on as the doctor began to page through each of the files that contained pictures, names, addresses, medical histories, complaints, interview records and notes regarding payouts. When he had completed the first file and set it aside, Jeff said, "Excuse me, but can we do that again? I'd like to use my cell to photograph each page of each file."

The doctor looked up at the tall captain who gave the briefest of nods downward. After all, according to his extensive research on the man, this Shenero character could do whatever he wanted, as long as it didn't involve steering the vessel.

"Yes, of course, but I can get you copies of these," the doctor offered.

"Photos will be fine," Jeff retorted. He had his own plan.

When the doctor finished, Carmen asked, "Did they have any common area of housing?"

"None at all," the doctor answered. "That was one of the first things we looked at. Typically, the first rooms to go are the luxury suites and the balconies. The last are the cheaper seats, the interior cabins. These people were in every area of the ship, top, bottom, middle, front, and rear. The only common thing is they all visited the gym."

Carmen asked, "I suppose you sanitized it."

The doctor answered as though it were a ridiculous question. "Yes, of course."

"I'd like to check your cleaning procedures, if you don't mind," she requested.

"I'll get you in touch with the head of our cleaning crew," offered the doctor, reluctantly, not normally given to flagrant requests by outsiders.

"How much do you normally pay on complaints such as these?" Jeff asked, looking up at Larsson.

The captain said, "Worldwide, it depends on the country that owns the ship." Pointing to the stack of folders, he added, "In these instances, it's the equivalent of 50-100 thousand dollars. One of them went for a quarter million. The couple had a good attorney. But you have to understand this goes on all the time; payouts, I mean. This ship nets two million dollars a week on items sold like souvenirs, jewelry and clothing, along with auctions, certain performances, contests, gambling, special classes, drinks at dinner, room moves, and a score of extras. We can't afford not to have these people stay quiet, especially when they have a legitimate complaint."

Late the following afternoon, the ship pulled into the Port of Seattle to spend the night. Disembarkation would occur by 8:00 am the next morning with boarding at 5:00 pm, or earlier, if a customer had seen enough.

Once the rain had ceased, Jeff and Carmen made their way down the elevator to the I-95 corridor, the main corridor of any cruise ship, designated Level 1 on this ship, and the only one where a person could see from one end of the vessel to another. The crew's quarters were situated on Level A, one level below the I-95 corridor. The level included their own exercise facilities, three restaurants to call their own, numerous prep kitchens, and storage for extra luggage. After the lengthy walk, the pair reached the gangway. The tide had come in, so they walked downward to reach the land. In the afternoon, the situation would be reversed.

"Space Needle first," Carmen declared, making their way through a sea of bodies all headed for their designated locations, although it was not unusual for hundreds of people to stay aboard a vessel during a stop for a variety of reasons.

"Seafood for lunch," Jeff responded. "There's a place I read about online we must try." He fully expected prices to be jacked up, as is normally the case when tourist ships rolled in, especially when two others were already docked ahead of them and another on the horizon.

Boarding a bus that had signage reading SPACE NEEDLE, the pair relaxed during the short drive to their destination. Jeff wanted to walk through the Science Fiction and Fantasy Museum Hall of Fame, which was part of the Museum of Pop Culture located adjacent to the Needle. Carmen had no interest in science fiction, whatsoever. Jeff needed the visit. He wanted to get himself thinking outside the box and what better way to do it than to leave the planet entirely, an accusation commonly used to describe Jeff's character in general.

On the bus ride, Jeff pulled out his phone. Carmen expressed her annoyance. "Why are you playing with that? You know I hate it when we're out somewhere."

"Texting someone. I won't play with it after this," Jeff retorted, sharply, totally absorbed in the activity and somewhat annoyed at having his concentration broken. Once he had completed the task, a pang of guilt swept over him. Taking hold of Carmen's hand, he said gently, "Sorry, honey, I didn't mean to speak so gruffly." She squeezed his hand in return.

A product of the 1962 World's Fair, the citizens of the city voted to retain the earthquake-proof 605-foot tall Space Needle as a public landmark. It bragged a 360 degree observation deck which could be reached after a four minute elevator ride. The landmark served to attract visitors from around the world.

Bypassing the tourist trinkets, the couple rode the elevator to the observation area to enjoy a spectacular view of the city including the view of their own ship. She led him to a built-in telescope and began to look through it when his cell phone vibrated in his pocket. He nonchalantly strolled to another area where he surreptitiously pulled out the phone, glanced at the text, punched in a few words to send, then quietly returned to her side.

From the Needle complex, the couple traveled to Chilulu Gardens, named after the Dale Chilulu, famed sculpture of enlarged spectacular displays of glass to awe the imagination. This is what Jeff sought-a challenge to the imagination. How each exhibit was carefully packed and crated and the expense involved in shipping the display around the world was open to discussion.

Mindful of the time and after touring the gardens, the pair took a bus ride to Pike Place Market, and finally relaxed for a seafood lunch seated outside on a wharf. The choppy waves were blocked by the rise and fall of the rocking ships in the harbor to provide the sound of gentle wash against the pylons and the shore. Mount Rainier jutted its 14,000 foot snow-capped peak 60 miles to the north.

On the table in front of them stood three pails: One filled with lobster tails and crab legs, another with bottles of beer in ice, and a third for trash. Numerous deconstruction tools lay available for their use.

Looking out over the water, their ship in sight, Carmen wiped a morsel of food from the corner of her mouth with a napkin and asked, "Who was texting you?"

Caught by surprise, Jeff had to smile. With Carmen, honesty is the best policy. "Returning a text," that's all.

"No, that's not all. From whom?" she inquired. For an instant, she thought she might go into the field of dentistry considering all the teeth she had to pull to get Jeff of open up.

Once Jeff told her, she mumbled, "That's what I thought."

Back on track, speaking softly, he chose another subject. "What did you find out from the cleaning crew?"

Carmen answered, frankly. "They were thorough. I don't think either of us could have done a better job. I did take a lot of photos of the gym. Crew members have their own gym, but the complaints came from guests, not from crew members."

"Do you think they might have gotten something similar to Legionnaires disease from the saunas," Jeff asked. "Coughing was one of the symptoms."

"Maybe," she replied, "except that only two of them used a sauna after their workouts. Gastric upset was also a complaint, but that could be from overeating, symptoms of allergy, various infections, medications, psycho-somatic complaints; a lot of things."

"Any common machines they preferred?" he said, continuing with the interrogation.

"None"

"How about the floor mats? I know these people don't have the materials and facilities to pursue the relationship between floor mat-related microbes and humans, but do they sterilize them?

"They're sterilized daily," she responded. "Come on, Jeff, we had to show our Covid vaccination cards when we boarded. They take cleanliness as serious as humanly possible."

"You reviewed their list of medications. Did anything stand out?" he inquired, trying to take all the bits and pieces and see if a picture emerged.

"Nothing in common. What I saw was a fairly normal distribution of doctor-prescribed meds stuff. Some of them never took anything except for aspirin and the usual OTC stuff."

"That's all good news," Jeff concluded, grinning.

"How so?" she asked, with narrowed eyes, wondering how not finding anything can be considered good news.

"It limits our options," he replied.

Carmen had become tired of it all. Damn it, they were on vacation. She looked Jeff in the eye and accused, "Instead of trying to work all the time on this cruise, maybe we can have some fun, too. I feel like I got suckered into playing a bad hand."

"This is fun," he answered, without thinking. Reflecting on his reply, he thought: What was it he'd overheard someone say about him during a gossip session? *Shenero's a high-risk-high-gain person. His mouth gets him into trouble. But you can put your money on him. I mean, he'll stick his neck out there as far as he can and the son of a bitch will bite the man who's holding the sword at his head.*

But Jeff had to share more of his thoughts. "This drug thing has me stymied."

Carmen sighed. "It's not your problem, nor is it mine. Vacationing is the only thing we need to be concerned with."

"What are the ways people can get drugs here? All you'll get from the doc is OTCs, which you can buy in any shop, and if dealers walked up to people and asked them if they wanted to buy, security would know about it in a flash. Therefore, the request has to come from the customer, but there's nobody to ask."

"Unless there is somebody to ask," she began, getting pulled into the quest for knowledge. That had always been one of her characteristics. It's what led her to medical school and what attracted her to Jeff. The man was the definitive searcher, an investigator on steroids. Anything that smelled like a puzzle would pull him in like a bee to a flower, and it would not have to do with microbiology whatsoever.

Jeff recovered immediately and deflected by saying, "Next stop Ketchikan in a couple of days. How about if you pick a performance you like tonight and take me along on a date?" Jeff offered.

"All right, deal. I also get to choose what we do afterward, too," she teased. She had become the dealer.

Jeff agreed. They both needed more intimate time together.

THREE

The review of the photos proved fruitless. To ensure they had covered the bases, they visited the gym itself with no new revelations. To Jeff, that meant more good news because it eliminated another piece. He tried to work a puzzle in reverse: There was the outline of a picture in front of him, but he couldn't see it clearly because there were too many distractions, too many pieces piled on top of it. He needed to remove as many pieces as possible.

To Jeff's delight, the doctor could shed no light on the gambling habits of the complainants and LaMonde could offer nothing of assistance regarding what he knew of their eating habits via interrogation. It wasn't an absolute in either case, but the information helped. Two more pieces gone.

All the cases hinged on symptoms common to asthma and allergy, including headaches and gastric upset resulting in loss of sleep, possibly caused by excessive mucous drainage. These were not uncommon symptoms aboard a new environment, such as ship, with passengers wearing various colognes and perfumes in crowded venues, but deep coughs were a step beyond the common complaints. None were smokers, or at least had no recent record of smoking. Unfortunately, the limited facilities aboard ship obviated the ability to isolate bacteria such as pathogenic staph or strep. Even lung volumes couldn't be ascertained, which might reveal information about bronchiole irritation. Frustrated, both investigators wondered how one can reach a destination while flying blind.

Both were out of ideas and Carmen thankfully gave up the effort and began to enjoy the cruise. For Jeff, he needed to rest his mind, to allow the brain to sort through the trash and reorganize.

Spending more time on deck at the rail and washed by a cold wind, the couple enjoyed watching dolphins cavorting alongside the ship, keeping pace, diving, and jumping, showing off for the throngs lined up along the individual balconies at every level like different colored birds lined up on lines of wires, one above the other.

Ice floes began to appear in the colder waters, carried down from the glaciers melting in the northernmost climes of the planet. In Jeff's view, the Earth was going through one of its normal geological warming periods. Man happens to be here during the change and is taking credit for it. He occasionally wondered if the human race would survive its own ego, or end up like the sponge, a life form that dead-ended at the far tip of the multi-branched evolutionary tree.

Bishop's voice came over the loud speaker explaining that the blue color in the floes was an indication of intense pressure that had been put upon the ice at one time to convert it into a form of water not seen elsewhere. The announcer then asked the audience to look off to the northwest where the occasional streamlined body of a blue whale could be seen spouting, shooting water over thirty feet in height.

Amidst it all, the announcer said, "Will Doctor Jeffrey Shenero please call the central office."

Jeff and Carmen wondered about a possible problem. Might there be an urgent message from the lab at home, an accident perhaps, a tragedy? If so, there was nothing they could do about it at the moment.

Jeff quickly located a red deck-side phone and made the call, spoke briefly, then hung up. "The doctor wants us," he said, feeling both relieved and confused.

"No, he wants you," Carmen replied. "I'm staying here."

The announcement rubbed Carmen the wrong way. It should have requested Doctor and Mrs. Shenero or Doctors Mr. and Mrs. Shenero. Not for the first time she wondered why Jeff hadn't ever asked her to marry him after all they had gone through together and all the love they espoused for one another. They lived together, worked together and breathed the same air. The answer was obvious. Jeff was a coward; she knew it, he knew it, and he knew she knew it, which was a place he didn't want to visit.

That announcement would change their lives, because whether Jeff liked it or not, she would marry him this trip by the ship's captain, come hell or high water. Jeff had no problem getting married once. Never mind his wife left him for a real life, one that didn't get her embarrassed because of her husband's eccentricities and his big mouth. Carmen could be as stubborn and resolute as her partner. So far, that's all he was, a partner. She wondered if she served as a convenient person of interest to Jeff or if he had true love for her. Never mind hot passionate love. She wanted long term commitment.

The infirmary was located on Level 2 with services available 24/7, but these were limited to everyday problems, not surgeries or dental procedures. For those, the patient would have to wait until the ship reached the next port. Typically, non-surgical procedures include emergency cardiovascular care and minor procedures. The medical staff are trained and prepared to deal with influenza and GI issues, such as occurs during a norovirus outbreak.

Jerry Richards had come from New Jersey. A computer engineer in his mid-forties, he stood a little less than six-feet in height and in need of some exercise, but had a clean look about him. Conversational and conservative, Richards opted for an interior lower-priced stateroom. This was his first sea cruise. He began noticing the cough the second day of the voyage. It had worsened and he complained of nasal congestion and difficulty in breathing. Yes, he had been to the gym for a light workout and, no, he had not incurred motion sickness or eaten any food that did not agree with him.

The doctor and Jeff interviewed Richards, taking notes and pictures and creating a file. He said yes and no at the appropriate times, and in the end, confirmed a case similar to the others. His eyes watered, he had intermittent cough with inflammation of the nasal passages. The medical offices could and did screen for drugs. International regulations called for zero tolerance among crew members. They found no issues with Richards' blood after he readily gave consent to have it tested. Once the file had been compiled, Jeff recorded each page. When he reported the meeting to Carmen, she asked, coldly, "What now?" still miffed at being left out of the meeting, but glad she didn't have to be part of an investigation she wanted no part of anymore.

"We get ready to play in the small town of Ketchikan that is snowed in for nine months of the year until the cruise ships hit port. Then sell, sell, sell and shop till you drop," Jeff quipped, sensing her mood and trying to make light of the present circumstances.

Ketchikan is not part of the Alaskan mainland. It belongs to a portion of the state that flows down the western edge of Canada like an amoeba extending a pseudopod in search of food. It was a part of the Inside Passage, as it is called. The city brags a population of little over 8000.

The average high temperature is approximately 50 degrees Fahrenheit and the air is always wet from either snow or rain. Ketchikan sells a lot of jewelry and leather goods when the ships come in, enough so that the citizens can buy sufficient supplies to hole up for another long winter. As the story goes, one annoyed tourist stopped a youth on the street and asked him if it always rained there. The youth replied that he didn't know about *always* because he was only sixteen.

Cafes ran the gamut from Chinese and Mexican dishes, to fish and burgers. Carmen watched Jeff eat an elk burger and down a beer. Then he sat with her as she ate Chinese dishes and drank tea. Afterward, the couple took a short bus ride to watch a lumberjack show where the men, and occasional women, threw axes at targets, chopped logs, and climbed trees, before returning to the ship, hoping the disease had not spread to other vessels. What's bad for one can be bad for them all.

Late that night, the couple sat on their balcony looking out at the moonlight reflected off chucks of blue ice and the sea itself. They sat quietly for several minutes, each wearing a windbreaker and wrapped in a blanket. Over her mood, Carmen said, "I suppose it makes sense if we accept that our subjects all had a rare disorder that got triggered onboard ship."

"True," Jeff agreed. "Ships like these have been around for a long time. Okay, they've gotten larger, but why all of a sudden on this line?"

"And the patients come from all walks of life," added Carmen. "We've got a retired elementary school teacher, an attorney, a young couple on their honeymoon, a door-to-door salesman . . . mostly from different parts of the country."

"Let's talk about Juneau, instead. That's coming up next," Jeff said.

"I'm hungry," Carmen interjected.

"What? Do you know what time it is?" Jeff queried.

"And?" she asked.

An hour later, full of cake and ice cream, the weary couple hit the sack planning to sleep in. Unfortunately, it didn't work out that way.

At 3:00 am, Jeff's cell phone lit up and chimed, indicating a call was coming in through the ship's WiFi system. The name on the screen read Emily Kaufman.

"What is it?" Carmen muttered.

"It's Emily Kaufman?"

"Who?" asked Carmen. "Oh, wait. Remember she got married a couple of months ago and said they had a quiet wedding, but she'd fill us in later and you wished her the best."

"That's right." Jeff mumbled, rubbing his face and texted back that she could call him if she wanted. Computing the time difference, he thought it must be around 6:00 am in Boston.

Within a minute, Emily did call. "Doctor

Shenero, how is your vacation?" she inquired, to break the ice. "I called your office yesterday. They told me you were on a cruise."

Jeff turned on the bed lamp. "Smooth as silk," he replied, ignoring Carmen who had rolled her eyes at his simplistic statement. "Having a great time. How's married life?"

Emily briefly told him about how she and Arnold were meant for each other and then said, "Doctor, we're in the lab confirming results, but I'm certain we have a breakthrough. I mean, it was totally accidental, but I guess that's the nature of breakthroughs, isn't it?"

"This must be serious because you're starting to ramble," Jeff said. He heard Arnold's voice in the background urging her to tell him.

"Yes, yes," she said. "Doctor, it's about the toxin produced by *Jeffrus shenerii*. Well, it does a lot more than we thought it did. You know how when we get a new toxin we test it against anything we can get our hands on, from bacteria, to protozoa, to plants and mice and even sea life. Well, a number of our people have small boats in slips in Boston harbor and one guy brought in a glass jar with barnacles covered with Zebra mussels that he scraped from the bottom of his boat. You know what zebra mussels are, right?"

Jeff scratched his head and saw Carmen propped up on her pillow, her hair looking as though she'd stuck her finger into an electrical socket. "No," he admitted, hoping this conversation was going somewhere fast.

"You don't?" Emily announced. "Zebra mussels are the scourge of the seaways. They grow on anything, rocks, metal, even other life forms like barnacles, such as in our harbor here and in Seattle and the Mississippi, and so forth. They're destroying the natural ecosystems at an incredible rate. The barnacles themselves are dying because they can't get food. The mussels extrude this protein-foot that allows them to stick onto things. Doctor, all we have to do is to come with a way to apply this to patches of zebra mussels and we can save a harbor and a zillion ships. "

Jeff finally grasped what Emily was telling him and asked, "But obviously the same toxin will kill other life forms."

"No, not at all. That's the beauty. The toxin degrades in salt water within a short time and disappears entirely after doing its dirty work on the mussels."

"Emily, the Mississippi River is fresh water," Jeff argued.

"Only the top portion," she countered. "The bottom is lower than the gulf, so salty sea water comes in and layers along the bottom. It's not perfect and we have a lot of work to do, but we feel good about it."

Like any good researcher, Jeff knew that a moment of excitement in a lab is a merely a brief flash of light in a long dark period of drudgery. Still, he had to admit, Emily was onto something and he latched onto her excitement. First the telomeres, now this. "Emily, I want you and Arnold to send me what you've got and, for what it's worth, I'll look at the data. I know you have an army of good minds out there, but I'll be there for you both, if you need me."

"You will? I was hoping you would say that. It would mean the world to me . . . to us, doctor. There's another thing too," Emily quickly inserted. "When we prepare nutrient agar with 1% petroleum distillate added, the mold grows rapidly and it produces spores. They have an odd bronze-like appearance, almost umbrella-like and appear in long chains that easily separate when exposed to the slightest breeze. We'll forward the pictures to you. Anyway, say 'hi' to Carmen for us."

"Say hello to her yourself, Emily," Carmen said, taking the phone from Jeff's hand.

Carmen spent a half hour talking science with Emily and then with Kaufman, roaming charges be damned. When she closed the call, she found Jeff sound asleep laying on his stomach. Staring at him, the thought about how much she loved him. She thought about the meaning of their years together. She had sacrificed her medical degree to be with him.

She made a final decision. They would absolutely be married on this voyage. The man was like the magician on stage they had seen the other night, a man who puts up a good front to slither out from a trap, always making a success-ful escape. Read: Jeff Shenero, marriage escape artist.

Carmen returned to bed and half-slept, smiling, thinking, finally coming up with a plan of action, careful not to force an event only to be sorry later. With Jeff as the subject, that might be a legitimate concern.

FOUR

Before whale-watching, taking a helicopter ride to see Mendenhall Glacier and going dog-sledding in Juneau, Carmen thought she might add a little real life excitement to Jeff's life by taking him jewelry shopping before hitting port. Nothing serious, only something to eat away at his mind.

The overly bright main promenade could have been a small shopping mall anywhere; a ring of small stores stocked with books, souvenirs, dresses, sunglasses, deck wear, athletic equipment, handbags, cell phones, and, of course, jewelry. No fast food restaurants here with too many free food options available. This one had a 5000 square foot supervised play room for children with everything from slides for toddlers to wall climbing for teens.

Leaving the souvenir store, Carmen meandered toward the area where a number of people were looking into the showcases of fine jewelry, winking at the young sales girl as they approached. Jeff, who had been inclined to head toward sporting goods, failed to notice the sales girl give a knowing smile.

Carmen parked herself in front of the case with rings, saw one she had handled on a previous visit, and said to the girl, "Could I take a closer look at that one, please?"

"Of course." The girl reached into the showcase to remove the diamond ring Carmen pointed to.

"Mind if try it on?" Carmen asked the girl, who looked to be in her mid-twenties, unmarried, and eager to please.

She had Jeff's attention.

"Absolutely," the girl said. "We can even size it for you and have it ready by the time you leave the cruise. Our experts are the best."

Carmen slid the ring on her wedding finger and held it up for Jeff to see. "What do you think, honey, isn't it gorgeous?"

"Uh, yeah, it does look good on you," he replied, his discomfort evident.

"It's a little loose, though," Carmen said to the sales girl. She removed the ring and made a show of looking at the price tag attached to the ring. Holding it up to Jeff, she said, "Definitely affordable, don't you think, sweetheart?"

"You're not thinking . . . ," he began.

"What if I am?" Carmen asked.

"Uh, maybe we should talk about this later,"

Jeff offered, blushing somewhat.

"You bet we will. But before that, we need to look at the men's rings."

Carmen handed the diamond ring back to the smiling girl, evidently enjoying herself, and who, doubtless, would pass on the story in short order. Carmen led Jeff to another section of the showcase where she, more than he, looked at men's wedding bands.

Minutes later, they headed toward the door leading to the deck where she quickly found a couple of lounge chairs for them to call their own and talk about something he had no desire to discuss.

Five seconds after they put on their light-weight nylon windbreakers and relaxed in the breeze of the moving ship, Carmen said, "They're called wedding rings, Jeff."

"I know what they're called," he retorted.

"And?"

"And what?"

"Are you that naïve?" she queried, beginning to get upset again.

"Are you asking me to marry you?" he inquired, sheepishly.

"No, stupid, I'm asking you to ask me. Mother of God, help me with this idiot," she said in Spanish.

"Carmen, maybe I'm not ready for marriage," he confessed.

Enough with the game playing. "Well, you

know, my love, it's been nice, but I think it's time for me to find a good honest man, a real man." At that, she got up and walked away. This was as good a time as any for her to grab a few things and head to the library for an all-night reading session before hitting Juneau in the morning. Jeff could do what he wanted. Screw it. She'd show him cold and objective from now on, if that was how he wanted to play it. The days were over when he wanted to keep her as a play toy. You can only work together and say loving words and shack up for so long before something breaks. Well, it broke.

On the way to her destination, Carmen passed members of the night crew, gloved men and women actively cleaning and polishing miles of railing and surfaces, removing fingerprints, sanitizing. Worker bees tending the hive. Maybe tonight she'd run into a real man who knew how to treat a woman right.

At 3:46 am, Jeff found Carmen asleep in the library with a book in her lap. He stroked her hair gently to waken her and said, gently, "If you like that ring, then it's yours, although I think we can do better than that when we get home."

His soothing stroke and gently touch brought her out of REM sleep. Taking a breath, she began to focus on reality, processing the words he had spoken. Smiling, she cooed, sweetly, "That one will be fine, dear," not giving him any wiggle room.

"I'll set it up with the captain tomorrow, after we hit port," Jeff replied. "Now I need to get a little sleep. This is a big ship. Looking for you took some time."

The wedding took place in the ship's chapel, shortly after departing Juneau. Jeff invited La-Monde to be his best man and knowing no one else, Carmen invited the sales girl who had sold her the ring to be her witness. Delighted to receive the invitation, the girl accepted the offer, believing it to be a good omen for her.

That evening the couple sat at the captain's table once more as his guests. At the beginning of the dinner, Larsson stood and addressed the other diners, all of whom were dressed for an elegant dinner. He toasted the newlyweds who stood and raised their glasses in salutary congratulations, then returned to the meal.

In the morning, the ship reached Glacier Bay National Park and stopped for a period of time to watch a glacier calve, and to marvel at the wildlife, which included the humpback whale, harbor porpoise, harbor seal, sea lion and sea otter. Bird watchers with binoculars and checklists made frequent shouts of discoveries of some 260 species of birds inhabiting the bay. After a full day of stoppage, the boat moved on toward Sitka.

Approaching the small community, the announcer said, "Sitka is a Tlingit Indian name for Baranof Island. The Tlingits are reputed to have settled Southeast Alaska some 11,000 years ago preceding the Eskimos and earlier migrants that arrived from Asia up to 40,000 years ago. Sitia has a population of about 8400 and gets less than three months of sunshine each year."

Looking out at the ice and snow, Jeff remarked, "I shudder to think what it must have been like when the very first humans came across the 600 mile deep land bridge from Asia when there was almost perpetual darkness, to cross mountain ranges in terrible blizzards with food almost impossible to find. And we complain about a little snow or heat. Have we gone soft," Jeff concluded.

The monster ship slid in past the dozens of trawlers and smaller craft to gently touch the dock. In a short time, the announcement came: "Ladies and Gentlemen. You may depart the ship at this time." This was followed by the usual admonitions of caution.

The couple cavorted on their own for five hours, visiting the art galleries and absorbing the Russian heritage of the city. At last, returning to their stateroom, tired from hours of walking, they found a letter slipped beneath the door. Picking it up, Jeff closed the door, took off his woolen cap and sat at the edge of the bed. Carmen sat next to him. The envelope had the name *Dr. Shenero* handwritten on it.

Opening the envelope, Jeff pulled out the folded paper fax received by the ship two hours before.

It read: Dr. Shenero: This missive is in response to your short cover letter and the ten files you sent to our office via phone. Our investigators have found that most of those described are members of an extended family and there is a possibility that this is a scam. Included in this familial group is the one person onboard ship whose file you also sent. Unfortunately, there may be other possibilities for the complaints, such as similar genetic sensitivities, and until we have more information, we cannot proceed further. Any assistance you can give us will be appreciated.

Signed,
William Butler
Washington, D.C. Bureau Chief
Federal Bureau of Investigation
601 4th St NW, Washington, DC 20535

Jeff flopped back onto the bed. "Thought so," he muttered. "We can't ask security to interrogate the man. He'd deny it and raise a stink."

"Once we get underway, the next stop is Vancouver Island and that won't be for a few days. Maybe by then we might be able to make some headway on this case," Carmen offered.

She realized that the stress of not being married after years of partnership had caused her to act out on the voyage and not want to get involved with the investigation. Now that she had landed her man, she felt great relief and joy, prepared to dive into the matter whole heartedly.

"Here's an idea," Jeff said. "How about if I do call security. The captain already told us to mention his name if we needed anything at all in this matter. Everybody's returning from Sitka so they can have one of their people keep an eye on Richards' room and let us know when he gets in."

Carmen caught up with the story. "I already turned in my ring to be sized, so I'm single again. I go down and knock on his door by accident and ask him if he could he show me what's what."

"Sweetheart, 'what's what' can have a lot of meanings," Jeff teased.

Carmen ignored him and continued, "We become friends and start to hang out. He wouldn't have seen me at the big wedding dinner because that was above his pay grade. I'll mention his cough to him. At some point I might get him to confide in me about how he got it."

"Perfect. Your Spanish accent adds flavor to the pie. Do you think he'd feel less threatened if you let him know you have money?" Jeff asked.

"Let me think about it. I may have to play that one by ear," she replied.

"What if he already saw us together in Sitka? It could be a problem," Jeff said. He thought about the omen. So far, this sounded more like a dumpster fire than a skyscraper burning down.

"I don't see why? I have a right to make

friends, don't I?" Carmen grinned. *This could be fun,* she told herself. *Back off Carmen. Don't be so cavalier. It could also be dangerous.* She recalled what Jeff had once told her. "It's all right to have weaknesses. Take care they're not exploited."

A half-hour later Jeff got the call that Richards had returned. Carmen took a quick shower, remained in her jeans and sneakers, but changed into a low-cut see-through blouse with black bra. She ran a brush through her hair, put on a red scarf, adding some deep red lipstick, and a dot of perfume.

FIVE

"Oh, hi," Carmen said, in heavily accented Spanish, "I'm sorry, I must have the wrong room. I got a number from someone and thought I could remember it. I'm all turned around. I don't know where I am, Could you show me . . . how do you say, 'what's what'?"

She held her hands out in front of her as if in apology, but with the actual intent of showing Richards she wasn't wearing a ring.

Richards appeared exactly as Jeff had described him and wearing the jeans and sneakers he had worn during the interview. Now he wore a dark red short-sleeve pullover.

"What cabin were you looking for," Richards asked. "Maybe I can help you."

Carmen rummaged through her purse and said, "I had it here somewhere. Well, I guess I'm out of luck."

Carmen turned to go when Richards said, "If you want, I can show you around, if you have the time."

"Are you sure. I'm so bad with directions. I've never been to this part of the ship," she added.

Two hours later, Carmen returned, having gone to the ladies room once to use the WiFi system to text Jeff. She informed him that she and Jerry were getting to know one another. She had only a single drink of wine alternating with sips of water compared to Richards' two vodka martinis. The conversation centered around generalities such as perks on the ship, where they were from and some of the crazy friends they had made.

When she returned, she reported to Jeff that she had told Richards she thought he had an interesting childhood, traveling with his military family, but didn't want to catch whatever he had that made him cough. Richards had told her it wasn't contagious. She had asked him how he knew and he said he just did. They had set another date for the next night.

On the second date, Carmen and Richards ate a late dinner at a family-style restaurant. After dinner, he guided her to his side of the ship to revisit the same club next to a large capacity movie theater/auditorium that played a different movie each night.

The couple found a table away from the band playing slow jazz. Ella Fitzgerald and Louis Armstrong look-alikes were performing *"Sing a Little Song for Me."* The hour embraced a crowd of perhaps 80 patrons.

After Jerry ordered two vodka martinis, Carmen warned, "Jerry, I have something to confess. I'm a lightweight drinker, so watch that I don't drink too much, all right? It's a genetic thing." At that, she recklessly took a strong pull on her drink, set it down, and pretended to push it away with her hand.

"Will do, Carmen," Richards replied, laughing at her antics. "You were telling me about an abusive husband last night. It sounded like it's in the past. Is it?"

Carmen had given Richards her first name to avoid confusion later. "I'll drink to that," she said, enjoying her lapse into heavily accented Spanish, as the raised her glass. "The *pinche cabron* was into drugs, too. I hope you don't do any."

"Never," Richards admitted. "Alcohol is fine with me." His cough had disappeared for the evening and his eyes were clear.

With her medically trained eyes, Carmen observed that the upper portion of his nose had a slight swelling, as though he had been snorting cocaine or got popped with a fist.

Her date spent some time telling her about himself, explaining about how to build better computers and programming them. Carmen tried to keep her focus and pretended interest. Electronics was not one her specialties.

Jeff had learned that Jerry Richards had another doctor's appointment the next afternoon, so Carmen put the squeeze on him. He couldn't go into the medical office free of symptoms, but he had to stay that way to lure her. He had no choice but to continue with the act, if that's what it was. What he might be up to was probably a lot more important than scoring with her.

When Jerry did visit the doctor on schedule, his symptoms had returned in full and hadn't cleared by the time Carmen came to his cabin for their third date. When he opened the door, dressed for an evening out, he spoke nasally and coughed after every few words. When Carmen saw that she said, "Jerry, you told me you didn't do drugs and look at you. I need to go."

She turned to leave and Richards gently took hold of her arm. "Wait, please, let's go down for a few drinks first and talk, then you can go if you want."

Carmen humphed, "Next thing I know you're going to start beating me, probably because I'm rich and live in a penthouse suite and you're a substance abuser."

"Please, for a few minutes, Carmen, give me a chance to explain," the man implored.

Carmen hesitated before replying, "All right, for a few minutes, but if I think you're doing drugs, it's over."

The couple ate dinner again then returned to the usual nightclub. Carmen used the swizzle stick to stir her half-finished third drink and began to giggle. This time she was drinking martinis. "Oh, Jerry, you can be so much fun. By the way, what did the doctor say about your problem? Come on. You said you'd tell me."

Richards said, nonchalantly, "He thought it might be an allergy and gave me some anti-histamines. He said it should clear up once I left the ship. See, nothing complicated."

"Oh, honey, that such good news," Carmen slurred, leaning forward in her low cut blouse, her cleavage serving as a powerful eye magnet. "I'll tell you a big secret of mine, if you tell me one of yours. I can guarantee I'll never remember anything you tell me, anyway, by tomorrow morning. My friends say I'm brainless."

Carmen appeared to make an effort to put together the next words. "Jerr, hon, that's one of my secrets. You want to know another one? I like bold men. And maybe someday I'll tell you how I got my money because I got stories to tell."

She had the urge to slap herself back into reality when she saw the grin on Jerry's face, as though he were making headway with this gorgeous creature the weaker she got. *Don't let your weakness get exploited.*

"Gee, you were supposed to tell me your secret first," she concluded, and downed the rest of her martini, gently sucking on the olive with red, pouted lips, starring goggle-eyed at the man across the table from her.

Richards settled back in his seat assessing the situation, tossed down the rest of his drink, ordered two more, and leaned toward Carmen. "Powdered white chili peppers," he said at last. "You inhale them. They get absorbed and none of it can be detected because nobody looks for that. But they cause a lot of symptoms that make the doctors all go crazy. You can measure the symptoms, but not the cause. In the end, the cruise line always pays. I can tell you that for a fact."

Carmen shook her head, slowly, swaying, her eyes unfocused from the vodka. She understood it all, but she had passed her drinking limit. In her enthusiasm to be a spy, she failed to order a glass of water to drink alternately with the alcohol.

Feeling secure in his conquest of this jewel of a wealthy woman, who ached to take him to bed, he said, "Money, honey. Look at the billions these people have. They can spare a few dollars once in a while."

Carmen laughed out loud and leaned forward again toward the grinning man to be as intimate as the table would allow, noting where Jerry's eyes went. The noise of the band caused her to shift from a seat opposite Jerry to a seat next to him. She leaned in a couple of inches from his face to ensure he received a little whiff of baby powder fragrance. She need to reaffirm his statement. "I get it, Jerry. You pretend to be sick and stick them for money later in a lawsuit. You have to keep it up for a while after you leave, right?"

"No, I am sick, Carmen. I have a lot of relatives who got sick too. It's genetic," Jerry answered, toying with her, pulling her strings in different directions, telling, but not showing.

Their drinks arrived. Sensing Richards might be thinking about asking her back to his cabin, Carmen said, "Let's toast to Jerry's illness," and raised her glass. An instant later she set it down, swayed into him slightly, and said, "Oh, Jerr, I don't feel so well. I'll be right back."

At that point, Carmen stood unsteadily, using the table for support. She didn't feel well. She had always been a lightweight drinker, preferring wine over anything else.

Fortunately, Jerry's back was to the club's entry, but as she stood up to leave, Richards gently grabbed her arm and pulled her down to his face, whispering, "Honey, that's pocket change. You ain't seen nothin' yet."

He released her arm to let her go, then pulled out his phone to begin texting, not noticing Carmen walk out the door of the club, thinking she needed the ladies' room. Once outside in the circle of stores and using the ship's WiFi, she texted Jeff: ONMYWAY. Somewhat unsteadily, she grabbed the nearest elevator, thankful to be the lone occupant.

After a slow ride, she exited the elevator to find she had pushed the wrong button and had gotten off one floor too early, according to the signage. The door closed behind her and not trusting herself to take the broad staircase even one flight, she punched the button and waited. Within a few seconds, the elevator stopped and the door opened. A middle-aged couple dressed for the evening stood in front of her. "Going down?" the man asked, holding open the door.

"Going up, actually," Carmen responded.

"Sorry," said the man, who let go of the door.

Carmen listened to the elevator stop three more times before reaching the bottom. Now, she really did have to pee. She looked at the stairway again, and declined its invitation a second time.

At last the door opened and she rode it the single floor to her level. She carefully negotiated the corridor to their stateroom, trying not to bounce from wall-to-wall in a hallway not much wider than the width of a wheelchair. When one did come through, a person coming from the other direction would have to step into a small alcove in front of a cabin doorway to enable it to pass.

Carmen's mind swirled with bits of conversation, then returned to thoughts of herself. She realized what she had done, what she had become. This was all completely out of character for her. She was a dutiful educated office manager, investigator, scientist, married woman, and a lot of other things. But within the past couple of days she had found a new role for herself as a manipulative, deceitful person. To make matters worse, she felt good about it, comfortable in the role, as though it were completely natural for her to act in that manner.

She found the door unlocked to see Jeff seated at a small writing table working on his laptop. He turned toward her as she entered, anxious to hear her tale. "I was getting worried," he said. "What took you so long?"

"Elevator troubles," Carmen said, throwing down her small purse on the bed. She unbuttoned her blouse and reached down inside her bra to pull out the miniature microphone bluetoothed to the hidden tape recorder inside the waistband of her jeans. Then she entered the bathroom. Emerging minutes later, she slurred, "All right, let's see if we got it. I'd hate to do it again," Carmen slurred.

Jeff came over and put his arm around her. He said, "Baby, you overdid it. Sit down."

"I'm tired of sitting. I need to stretch out." Carmen said. She lay down on the bed with Jeff seated on the edge. Replaying the last portion, she stopped the recording at the end of the confession, which came out loud and clear.

"Damn you're good," Jeff said, giving her shoulders a squeeze and kissing her on the cheek. "The problem is, I don't think there's anything solid here. He mentioned everything from allergies to pepper to genetics, but let's get this to security, then we'll tell Captain Larsson and LaMonde. I'll let Butler over at FBI know, as soon as I can get to the message center."

Carmen went to the bathroom to wash her face and drink a glass of water. When she returned, she said, "It's a partial admission. It doesn't directly implicate the others."

Jeff added, "True, if there were he might rat on the others. Too bad security can't check his person or his luggage. It's a great idea, the pepper thing, though. It makes sense to me. What do you think?"

"I think poor Jerry will spend the rest of his life wondering about how Carmen fit into all this," she concluded, her mouth downcast in a mock show of sadness, her head spinning. She needed to fix the problem.

"After we take care of business, I could use a drink," Jeff suggested to lighten the mood.

"Not for me, thanks," Carmen replied. "I think I'll lay off the stuff for a few days. All it does is make a person talk too much."

At that, they both laughed. Comedy relief in a tragedy. Carmen finished putting herself back together, looking forward to some late night coffee, bed, and a good night's sleep. She would definitely ensure that cell phones and ringers would be turned off. With her husband around, anything was possible.

"I'll have a pot of coffee brought up," Jeff offered.

Fifteen minutes later the couple sat on the veranda outside their suite looking out at a bright crescent moon hanging over the water. Occasional pinpoints of light glowed from land in the distance, like unwinking stars. The cold air helped to clear Carmen's head. She held a large hot cup of mocha coffee in both hands sipping it slowly, emotionally drained, recounting the evening. Something nagged at her.

"In the morning, we need to listen to everything," she said.

"Over two hours worth?" Jeff inquired, very certain he didn't want to hear about how Jerry grew up while listening to Carmen cooing over his every word.

Carmen confessed, "Not really. Since the recorder is voice activated, it shouldn't be that long. There's something he said that's bothering me and the more I think about it the farther away it runs."

After a good breakfast and back in their room, Carmen played the recording of her evening with Richards. She let it play until after the confession and after a slight pause, she announced she didn't feel well and Jerry had replied, "Honey, that's pocket change. You ain't seen nothing yet."

"Play the last part again," said Jeff.

She did as he requested. They could have saved a lot of time by simply listening to the last five seconds.

The ultimate conspiracy theorist, Jeff could take a good molehill and turn it into a bad mountain, but somehow it worked out for him. He said, "Jerry's playing a role like you are. This guy is not all he seems. Something bad is going to happen. If we give that confession to the authorities and call it a day, that won't be the end of it. Even under pressure, there's a good chance this guy is not going to turn in the others. He's too hard core."

"What do we do, nothing?" Carmen asked, her eyelids getting heavy.

"You're going to need to see him again," Jeff suggested.

Carmen sat bolt upright. "Oh, no. That is so not going to happen," she declared with certainty. "I walked out on him and said I'd be right back. He'll be mad."

"I'm going to call security, identify myself, and ask if they have the capability of capturing fingerprints, then we can go to sleep," Jeff suggested. Without waiting for Carmen to reply, he made the call.

SIX

Reluctantly, Carmen knocked on the door, but got no reply. On a hunch, she went to the nightclub she and Jerry frequented and surreptitiously looked in to see him seated with another woman at the same table they had used. Both had drinks and finger snacks in front of them. Appraising the woman, Carmen saw her to be a little past middle-aged, not bad looking, well-constructed and wearing a modest dress that didn't show much except for neck and upper chest. Her well-styled brunette hair came to her shoulders. Jerry seemed to be doing most of the talking. The way he was gesturing, it looked as though he were pleading a case. Were they discussing her?

Carmen felt relieved and frustrated at the same time. To interrupt them would create an unpleasant situation. She felt relieved not to have to deal with having to explain herself to Jerry, yet she wanted to get it over with. She allowed the night belonged to him and would try to see him again the next evening. On an impulse, she pulled out Jeff's cell phone he gave her for a backup. It had three cameras and an excellent zoom feature. She casually took pictures of the surrounding stores, then turned to focus on the couple while trying to look like a tourist taking pictures for her new picture book, *Reflections off a mirror.*

Why wait until tomorrow evening, she told

herself. She'd knock on his door late morning, say, before lunch, and presumably, if this woman had been his date for the night, she would be gone by then. He might be, too. It's worth a try.

She found Jeff in the gym finishing a workout and told him what had happened. He agreed to her idea of her trying to see him earlier the next day and within a half-hour, the newlyweds went to the dining room for dinner and a chilly roof top stroll in the park.

Despite the relaxing walk, Carmen slept poorly that night thinking about various possible conversations she might have with Jerry the next day, working out responses to his questions in detail, like anybody working hard on a project at hand.

A little after 10:00 am, almost robotically from lack of sleep, Carmen went down to Jerry's cabin and knocked on the door. He had either gone or didn't want to open the door. So much for all night deliberations. She met Jeff in the library where they browsed through the books, then went to the gym, ate lunch, and tried to kill time by going to the movies. Neither of them could enjoy the film. During the movie, Jeff looked at a new watch he had acquired and punched the face to scroll past the oxygen monitor, the EKG sleep memory graph, the heart rate monitor, stop watch, countdown timer, alarm, jogging and step counter, altimeter, barometer, GPS, compass, phone message center, and music stations, but he never could find the time, so he pulled out his cell only to get admonished by nearby patrons.

At 6:00 that evening, Carmen made a second try, thinking that neighbors must wonder who she was, as if it mattered. When Jerry did open the door, he stood shirtless, wearing jeans, with a towel in his hand. Before he could say a word, Carmen said, "Sorry, Jerry, I came by to apologize."

"Come in," he said, sweeping his arm inward, coughing slightly.

He must have visited the doctor again to go on record, Carmen thought. She suspected Jerry had a good frame with his clothes on. With his shirt off, she thought that a year of hard working out could transform his body into something admirable, although not to her. He could never work out enough to equal her husbands' rock-hard bod and well cut musculature. She also noticed the bed had been made, so no evidence there of any recent activities.

While Richards slipped on a pullover, Carmen began, "Jerry, I don't even remember going to bed. All I remembered in the morning is that we had a good time talking. I'm sorry I didn't come back."

Struggling for words, she added, "I told you I couldn't hold my liquor. Besides . . . well, this is embarrassing, but, I have . . . female problems I had to take care of."

"You mean like an infection?" Richards grinned.

Carmen laughed. "Yeah," she said.

"Till how long?" he inquired.

"I don't know. It flared up this trip, but the ship's doctor only gave me OTC stuff to take. Big deal. I need something stronger. Anyway, I came by last night, but I guess you were out."

"To tell you the truth, I went out looking for you, but I guess you were holed up somewhere," Richards divulged.

Carmen thought. *Liar. Maybe he doesn't want to admit he went out on you, which means you can't trust him like he can't trust you. Forget it. I need to get him to tell the truth.*

"You don't remember anything about the other night?" Richards asked, combing his hair in the mirror. If he had plans to go out somewhere for the evening, this could delay her own plans even further.

Carmen shook her head. She had let down her black hair and the shining ringlets danced across her shoulder blades. "I had this sense that we talked about a lot of money, at least I think so, but I can't get there. It's gone. I like alcohol, but it doesn't like me."

Fully expecting him to reject her offer, she plunged into the deep end. "Anyway, if you're open for a little while and don't have somewhere to go, maybe I can treat you this time."

"Only if you promise not to run away again,"

Richards said, with a sparkle in his eyes.

"Deal," Carmen agreed, with a beautiful toothy smile.

On the walk, Richards added to the list of jokes he had been telling her by saying: "Three engineers are on their way to a convention when their car stalls. The mechanical engineer says, 'I have my tools in the trunk. I can fix it'. The electrical engineer says, 'I have my multimeter with me, I can diagnose the problem', and the software engineer says, 'Nothing complicated. Let's get out of the car and get back in. Everything will be fine then'."

Carmen didn't think the joke very funny, but she laughed out of politeness. "Cute, Jerry, I'll try to remember that," she said, occasionally chuckling, as though the more she thought about it, the funnier it became. She had heard ribald versions of the same story that were quite humorous, the memory of which actually did provide the mirth required for the occasion.

By her third drink, Carmen fared better than on the previous occasion by sipping wine, alternating with sips of water, when Jerry asked, "What's it like up there with the wealthy?"

"How did you know I'm there?" Carmen seemed genuinely puzzled.

"You told me when you yelled at me," Jerry laughed. "You also said you'd tell me how you got your money."

"I did?" Carmen slurred. Looking around,

she left her seat opposite him and took the chair to his right, leaning toward him she whispered, breathing alcohol on him, "You won't tell?"

"Promise."

"I told you my husband was into drugs. Well, he flew for the cartels. He never stole from them, but over the years they paid him millions in honest hard-earned dollars. I knew where he stashed it and it wasn't in a bank. Millions, Jerry. All the money belonged to him and when his plane crashed, it became all mine."

"Where was that?" Jerry inquired.

"Guadalajara, Mexico, where I grew up. I told you that on our first date," Carmen replied. *And went to medical school,* she didn't add.

Suspiciously, Richards said, "I know Guadalajara. Have you ever eaten at La Chata on C. Manual Cotilla?"

Carmen smiled, "Silly, you're confusing that with Restaurante Allium, the open air restaurant on that same street right next door to the nightclub Villa Acapulco."

Carmen had passed the test. Still, Richards wanted to find out more about her. "Besides Mexico and the U.S., where else have you ever traveled to?" he asked.

"That's all," she answered truthfully.

"Because over the past ten years I've spent time in Russia, France, England, and various countries in South America. My business allows me to travel."

"What kind of business are you in?" Carmen inquired, feigning forgetfulness, knowing he had told her he worked with computers.

"Selling advanced shortcut software that allows you to save time," Richards replied.

Carmen gave a look to indicate she didn't understand, but at least he was warming up.

At that point, Richards repeated what he had told her about his money-making scheme. Carmen resisted the temptation to place a hand on his inner thigh and move it around lightly, something she enjoyed doing with Jeff; in fact, her heart began racing at the thought. She quickly realized there is more than one way to have sex and she wanted none of it with him. She needed to stick with the program. Taking another sip, a larger one this time, she gave him a light kiss and replied, "To most people, that's a lot of money, but in the grand scheme of things it's nothing "

"Exactly. That's lunch money. Here's the real deal. You hack into the cruise ship's computer system that controls the money flow and direct it elsewhere."

"Oh, is that all," Carmen quipped. "You're a computer guy, why don't you do it yourself? Here you are settling for chump change like thousands when you can have hundreds of millions or billions."

"Honey, I'm a shopper, not a doer. Besides, a lot of small change can add up. Look, any computer system can be hacked. We . . . I need a very good hacker for the job. It costs money to make money. Hacking is like medicine, real estate, law, or construction. You can't know it all so you pick a specialty. If you want to turn off the lights of a city, you go to one kind of guy. If you want to steal credit card data from Walmart, you get another guy. All of the targets have common codes, but also specific codes. I needed to find somebody who worked with codes similar to those used by cruise lines and line them up to work in my specific area. Does that make sense?"

"Sort of," Carmen admitted. She picked up on his usage of the word *needed,* as in past tense. Did that mean the job is over? She also admitted to herself that it may not make sense to a layperson such as herself, but an expert might be able to make something of it.

Jerry continued, "The people I have lined up are specialists in this area. They've done it before. They also travel a lot internationally for obvious reasons. They'll immediately confiscate 40% of the take, but want a million up front. It's almost there. I need to raise capital. Another 100 thousand. Most of it has been accumulated fairly easily over the past couple of years. That's the bare bones I'm going to tell you."

"If they're that good, why do they need you at all?" Carmen asked.

"Because I know pass codes and short cuts. They need me and I'm not good enough to do it by myself. I'd leave my electronic fingerprints all over the place. It's simpler to pay somebody else to do it. These guys won't leave a trace, except for something that might smell Russian and that's par for the course, these days."

Carmen had to be careful of entrapment, although, actually, he had opened the door. She sat back in her chair and said, "I'm going to make you an offer, but first I want a selfie with you."

Without waiting for a reply, Carmen reached into her clutch and pulled out her phone by the edge and handed it to Jerry. He took it from her, suspicion clouding his face. Carmen said, "What's the matter, Jerry, afraid I'm going to make an eight-by-ten of it and hang it on my wall?"

Carmen could see him process the request. Handing the device back to her, he said, "Sorry, I never did like pictures of myself."

Distracting him, she said, "Guess I'll just have to remember you," taking the phone by the edge and replacing it, trying not to smudge any prints.

Now the hard businesswoman, Carmen said, "I like to invest in people, but frankly, I'd loan you the money for a piece of the pie, but I don't think you have anything to give me for collateral."

"Will the title to my Lamborghini serve as collateral?" Jerry offered, a big grin crossing his face.

Fully prepared to accept that the man had nothing but bluster to back up his words, Carmen was taken aback at his statement. "And you happen to have that with you," she stated, flatly.

"Correct. I don't have liquid cash and that's what some people want," he replied. He pulled out his wallet and slid out a laminated photograph of a yellow Lamborghini Urus and another with a photo of the title with his name on it.

"Impressive. What's it worth?" Carmen asked.

"It's a year old and worth about $150 K. Look it up. Obviously, it's paid for because the title is in my name. I also carry the real paper with me for negotiations like these. I always come through with my end of the deal because I still have the car."

"How much do you need?" she asked.

"It'll go nicely next to my Porsche 911 Carrera," Carmen said.

Jerry laughed. "Nice thought, but you'll never get it. You'll have your money back in a month."

"With 15% interest," Carmen threw in.

"With interest," Jerry agreed.

Carmen leaned back and nodded up and down with large slow motions. She turned down her mouth as a show of understanding and said, "Tell you what, we'll talk details in two days right here. That'll give me time to move some money around, that is, if you're interested in a bank transfer."

"Are you going to remember anything about this in the morning?" he queried.

Carmen replied, "Notice I didn't get slammed. Plus, if I drink lots of coffee, I'll be fine. I have my own medical problems to deal with, so I'm going to try and get some rest. You know, a female type of medical problem."

"Like an infection?

"Si."

She left early, rightly trusting that Jerry's mind had shifted from sex to serious financial matters. Once in the cabin, she replayed the conversation, and, as they had done the first time, Jeff recorded it onto his cell phone for backup, not touching hers.

Jeff said, "Nothing solid, again. For all we know the entire family suffers from some genetic problem, got paid because they picked up some unidentified infection onboard ship and contributed the money to Jerry for his scheme to hire the hackers. Yes, they're contributing to a criminal enterprise, but it doesn't yell scam to start with. Does that make sense?"

"My head hurts," Carmen responded.

Jeff had promised to call LaMonde if anything developed on the disease front. Although the game was far from finished, he decided to call the chef on the cell number he had been given and bring him up to speed. He would leave out the part about computer hacking and the negotiations in progress with Carmen. He made the call to an avid listener and cautioned him that it was a work in progress.

Next, Jeff called Captain Larsson, who said he would make himself available to them. The couple met him at the bridge along with the head of security, John McKenzie, whom they had already met. Three white-shirted officer worked at the various screens when they entered the room. One of them wearing a name tag ORTIZ, sat in Wentworth's seat.

Most cruise ships cost from half-a-billion to a billion dollars to construct. One this size costs a lot more. None are lacking in communication equipment. Anybody with sensitivity to EMF radiation would be advised not to enter the room packed with electronics, radar screens, satellite connections, WiFi, Internet, ship security systems including cameras, meteorological data, and basic phone lines to everywhere in the ship.

Carmen carefully removed the phone, almost pouring her purse onto a table, tying to keep her makeup in the handbag at the same time. McKenzie reached into a briefcase and removed a roll of 2-inch wide clear Sellotape and tore off a portion at the seam. He then carefully placed it over the front of the phone, pressed it in place and peeled it off. Fingerprints were visible on the tape, which then got placed onto another piece of clear tape and put in a bag on which he wrote identification numbers. He did the same thing for the reverse side. He then asked Carmen to press her fingers and thumbs of both hands onto other pieces of Sellotape which he also labeled. He handed all envelopes to the operator.

McKenzie said, "Go ahead and send me those picture, ma'am."

"I have several on this other camera. Some with Jerry and some with the other woman he met," she offered.

"Send them to Captain Larsson's computer, please," McKenzie requested. "And, the recording device, if you don't mind," he added, holding out his hand. He received the device and turned it over to the operating technician.

McKenzie said, "There is no emergency on any of this because we'll have to work with authorities to build a case. I'll turn in the evidence in person once we reach port in San Diego. In the meantime, Captain Larsson will work with your husband and Mr. Ortiz to send what you gave us to our people and to your husband's contacts."

Jeff said, "Question. Does she have to meet this guy to hear more details of his plan and try to close the deal, or do you have enough to prosecute?"

McKenzie said, "Prosecution is not in my realm, and honestly it's all hearsay without solid evidence. It would be nice to find out who this Russian hacker is."

Larsson said to the couple, "I'll leave that decision up to you two. You've both done admirable jobs."

Jeff felt great respect for Carmen. She had gone the extra mile. Enough. Even if these hot shot hackers were caught, more would move in to fill the vacuum. All the evidence pointed to bailing out. He said to Larsson, "Tell you what, let's send what we have and get that off the table. It'll probably take them a week or more to put anything together and by that time we'll be back home."

Ortiz said, "What's the number, sir?"

Jeff told him and Ortiz made the call. The answer came over the speaker. Jeff identified himself, provided the necessary passwords and asked for William Butler. He turned to the others and said, "Butler is the head of the FBI's Washington D.C. field office. He and I go back a ways."

A talking head appeared on screen. The head possessed razor cut gray hair. He could have been the neighborhood banker who slept well with less bags under his eyes than the banker. "Yes, Dr. Shenero. Nice to hear from you. What information do you have for us today?"

Jeff said, "We're going to send over some pictures, fingerprints, and electronic recordings that directly relate to the shipboard scams we spoke of earlier." He explained about his presence on the ship and the people accompanying him, introduced Carmen, who had done all the hard work, then asked Butler for the bureau's fax number.

"Great. We'll watch for them, and stay out of trouble," Butler replied, knowingly, then provided the number.

Larsson gave the nod and Ortiz went to work.

Jeff and Carmen went to the outside railing to shiver in the cold air of an overcast day with their arms wrapped around each other ready to return to their vacation. Case closed.

SEVEN

At approximately 11:15 two mornings later, a call came over the ship's speaker: "Will Dr. and Mrs. Jeffrey Shenero please call Extension 264."

Of the thirty people attending the auction of paintings ranging from $50 to several hundred dollars and more, two of them rose and left the room.

In the corridor, Jeff said, "That number belongs to the security line."

Carmen grinned, "I'll get it this time."

Jeff followed her to a red wall phone. She picked up, spoke and listened, then hung up. "McKenzie wants to see us."

"That's interesting. I wonder if it has anything to do with our landing in Vancouver in a couple of hours," Jeff said.

A different officer clothed in white, with the

name of Wentworth printed on a name tag, sat at one bank of instruments, when the pair arrived minutes later. A dark eyed handsome man, he stood of average height and had not gone to flab after retiring from the navy where he had spent years navigating aircraft carriers in both the Pacific and Atlantic theatres.

Butler is on hold for you," Larsson said, with a dour look, as though a bomb threat had been called in.

Butler's face came on the screen. He said, "We have some information. We processed all the data you sent us and got some positive results. "

Awestruck, Jeff couldn't stop the short nerve that connected his brain to his mouth. "Already?" he interrupted.

Butler smiled, "Yes, Jeff. Despite what you may believe about the slow movement of government, there are times when we can make things happen very quickly. Even pull strings if we have to. Jerry Richards is as he seems, at least according to what we can find, or not find. He's traveled to the countries he said he traveled to, lived in each of them for a period of time, and he has no criminal record.

"The woman he was with, however, is a different story. Captain Larsson told us she came onboard as a married woman with the name of Sandra White. Her husband is named William White. We don't have a picture of him, but we've got a 95% match of her through the use of facial recognition technology--great close-ups, by the way, Carmen. Her true name is Marina Sobol, a Ukranian. She's vying for top honors on Interpol's list of bad girls. We have no record of her being married. She's strongly suspected of being part of schemes for fraud and computer hacking on a grand scale, an arm of a larger network, actually, that is bringing chaos to Western countries, including our own."

Carmen voiced all their concerns, when she asked, "Which means she and Richards knew each other before the trip."

Larsson asked, "We're going to need to arrest them before we dock in Puerto Vallarta, unless you have other plans for surveillance."

Carmen stared at the screen as though she were in a trance, exclaiming, "It wasn't on the recording, but something Pierre LaMonde said during our first meeting. He told us that cruise ships bring in an incredible amount of money each week for sales of souvenirs, books, clothing, and money spent on a wide variety of activities that don't come with their ticket. Could that be part of what they're up to?"

Jeff gave a slight grimace. "But there's no cash. If there were, I should think he would hire a safe cracker, not a computer expert."

A voice could be heard on Butler's end. The bureau chief turned his head to speak with another man, whose face appeared on the screen.

He identified himself as their resident computer technician. "Thank you for that—Carmen, is it? The way I see it, they can't do what they're planning from the land, simply because they have to tie into the onboard ship's computer that transfers the credit card money to the central bank. In layman's terms, if you ride the express train to the bank, you end up inside the vault and you can make your transfers outward from there. "

Jeff queried, "Then why did Richards even tell anything to Carmen, other than to maybe hit on her?"

"Probably because he still needed cash to speed up the process," Carmen conjectured. "Which explains why he wants me to buy his Lamborghini."

McKenzie said, "Apparently not, because Marina and her maybe husband and Richards had all made arrangements for the trip some time ago. That's why they're all here together."

Everyone fell silent until Jeff snapped his fingers and said, "Trial run. Marina and hubby needed to check out the system, but Richards wasn't giving them everything they needed to get completely in. He still owed them money, but was close enough to making full payment that Marina and hubby came onboard to check out what they would have to deal with later.

"Maybe Richards was supposed to come up with it all in a certain period of time or lose it all. Maybe they had other jobs lined up in the queue, so she put the squeeze on Richards for a final payment. This caused Richards to entice Carmen to put up her money."

McKenzie suggested, "They may wait for another cruise to pull it off because time is getting short. Richards is nervous. He's afraid Marina is going to walk. He doesn't want to wait months for the cruise lines to pay him for his soon-to-be medical claims. At this point in the game, he could lose the big stash they're all after, plus make a lot of relatives very angry that they invested in him and lost their hard-earned money."

Carmen said, "With my bank transfer he can close the deal."

Jeff suggested, "If he's confident you'll give him the money, I'll bet no bad guys are going ashore in the interest of time and they're going to work in somebody's room. There are still days of sailing left with a stop in Mexico."

Butler offered, "If we grab Marina and Richards, the husband will probably disappear in Vancouver. I'm going to send her picture along with Richards' to my people there to surveil them, if they do come ashore. The hallway cameras can tell us when they leave. We don't want to move too early or we might lose him. These people are very slippery and they're always on the lookout, but somehow she has to report to her reputed husband. We have to be cautious about picking her up on land, because somebody she speaks to doesn't mean it's him, and our hand is tipped.

"Captain Larsson, I'd like you to delay your departure, if necessary, until we have completed the arrests."

Larsson said, "I'll be happy to comply, but you should have plenty of time because we don't depart for at least two hours after boarding has been completed for a number of reasons. One of them relates to excursions that run overtime. These are out of our control."

Butler said, "I'd like you to watch both rooms. When we board, we'll make our move."

On an impulse, Jeff asked, "Captain, where is Marina's cabin located?"

McKenzie checked his tablet. "She's in 4-23."

"What?" Carmen exclaimed. She could not contain her surprise. "That's next door to Richards' cabin."

McKenzie checked further and said, with great concern, "Correct, there is an adjoining door connecting the suites, which means they must have requested this when they signed up for the cruise."

Larsson said, "John, please shut down all credit card and electronic transfers until further notice. If complaints are made, provide our apologies and tell them our systems are under repair until further notice."

Not having seen anyone leave either Richards' or Marina's room after the ship reached port in Vancouver, Carmen knocked on the door of 4-24, waited a half-minute and then knocked again. Nobody home? Preparing to knock a third time, Richards opened the door only slightly, saw her and said, "What do you want, Carmen?"

"Sorry to disturb you, Jerry. We came into Vancouver a few minutes ago and I wanted to know if you'd like to keep me company. We can talk business. The money's ready to transfer," Carmen said, contritely.

"Can't. I'm going to stay here. I don't feel well, okay?" Jerry insisted, making a move to close the door.

"Don't you want to close the deal?" she continued, pressing him.

"I said I'm busy. Maybe tomorrow," he repeated, forcing the door closed. She heard the dead bolt click into place.

The hall camera saw her turn and walk away. Before she reached the end of the corridor, she had to make way for three suited men coming in the opposite direction.

EIGHT

Returning from their Vancouver tour, the couple were in good spirits until they began coughing. They hadn't been in their stateroom more than a couple of minutes when John McKenzie summoned them to the security office. Captain Larsson was busy making preparations to get the ship underway and couldn't attend the meeting.

McKenzie's office had been a stateroom turned into a work center without an outside view, basically in the center of the ship. It held file cabinets and two desks, two computers, printers, and storage for various security devices. The other members of the security staff were housed elsewhere. McKenzie asked them to find an available seat and relax.

McKenzie said, "The two foreign hackers aren't saying a single thing, but Jerry Richards told us a lot. First, he saw Carmen right away as somebody from the insurance company who was trying to entrap him, so he told her the entire story about the pepper, trusting she would believe it, but would have absolutely have no proof. He teased her with the truth. In a word, she was too good to be true.

"We went through Richards' possessions and couldn't find the pepper or anything at all that could be used, as Richards had described in the recording. He admitted to the wire fraud because we caught him red-handed, but as for the other, he laughed it off. He admitted that his relatives were involved in a plot to hire the hackers, but in this case, the disease is real and he wants to file suit. You are not the only ones on your level to have episodes of coughing with eyes tearing. Can you add anything to this, Carmen?"

She said, "The disease does seem to be real and it appears to be communicable, despite what

Richards told me, which makes no sense from an epidemiological point of view. You can expect a disease to spread outward from a point source, but I was the only one Richards associated with who lived on the upper level, at least as far as I know. Being human, we think the worst, like something similar to norovirus," she concluded.

She did not have to mention what everybody present already knew. The fast moving virus caused hundreds of passengers to fall ill on Royal Caribbean's Oasis of the Seas in January 2019. And according to what LaMonde had told them during their day with him, three Carnival cruise liners, all refurbished only three years before, were being parted out on muddy beaches of Western Turkey at a loss to the company of well over four billion dollars.

Taking a standing position over the two seated guests, McKenzie said, "The captain wants to keep this outbreak under the radar as long as we can, but this thing can explode at any minute."

The role of the head of security onboard ships is not easy. He deals with numerous incidents such as drugs, missing persons, sudden deaths, a vast number of accidents, thefts, deception, and rape. All of this would be set aside if epidemic-related issues occurred because of time constraints.

At that moment, McKenzie received a call. He listened and closed the call. Rubbing his forehead, he said, "We have a client in a cabin at the southeast end of the ship, where there is more sway—as do all corners—who has a friend in a luxury suite who is complaining of coughing. The client took this to mean that her own back hurt when she got up the morning, so she filed a complaint. This means I have to take the time to prepare a report."

This suggested to Jeff that events had escalated to another level. Reality is what it is, but a poisonous snake can have a several fangs. He could make the case that most of our beliefs are based on rumor, not fact. He could lecture ad infinitum about it. People accept rumors more readily than truth, unless the truth teller can be completely trusted, and even he or she can have the facts wrong.

Listening to McKenzie, his mind began to wander. Somehow, the ship's air conditioning system had to be involved. He brought up the subject and McKenzie said, "I already spoke to several of the ship's engineers. They said there is no way to contain an outbreak like norovirus, or Covid-19, or influenza, because even if you quarantined people, the air conditioning system would recycle the air and send it to other areas of the ship tied to the infected cabins."

Jeff saw this as the missing piece because the air handling system serving the upper level of the ship was independent from the others because it recycled its own air and mixed it with fresh air. This knowledge gave him a measure of confidence that the disease wouldn't spread throughout the entire boat.

Something came to Jeff's mind during his ruminations and out of nowhere he asked, "John, can we visit the engine room?"

Becoming accustomed to Jeff's occasionally erratic behavior, McKenzie led them to a particular elevator and inserted a key, then pushed a button to take them to the first of three levels housing the machinery that operated the huge ship. They walked down a long corridor with a number of doors on both sides. He led them into one of them and found an older man named Barney, Chief Engineer, a 30-year veteran of the shipping industry, who wore a hardhat, ear protectors, and carried a clipboard.

McKenzie said, 'Barney, these folks want to see the ducting for A-9."

Barney replied, 'Okay, it's over there." Leading them, Barney started to walk and explained, 'Working these boats is like driving the first Model T car compared with what's out there today. They all got wheels and doors and an engine, and that's where the similarity ends. You need special training to understand how to read the gauges."

He led them to the air handling system that fed the uppermost enclosed deck when Jeff asked, "Can you show me the filter, please?"

"Sure," Barney said, and opened a horizontal door, pointing to the large HEPA filter. Jeff had his suspicions and requested, "Can you pull it out without touching it?'"

Barney shrugged, walked away, and returned with a pair of channel locks, which he used to grab the filter and slide it out about six inches. There, in the grooves of the pleated filter, stood small mounds of powdered white pepper.

"Kind of thought that might be the case. Can you please get a large plastic bag and put the filter into it for evidence?"

Turning to McKenzie, Jeff said, "There's your epidemic on the upper deck. See if you can get any prints off the leading edge. Richards had to pull it out to put the pepper on it."

"Good call, Jeff," Carmen squeezed his arm.

McKenzie asked Barney, "Nobody can come in here, whenever, they want, can they?'"

Barney said, "Of course not. However, yesterday morning we did have our usual walk-through of the mechanical room for passengers who were interested."

Within the hour, McKenzie had taken prints from the leading edge of the filter and had sent them to Butler at FBI who confirmed they belonged to Richards, matching the ones on the cell phone. Once the source of the problem was eliminated, the problem soon disappeared.

"I've got an idea about their drug problem," Carmen said, setting her drink in the cup holder in the poolside lounge chair.

"I'm listening," Jeff replied.

"Our room steward comes in about 11:00 am each morning. Suppose I'm there and you're gone. I'm lying on the bed when she comes in or rubbing my head or something like that. She asks me what the problem is and I tell her I'm on prescription medications for pain in my neck from a car accident and I forgot them at home, of all things. Now I'm suffering. I went to the doctor and all he would give me was aspirin or something weak like that and it won't touch my pain. Is there any way I can get something stronger. Money is no object."

"Go ahead," Jeff encouraged.

"If she says 'no' then we can rule her out. If I hand her three hundred dollars and she takes it, then maybe we have a shot," Carmen concluded.

The following morning, the young woman took the money proffered by Carmen. "I'll ask around, but they're very strict about those things. Otherwise, I'll give you back your money," she said, assuredly.

The following day, both had been out of the room when Jenny entered to make it up. Upon preparing for bed that next evening, when Carmen began to pull one of the swans apart, two small plastic packets fell out.

"Don't touch them. Let's get pictures," Jeff said, pulling out his phone. He shot the scene from close-up to far away.

"Who are you going to call, John McKenzie?" Carmen asked.

"Yes, I want him to see them as they are," Jeff replied.

Minutes later, the security chief arrived. The couple recounted the story of their plan and how it had unfolded.

"This could be huge, guys?" the man said. "We'll interrogate the girl and probably bust the ring and this method of drug transfer, given that this is what it looks to be. Unfortunately, the bad guys will find another way to deliver the goods. They always do. "

"Do you think I can get my $300 back?" Carmen asked.

"I'll put in a requisition for you, but it could take a few months. I'll have to find out who she gave the money to. Consider it money in the bank without interest," McKenzie said, taking the swans and the packets with him.

"Makes you feel good, supporting a drug ring, don't you think?" Jeff quipped.

"Absolutely. At least I'm doing my civic duty," Carmen bragged.

The long cruise down to Mexico gave the Sheneros' time to relax and unwind from their adventures, which were unbeknownst to the other passengers. It gave them time to go to the movies, watch various performances, enjoy the auctions and try different restaurants. At this point, there was nothing left to do but to eat like cruise ship passengers.

Chapter 5

TAKEOVER

ONE

Except for an occasional assassination, the city of Puerto Vallarta, located in the western state of Jalisco, is deemed safe for tourists. There exists an ample number of police armed with pistols, rifles, and submachine guns to watch over tourists. This, plus a training facility for the federal police only a few miles from the beachfront helps keep the drug lords from over-running the city, as occurred in Acapulco where hotel occupancy dropped to record lows.

Some 200 miles to the east, the city of Guadalajara is also a favorite site for tourists and a plane stop for those traveling farther south or farther north. The state also boasts vast acreages of sugar cane along with its processing plants.

Numerous cruise ships can be seen in Puerto Vallarta throughout the primary tourist season. This stretches from November into April or May when the temperature remains fairly stable between 85-90 degrees Fahrenheit during the day. This is perfect weather to eat shrimp ceviche and grilled red snapper while sipping on a Corona beer followed by smoking a Cuban cigar at a seaside cafe. Once late spring and early summer come about, the humidity increases and monsoon season begins, replete with hurricanes.

Jalisco is also home to the New Generation Cartel, one of the most ruthless drug cartels in the country and second only to the infamous Sinaloa Cartel, with designs to more heavily infiltrate Central and South America, as well as northward into the United States and Canada, porous borders or not.

The cartels' main cash flow is drug trafficking with secondary income sources coming from arms sales, hostage negotiations, and other sundry practices. Buying off police departments and entire governments is well within their capabilities. They also specialize in buying off politicians to acquire legislation in their favor. They're favored by many small communities which acquire paved roads and needed edifices. However, terrorism, does not rank high on their list of activities.

This was about to change when one of their newly hired terrorism experts by the unassuming name of Muhammad Mohammad, laid out a plan to highjack 8000 passengers and crew members along with their cruise ship. He quietly proclaimed that he wanted to be like Yasser Arafat, who had originated the art of hijacking commercial aircraft and mid-air bombings. He died a multi-billionaire.

The plan would take close to three years to actualize. The original plan did not include the presence of cartel members for the primary reason that they were not skilled enough to carry out the concept with the efficiency required for this world-class operation. It would be both intricate, yet clean and simple at the same time. More specialists would be needed outside the vessel than inside. Logistics would include airports, shipping ports, spies, armed intruders, hostage takers, explosive experts, electronic and communication personnel, people with shipping experience——all would be called upon.

Mohammad's final selection of a mere 10 on-ship personnel met with resistance by cartel members in that they *must* play a major role in the project. Call it an ego thing. Call it a trust thing. That's how they operate.

Aboard these cruise ships, and once in port, the gangway watchman or the chief of security, the Control Officer—in this case John McKenzie—would supervise the boarding process. In case of emergency, the international SSAS, or Ship Security Alert System is triggered during a serious threat of any kind, including attacks by terrorists, such as occasionally occurs off the coast of Somalia, an area notorious for ship hijackings. From the signal over from his walkie-talkie, a beacon is activated that transmits to the local authorities, the land-based company security officer, and the naval operations center sponsoring the ship to result in the dispatch of the military, as well as hostage negotiators. Ships in the area proximal to another that has activated the SSAS alert are not notified of the alert. If so, this would introduce unforeseen variables and might hinder plans to retake the threatened or captured ship.

While always alert for armed intruders coming up the gangway, there is no way to tell if onboard passengers are a potential threat. Aside from many freighters, the good news is that the control room of the ship is secure at all times.

The bad news is that, for this plan to work, it didn't matter. In terms of financial gain, it would make no sense to hijack an empty ship and hold it hostage. Blow it up and they'll build another. The world's cruise lines lost numerous ships during norovirus and Covid episodes only to construct new ones. However, when the ship is full of passengers, this presents a different picture in the eyes of the world. History has shown that individuals or governments will pay a million dollars each for hostages, even though they publicly announce they will pay nothing. If 8000 hostages and a two billion dollar cruise ship is at stake, the ante is considerably higher.

Billions of dollars in ransom money would catapult the Jalisco-based cartel onto the world stage. It would give them enough cash to recruit anybody anytime and would enable them to sweep across northern Mexico and more rapidly take over the United States completely, not only in terms of absolutely flooding every corner of the country with narcotics, but in terms of buying off everybody they damned well pleased to pay. Either that, or eliminate those who stood in their way. Call it business as usual.

If entry by armed persons were attempted, as soon as the gangway was retracted, the doors to the ship would be immediately closed and the authorities notified. Therefore, entry would have to occur toward the end of the boarding period to maximize the number of hostages on the ship, which meant that, for the takeover to be successful, several factors would have to come into play. Mercenaries would have to be embedded as part of the passenger cluster, who would leave the vessel to be replaced by others who would board in their place. Look-alikes would be preferred.

The main I-95 corridor began to fill with passengers awaiting the announcement to disembark. A series of announcements admonished the travelers to follow standard safety precautions: do not stray too far from the beaten path, protect your valuables, pay close attention to the return time, take note of the bus you were on, and so forth.

These operations typically went smoothly and so, when the doors were opened, the crowds moved leisurely down the gangway in no particular hurry. At the bottom, Jeff and Carmen moved along with a knot of passengers being directed by numerous personnel to available taxis and buses. The latter ranged from 12 to 92 passengers. In their instance, they climbed aboard a bus that held some 25 tourists. Bus No. 8.

The couple found themselves in the middle of the pack and during the shuffling for seats, a middle-aged man wearing a white panama hat stepped on Jeff's toes. Turning to Jeff, he said, "Pardonne," with a French accent. (Because the tour originated in San Diego, most of those aboard spoke to each other in English or Spanish-accented English, one couple on the bus spoke French and another couple spoke Japanese, or possibly Chinese or possibly Korean.)

"No worries," Jeff replied, smiling. Finding a window seat toward the back half of the bus, he slid in with Carmen following him. Behind them sat a clean cut couple perhaps in their mid-forties, joyful, excited about their grand adventure. No cell phone photos for their memories. Each carried an expensive camera with a telephoto lens slung around their neck, one a Canon, the other a Nikon.

A minute later, the driver stood up and announced that he, Enrique, welcomed everyone to Puerto Vallarta. He announced, with great enthusiasm, "This is Bus No. 8. Be sure to come back to this bus at 5:00 pm. Now, I want everyone to say 'hi' to everyone else, and let's have some fun!"

His enthusiasm became infectious and, after passengers had done as requested, and after Jeff and Carmen had shaken hands with couple behind and in front of them, Enrique closed the door and began the short drive from the port to the beach.

After 9:00 am, when the buses did unload at the beachfront, El Malecon, only minutes later, Jeff and Carmen grabbed a taxi to take them a few miles south to a 14-tier zip-line in a jungle area where the movie *Predator* was filmed. Their last zip-line took them over a deep gorge and landed them at ground level where taxis awaited and videos of their adventure could be purchased.

Returning to the city, the couple ate at a waterfront café popular with tourists where they re-met the couple from Montana named Marianne and Charles, she with a slight French accent, he a Brit. Professional photographers. Nice folks, Good vibes, eating like they'd never tasted good Mexican food before. Before them stood two 14-oz extra-strength margaritas. Jeff quietly told the waiter to add their tab onto his.

Similar to the luncheon in Seattle, the harbor and its four parked cruise ships was visible. On the horizon could be seen a fifth ship, even larger than their own, waiting its turn for a berth.

Impressed by the huge vessel, Jeff called over the waiter. "What's that big ship there? Do you know?"

"Yes," came the reply. "That's an Oasis Class ship, the largest of its kind. We've been waiting for it to arrive. We finished dredging the harbor six months ago to make it deeper just for them. It has close to 10,000 passengers and crew with 16 decks. It has an entire theme park on its roof."

The couple sauntered along the sidewalks, amidst heavy tourist foot traffic, cormorants diving for fish, occasional pelicans pecking for food, old VW buses mingling with new Mercedes sedans on the street. Hawkers tried to sell them everything from discount tickets to various events to Tee-shirts, to time shares to Girlie shows. They marveled at the Huichol beaded art that challenged the imagination with its intricate designs. Some model animals, such as a life-size jaguar, were covered with a hundreds of thousands of beads of all colors laid onto a bed of beeswax. Prices varied from tens of dollars to several thousands, with shipping optional.

Following their examination of the Huichol art, the couple visited a number of stores all proudly displaying the Mexican fetish for silver, stores specializing in silver items of every ilk, from jewelry, picture frames, and serving sets, to ornately carved silverware. Finally, keeping an eye on the time, the couple walked the half-mile to the bus drop-off point.

TWO

People tend to take their original seats on a return trip. When boarding the designated bus for the return to the port, this did not occur, for the large part, although Jeff and Carmen occupied the same seats they had taken on the way out as did their Montana friends. Looking around him, he leaned over and said, quietly, "This is Bus No. 8, right?"

"Yes, you know it is, we both spotted it at the same time," she replied, wondering why he had asked the question.

"Well, if you look, you'll notice that most of the passengers are gabbing like they spent the day enjoying the city, but a few look stone-faced like they're riding a New York subway. Okay, no big deal, but why do we have a different driver. Something doesn't feel right. The guy who stepped on my foot isn't here, but somebody who looks like him is wearing his hat. We were all instructed to come back to the same bus for check-in purposes."

Not understanding Jeff's point, Carmen casually looked around, as though gazing out the farther windows and thought Jeff might be playing a game. "Okay, we have some look-alikes, although I do see a few Hispanic looking types in the mix that I didn't notice before. Maybe aliens changed places with some of our people."

Jeff exhaled in exasperation. He stood up to walk up a few feet to the driver and asked, "Where's Enrique?"

"Who?" the driver asked.

"The other guy who drove us," Jeff answered.

"Oh, he got sick and they asked me to take his place," the driver said.

"Aren't we supposed to have the same passengers we had on the way in? Isn't that the rule?" Jeff persisted.

"I don't know anything. I just drive. Please take your seat," the driver replied, gruffly.

Jeff returned to his seat and repeated the conversation to Carmen, who said, "Honey, it's not a rule, for Pete's sake. Will you please stop with your paranoid suspicions? Sometimes you make me crazy." But she did look around again, this time more boldly and patiently, examining faces. A few passengers saw her and turned away. She began to take her husband more seriously.

Turning her head back, she saw Jeff lean forward to ask the man in front of him, who was not the same man who sat there on the way out, "Say, how did you like Sitka? Did you go on the train ride?"

"Yes, it was cold, but great," he answered. Turning to the woman seated next to him he asked, "Don't you think so, honey?"

"Absolutely," she said, smiling.

When Jeff leaned back, Carmen whispered in his ear, "There was no train ride in Sitka."

"I know," Jeff mouthed in reply.

"Got it. My turn," Carmen whispered. She leaned across the aisle, and, with a great smile like a ditsy broad, chirped in Spanish to the nearest man, who differed from the man who had initially occupied the seat. This man had a full head of slicked back black hair and to her, was quite handsome. Dressed in a lightweight sport coat of expensive cut, he wore a tan silk collar-less shirt beneath it and well-tailored dark blue slacks and polished black shoes. She didn't remember seeing him on the first bus ride into the city. "I'm from Guadalajara. My husband is from the United States. Is this your first tour? What part did you like best?"

Another man seated at the window next to the man she spoke to said something and her subject turned away to speak with him, instead.

A woman seated in front of the two men on an aisle seat turned to glance at Carmen when she asked her question. She might have been 5'5" with a nose that could be described as hawk-like had it been longer. Her black hair had been styled such that it fell across the right side of her face, partially covering one eye. Carmen immediately thought of a witch riding a broomstick.

Jeff's anxiety began to take purchase, to become his master. Whenever that happened, his power of reasoning increased almost as though his brain were being shunted into self-preservation mode.

If it looks like a fish and smells like a fish . . . Jeff thought, carefully watching the encounter. Approaching the parking area near their ship, he texted McKenzie. JOHN: I'M ON BUS NO. 8. ON RIDE BACK WITH CARMEN. SEVERAL PASSENGERS APPEAR TO BE NEW LOOK-ALIKES FROM RIDE OUT TO PV BUT SEVERAL NEW HISPANICS. NOT ALL SAME PEOPLE WE CAME OUT WITH. THEY AVOID SPEAKING WITH US. ALSO NEW DRIVER. WHAT TO DO?

The return text read: UNUSUAL BUT NOT UNHEARD OF. WILL MEET YOU AT BOARDING.

Curious, Jeff thought. *Am I spinning a web from a thread?*

Jeff showed the text to Carmen and directed, "McKenzie doesn't seem concerned. Humor me. You're in the aisle seat. Why don't you walk up and take pictures of everyone in the bus like a happy camper wanting every memory of their vacation. I'll take video. Who's going to stop us without showing their hand?"

With great reluctance, Carmen stood with her husband and snapped memorable photos of the bus passengers.

The bus came to a stop and the single door in

front opened. As they were about get up, several other passengers stood to crowd the aisle ahead of them leaving the bus to converge on the entrance to the gangway like a funnel narrowing to a small exit point. Passengers from other buses flowed into the mix, including a man pushing a woman in a wheelchair directly in front of them. Jeff had Carmen by the hand and tried to get around the man to no avail.

At last, showing their passes at the bottom of the gangway, the couple proceeded to move up the ramp to join the line like a row of slow moving ants. Jeff commented, "I don't think we're in any position to do much at this point. This could be embarrassing. I sure hope we got this right or I'll be crawling under a rock to hide."

"What the heck are you even talking about?" Carmen queried, completely confused by the actions of her husband.

"I think we have a takeover by terrorists," he replied.

"Dear Lord. And do what about it?" Carmen inquired, deeply concerned as much for his sanity as for what he had said. She pulled her arm free from his grasp, accustomed to his antics, but unable to stop them.

Instead of an average person morphing into a superhero, Jeff felt like he was morphing into a super jerk when he texted McKenzie a second time. ALMOST THERE. YOU ALL RIGHT?

"You and your conspiracy theories." Carmen

shot, having a moment of remorse for having married him.

"Yeah? Think how I feel," Jeff retorted.

The return text read: NO WORRIES. I'LL SEE YOU . . .

Jeff showed it to Carmen and said, "He got cut off. Let me see if I can get hold of Pierre. He said to call anytime."

Nearly stepping on the heels of the man in front of him, Jeff punched in LaMonde's number. Immediately, the chef answered, "Hello, Jeff. Are you back yet? Listen, we're prepping for new arrivals. Let me get back with you. Ciao."

"Pierre, I need to tell you . . . ," Jeff began.

But LaMonde had gone.

"How do you know there is problem, I mean . . . ," she tried desperately to understand.

"Because it's the only thing that makes sense," he said.

Passing through screening, Carmen declared, cheerily, "There he is. See, he's fine." She pointed off to the left where McKenzie stood with the same well-dressed man who had been sitting across the aisle from Carmen. The man held a large cell phone in front of McKenzie, who stared at the screen in rapt attention some 50 feet away near a wall. McKenzie wore one ear bud while his partner wore another. The security chief looked ashen-faced. Jeff waved briefly, but McKenzie's attention was focused elsewhere.

"No, he's not fine," Jeff said, quietly. "He looks like death warmed over. My guess is he didn't find out he won the lottery. I'm going to the bridge. If I'm right, they may be headed there. Stall them if you can. Faint, do anything to buy me time." He took off speed-walking down a corridor. Crowds waited by the elevators. He had no other option but to ascend eight flights of stairs with 20 stairs per flight to reach the upper deck and then sprint the distance of nearly three football fields to reach the front of the ship.

Obsessively, Jeff bounded up the steps two and three at a time, passing some, occasionally bumping into others. An eternity later, he reached the upper deck, pushed open the outer door and began weaving in and out, half walking, half running, heading north of the heli-pad toward the front of the ship, through the forest and playground, around the amusement park, past the pool, all out sprinting when he could, gasping for air, legs burning from the climb. The skyscraper was on fire. He wanted to be seen by the crew on his approach, so he opted to take the external stairway rather than have to pound on a locked door at the top of the internal one.

An instant of self-doubt hit him. The whole thing didn't make sense. Somebody wants to take over the ship, but he saw no weapons. He wondered what could be an alternate explanation for an event in progress. Obviously, the answer would point to his overactive imagination, his conspiracy theorist ideology, perhaps even the unusual setting of the ship all converging in space and time.

No. One thing he knew above all others. His total trust and faith in himself had always won out. He did have one last thought before he quit thinking. Was he running from the fire or into it?

A man passed through the checkpoint and walked over to John McKenzie, who stood in the background, overseeing operations. He eyed the man who looked relaxed, of average height, Hispanic in appearance with unremarkable features. He was dressed comfortably, almost business-like, as though he were part of the crew, or even a relative.

At the moment, McKenzie was replying to Jeff's second text, feeling annoyed at the scientist's persistence, when the man asked, "You are John McKenzie, SSO (Ship Security Officer), are you not?" the man asked in English accented with Spanish.

"I am," McKenzie replied, pleasantly.

"My name is Juan and I have something to show you," he said, pulling out a phone. McKenzie stopped texting to see a picture of his son and daughter-in-law seated in chairs next to one another. Both were bound with a gag in their mouths. A gun pointed at his son's head with the barrel touching the temple. A dead German Shepherd lay on the floor near their feet in a pool of blood.

"What is this?" McKenzie asked, shocked, looking into the man's eyes.

"It's self-evident," Juan said. He drew McKenzie to the side, plugged an earphone jack into the phone, gave one earbud to McKenzie and kept one for himself. Juan turned up the volume and the gag was removed from his son's mouth, who said, "Dad, they're going to kill us and the children if you don't give them what they want."

In the next scene, three children, all boys ages 5, 7, and 9, were playing on a swing set in the grassy yard.

"You're going to take me to see the captain," Juan ordered, smiling sweetly. To anyone watching, they were having a friendly business chat.

THREE

With Jeff off on one of his crazy larks, Carmen tried to refrain from asking herself, "What's the worst could happen?" which were code words for fate answering, "You want to see? Watch."

Mentally steeling herself to follow her husband's intuition, she rejected her first idea of creating a scene and opted to keep it low key, which had a better chance of giving Jeff the time he needed, or, on second thought, dismissing the entire affair. Carmen had to wonder, *Is feeling stupid better than looking stupid or does being stupid trump them all?*

She approached one of the security staff who stood watching the check-ins, a slightly over-weight, but pleasant looking middle-aged woman wearing a white blouse and slacks with a walkie talkie on her belt standing with her arms akimbo. Her name tag read KODESH.

"Excuse me, you're security aren't you?" Carmen asked, in all seriousness.

"Yes," replied the woman, pleasantly. "Can I help you?"

Carmen said, "See that man over there talking to Mr. McKenzie? Well, your Executive Chef, Mr. LaMonde, a friend of ours, was kind enough to introduce him to me and my husband. Anyway, when we were on the bus coming here and we stood up to leave a little while ago, he was standing behind me and reached in and touched one of my breasts. I'm certain it wasn't an accident."

"Really," replied Kodesh, smiling, always willing to assist a guest. "Let's go talk with him."

The two women walked the few steps to the men who were standing against the wall that depicted their own ship on azure seas with a setting sun turning white clouds into scarlet, red, and orange cotton balls. The crowd of entrants from the last arriving buses had diminished to a trickle.

Looking at Juan, Kodesh said, "Excuse me, sir, but this woman told me that you touched her inappropriately on the bus."

Juan quickly put the phone away, along with the earplugs. Confused, he replied, "What are you talking about? We're looking at family pictures and now I'm supposed to be a pervert?"

"Go ahead, Miss . . . ," Kodesh prompted.

"Carmen, and well . . ." She repeated her story. She scrolled through her pictures, seeming to take forever, finally finding the one she wanted. Showing it to Kodesh she said, "See, that's him on the bus with another guy."

Juan took the phone from her and looked at her picture. He didn't know whether to be angry or to act self-righteous. He broke out in laughter instead. "She was the one who started a conversation with me," he said. "Yes, I was sitting across the aisle from her, but I don't like forward women, so I didn't talk to her. And yes, I was standing behind her, but I never touched her. That's not my thing. I'm gay. My partner is right over there. He's the one sitting next to me in the picture."

Juan waved and a larger man came over. He stood a little over six feet tall and weighed a good 200 pounds, not fat, but strong and middle aged with hair so thin his scalp gleamed. A few pockmarks on his face gave it characteristics unfavorable to Carmen. Overall, a bad package.

The man came over to Juan who said, "Carlos, this woman says I touched her when we were on the bus and I told her I'm gay and you're my partner. Right?"

Ignoring McKenzie, Carlos looked at the three, spending time assessing Carmen's physical qualities and picked up the tale. He responded almost jovially. "Absolutely. We've been together ten years and I'm never seen him look at another man. I don't think he's ever had an experience with a woman, have you, dear? He certainly wouldn't touch or grope one."

Kodesh said, gently, without a trace of accusation, "Carmen, is it possible you were mistaken about who touched you?"

Carmen stammered, looked downcast and ashamed. She forced herself to blush. After a lengthy stammering of apology, all was forgiven and Carmen, trying to crawl into her shell, walked away down the corridor toward the first elevator she could find. If she had a hoodie, she would have pulled it over her head for shelter. Fortunately, the door opened upon her arrival and she entered along with four other passengers, where she took a deep sigh of relief, waiting for the heat in her face to dissipate. *I am so going to rip him out a new one,* she promised herself.

The elevator made two stops before reaching the top. Once outside, she speed-walked toward the front of the ship. Feeling shameful, she desperately hoped the sense of making a fool of herself would go away soon, thinking that this is so much bullshit. If it is, then, damn it, maybe the marriage should be annulled. Jeff's first wife had left him because of his erratic behavior. She could understand why.

Larsson laughed, interrupting Jeff's tale. "Jeff, buses are not my specialty, ships are, but I'm a human being and I get on the wrong bus occasionally when I'm not driving this thing. People do it all the time on excursions. It's human to make mistakes. Furthermore, I am fully aware of your eccentricities, if that is the right word, and your tendencies to exaggerate. However, I have a position of responsibility on this vessel. You don't. You're a passenger, who, I admit, has helped us greatly, both of you have, but at the present, your fantasies are becoming somewhat troublesome. Might I suggest you attend the theater or a show to lighten your mood?"

Jeff showed him the texts between himself and McKenzie, then said, insistently, "If that's not enough, try calling John. Go on, try it."

Larsson nodded to Bill Wentworth, who was also present, along with another officer with the name tag of EVANS. Three other men occupied the Control Room. Wentworth picked up a walkie-talkie and made the call.

"McKenzie," came the reply.

Wentworth made a general statement in the offside chance that Jeff might be telling the truth. "John, Jeff Shenero is here with a crazy story."

McKenzie gave a weak laugh, hoping the

two men still with him didn't know what the call was about. How would they know Jeff? He said, "Not too crazy. He's usually right. We'll catch up later." He switched off.

Short minutes before, McKenzie, distraught as he was, had caught movement out of the corner of his eye and glanced upward reflexively to see Jeff speed-walking down the corridor, atypical of a passenger's behavior and discouraged for safety reasons. He could only hope that the nutcase scientist was onto something. Then Carmen and Kodesh approached.

"All right, that's definitely not a normal response," Larsson stated, unnecessarily. "Still, you must have more to go on than that."

A knocking on the glass of a window drew their attention. Carmen stared in at them, waving. Larsson unlocked the door and she spilled in, sweat running down her face. She gathered herself and quickly confirmed what Jeff saw regarding Juan and McKenzie, then added the part about Juan and Carlos's gay relationship, which, on the surface, had nothing to do with any ship-related problem. It made her feel cheap when she recounted it.

Larsson saw Carmen in a new light, one who worked in tandem with her husband to create mayhem. He'd met people like that who rubbed off on one-another, often unwittingly to add turbulence to an already turbulent world. Where was their evidence? Hearsay? That she had accused one of their passengers of sexual molestation? He turned to Jeff and said, "Shenero, if you're wrong about this, I'll personally see to your hanging."

Jeff replied, "Captain, if I'm wrong about this, you won't have to. I'll hang myself."

Larsson made another call, this time to McKenzie's second in command, Collin Caldwell. Where are you now?"

"At entry, sir. We're about to close up," came the reply.

"Is Kodesh there?"

"Yes, sir, she's right here."

"Do you see John anywhere?"

"Yes, sir, he's standing away from us talking to two men who are holding a phone," Caldwell answered.

"I'm going to call him. See if he picks up."

A moment later the watchers noticed McKenzie reach for the com on his belt. The larger of the two men said something to him and he pulled his hand away.

Caldwell called Larsson back and related what had happened. Larsson said, "I have a man here who says there may be a problem. Grab Kodesh and go over there. See what's going on. Play it low key. Tell John I'd like to speak with him."

The two security agents casually approached the trio, their trained eyes assessing the two men. Caldwell said, "Sir, Captain wants to speak with you."

McKenzie tried to smile and said, "Okay, I'll get back with him in a minute."

Caldwell and Kodesh smiled and walked away. Caldwell reported, "Definitely not normal sir. I think we have a problem."

"Kodesh?"

"Sir, two men, bad demeanor, fake smiles, no visible weapons."

"Keep a casual eye on them. Let me know where they go next," Larsson said.

A minute later another call came in from Caldwell. "Sir, the three are entering the elevator. They're going up. They passed the fifth floor where John's office is located. I'm thinking they may be going to the top."

Which meant the bridge.

The funnel narrowed again. Jeff needed to compress his disparate thoughts into a quick summary. "Captain, help me to understand, please. This is what I believe is happening." He went into his observations, one at a time. This wasn't his wheelhouse, it was Larsson's. He couldn't take over another man's domain. He could only present his interpretation of events and let the powers decide what to do.

Still doubtful, Larsson, questioned further. "If a threat were imminent, John would activate the SSAS and we'd know about it here. Why didn't he? That's one of this primary duties."

"Maybe they didn't give him a chance to," Jeff answered. "Maybe, whatever they showed him or told him was so shocking that he wouldn't or couldn't do it?"

Larsson himself made the walkie talkie call to Compton. She did not respond. He patiently waited another couple of minutes, then tried again. They'd worked together for three years and she had never failed to respond before this. Perhaps she was in the shower. He tried a third time. She answered. Replying to his question, she said, "Of course everything is fine. What do you think this is, rocky shoals?"

For the first time, Larsson considered activating the SSAS. He'd spent his life working on ships and had never incurred so many coincidences. Then this Shenero character and his wife get thrown into the mix.

Now, from all indications, the second in command, Staff Captain Compton, had also been compromised. Which meant neither of them would be considered capable of steering the ship because of mental trauma, never mind that steering was virtually all electronic. The task would go to the quartermaster who also served as helmsman, navigator, and oversaw watch duties. The quartermaster could park the boat, if it came to that. These duties would belong to Wentworth or Ortiz. At least, his and Compton's shift times might have more flexibility.

FOUR

Jeff had always wondered whether crime would be less if it were recorded, but not reported. Take two identical small cities, for example. In one of them, information is deliberately withheld from the press about muggings, shootings, break-ins, rapes, holdups, car-jackings, and other felonious crimes. In the second city, all are reported. In the end, would there be less crime in the non-reporting city and if so, by how much?

Which gave him an idea.

To anyone within earshot, Jeff said, "My guess is these guys want to make their announcement to the world in their own way. How about if Captain Larsson disables all communications to the outside world, including the ship's WiFi, as well as their ability to make announcements to anyone. This would include among their own team once you shut down WiFi. The bad guys won't be able to speak to anyone to make their demands known, let alone be able to negotiate, or even to order the passengers around for whatever reason. Nobody in the outside world will know of their crime, let alone negotiate. If you do that, they'd be dead in the water with nobody to talk to outside the ship.

Although Jeff thought his idea was bold, it was not. It may have been original to him, but Larsson had been a seaman since he had joined the merchant marine 30 years before when he was 17 years old. Off-season requirements necessitated all cruise ship officers undergo training in dealing with terrorist attacks, although virtually all scenarios involved armed intruders. This one definitely bespoke of a new approach and had yet to unfold because it introduced new variables and uncertainties. The idea had been discussed at IMO meetings, along with a myriad of others, with the final decision to permit the captain and the ship's owner's the flexibility of making the final decision.

"Bill, activate the SSAS," Larsson ordered. He could always deactivate it later once the crisis had ended.

Borne out of necessity due to a rash of ship hijackings, all cargo ships, freighters, and cruise ships are required to maintain the alert signaling system via the mandatory security regimen imposed by the IMO, or International Maritime Organization. The IMO offers guidance in such matters. However, as each circumstance may be unique unto itself, flexibility in usage of the system is offered at the discretion of the ship's captain and the vessel's home company.

"Bill, inform HQ that we are going dark, then do so," Larsson instructed. To his mind, these weren't flagrant attackers out for a quick buck. They had put too much time and money into the plan to blow it with some action by a hothead. They would try to reason through the problem without having the benefit of outside assistance.

"And call Barney down in engineering. Apprise him of our situation," the captain ordered.

The two men made their calls, then Wentworth went to a separate keyboard and tapped in a passcode. All monitors went blank.

"Now we wait," Larson said, reviewing the state of affairs. All the pieces fit, but he couldn't fathom how they intended to take over the ship or how many of them there were or what their purpose might be. How did McKenzie fit into the picture, especially with some guy showing him something on his cell phone? What about Compton's strange out-of-character response about rocky shoals? The hint was there. Shenero thought there might have been 10 or more on the bus. No telling how many were embedded. With no detectable weapons, 10 against 8000 was not good odds. If it wasn't a takeover, what was it?

During his musings, he looked over at the newlyweds, Jeff stroking Carmen's hair, wiping her brow. The couple had done so much for him already. A feeling of guilt swept over him for doubting the man when he had first told of the possible takeover only minutes before. And what of his own dear Katherine? Always the faithful wife while he shipped out weeks at a time. Not complaining when they had moved to the States. She would be home from her work at the publishing house by this time, sitting down to read a good book with legs curled beneath her.

A knock at the window drew his attention. McKenzie stood there with two men and a woman behind him. He could have come through the internal door, yet here he stood in plain sight with three guests. Apparently, he had tried the passcode, but couldn't get it to work. Larsson had changed it on a hunch.

Why it is that bad news plays hurry-up while good news drags its feet?

"Open the door, Hunter," Larsson directed.

Evans did so and stepped back. One look at McKenzie's face told the officers that Jeff and Carmen had told the truth. In a way Larsson felt vindicated. Shenero would not hang. If this were a plot to take over his ship, it was the most nefarious one he had ever heard of. No guns blazing, no shouted orders, only their control officer in the company of three people.

"Obviously, you are Captain Larsson. You can call me Juan and these are two of my associates, Carlos, and Maria," said one of the men with the slicked-back hair, while the larger, more burly one, closed the door behind them. Juan appeared to be relaxed, poised, ready for a social drink and a discussion about golf.

Carmen recognized the woman from the bus. She wore jeans and a tan short-sleeve work shirt. Her large breasts were out of proportion to her thin frame. No rings adorned her fingers. A pouch crossed her shoulder with her head in the strap. It wasn't going to fall off. In her full disclosure, the woman was not someone Carmen would want as a friend. Never mind the face, she gave off bad vibes. The two found each other's eyes and glared. Electricity danced between them, as though Faraday or Tesla himself had created a connection, this one of loathing. Instantaneous hatred between the two occurred, like feral animals not liking the other's scent. No one else picked up the non-verbal exchange.

Tearing her eyes from Carmen, Maria said the next words, "We're here for business." with a voice like rubbing fingernails down a chalkboard.

For the first time, she saw why the woman let a portion of her hair cover the right side of her face. A jagged three-inch scar ran from the ear down the jawline, as though she had been in a knife fight with a left-handed person.

The intruders saw Carmen seated next to Jeff and stared hard at her for a moment before Juan said, "Well, Carlos, it seems we have a coincidence. Here is the woman who accused me of inappropriately touching her. I like that idea. Now we find her sitting next to some bald man."

In contrast to Maria's, Juan's voice sounded smooth and oily, almost greasy, like a courtroom attorney Carmen had once known who spoke like that even outside of work.

"Fuck you," said Jeff, acidly, fully prepared to launch an attack. He added, "At least I shave my head, what's your lover's excuse?"

Carlos gave Jeff a look that said it all.

"I thought you liked little boys, or is it little

girls?" Carmen replied, in her turn, winking at Maria, who gave her another murderous look.

Once Carmen said the words, she knew it was the wrong thing to say. She felt like a ventriloquist's puppet speaking the words her husband would have no trouble verbalizing.

Juan remained calm. With McKenzie standing in front of him and the glass window as a backdrop with the beachfront beyond, Carlos grabbed his left shoulder and fisted him hard in the right kidney. McKenzie grunted and began to fall, but Carlos held him erect and grinned at Jeff.

Jeff said, his voice dripping with poison and promise, "Your turn will come, asshole. Trust me on that. I already have plans for you. You know, lessons in life and all that."

Carlos grinned and hit McKenzie again, glowering at Jeff, murder in his eyes. Nobody talked to him like that and lived more than three seconds later. Nonplused without a trace of emotion, Juan stayed him with a hand. This is not what they were here for. The bald guy could wait.

Before either of the two men could respond, Larsson asked, calmly, doing his best to hold his anger in check, "What kind of business? Mr. McKenzie, what do they want?"

McKenzie, about to recover from the blow and speak, was interrupted by Maria, who stayed her partner. She stepped forward pulling out a phone. She casually walked the few paces over to the captain and said, "This kind." She held the phone up for the tall Scandinavian captain to see. Fearless, her head came to his shoulders.

Sven Larsson stared at his wife, Katherine, who sat bound to a chair at their home with a gag in her mouth and an unseen man holding a silenced pistol at her head. The video had to have been recorded because all links to the outside world were shut down. No roaming, no airplane mode, no nothing. If so, how long had she been a captive? A suggestion of good timing and excellent coordination entered the picture.

Maria displayed other pictures with McKenzie's family that Juan had shown earlier, and another with Compton's family.

"Do you want to listen? I have ear phones for you" Maria said, easily. Another walk in the park. "We want this ship and we want you to pull out of port. Now, or you'll lose it all. Then we'll let you know our demands."

"We're not scheduled to leave for another two hours. It's protocol. The Harbor Master wouldn't clear it," Larsson said, stalling, thinking. "We'd need a pilot boat to lead us out at the least."

"Does this look like protocol?" Maria replied, shaking the phone in front of Larsson. A mouse squeaking at a lion.

Juan watched the conversation and said, almost sadly, "I'll talk to him."

Walking over to Larsson, Juan said, "Captain, I know it will take a good hour to start your engines so I suggest you get that going."

When in port, the main engines are shut off, but auxiliary generators supply electricity to operate non-motion related functions, sometimes by tying into a city's power grid, sometimes using their own generators if the community is relatively small, like Cabo San Lucas or various islands.

Jeff watched intently. He could easily hurt the three. Obviously they believed themselves to be invincible, using whatever powers they had through the use of pictures and words on the phone. He had to know.

"What's going on, John?" Jeff finally asked.

"They've got our families under gunpoint and they'll murder them, if we don't comply. That includes Staff Captain Compton and I don't know how many other officers," McKenzie replied, gaining his strength back.

Waiting for the hour to pass, Carmen began to file her nails in anticipation of running them down somebody's face.

Jeff's thoughts alternated between the biochemical characteristics of the orange mold and what he would do to Carlos. The latter he put in the category of "We'll see when the time comes."

Juan reached down and pulled McKenzie's walkie talkie from his belt and said, "Here, use this to call the engine room. He won't be needing it anymore."

Larson made the call, then he walked to the Control Room, under the watchful eye of Juan. He retrieved a sextant and rolled up paper navigational charts that he brought back and unrolled them. He and Evans and Wentworth would have to discuss distances, directions, and potential hazards, because they would be sailing without instrumentation.

"What are you doing?" Juan asked.

"We need charts because we'll be flying blind," Larsson said.

"What are you talking about? Contact your headquarters." Juan demanded.

"Can't," came the reply.

"Can't or won't?"

"Can't."

"Yeah, yeah, you probably activated your emergency alert and I thank you for that. If you hadn't, I would have told you to do it. I've learned the system."

"Which was when?" Larsson asked.

Juan replied, self-assuredly, "When doesn't matter. Long enough to know your HQ keeps an open a line of communication with the ship for negotiation purposes and that your headquarters and certain authorities have been notified. We'll be expecting visitors soon. That would be the Mexican government, who in this case, would join forces with your heavy guns and negotiators based in San Diego."

Inwardly praying that he wasn't signing his wife's death warrant, Larsson chanced to give Juan a sad look and said, "That was then, this is now. You need to keep up on IMO proceedings. Our orders are to go dark when SSAS is activated. That means no navigation, no announcements, and no communications inside or outside the ship. We're flying blind right now.

"If you look around, all the monitor screens are dark. So is this entire area. My 1st and 2nd Officers, Mr. Wentworth and Mr. Evans over there, watch the screens for weather via radar and other means. They also have major navigation tools. No screens are on. Corporate shut us down. We still have fuel enough fuel to take us to San Diego, or stay in place, but we won't be talking to anybody and they won't be talking to us. Even when we pull into the Port of San Diego they may keep us shut down. You'd have to ask them why."

What he didn't tell Juan was that the bridge is kept dark at night anyway, with the exception of the monitor lights. This is to enable a clearer view of the oceans with binoculars as officers look for pinpoints of light that may belong to other seagoing vessels. Juan only need to hear about communications.

Juan said, "That's crazy, man. You can't operate this ship without navigation?"

Larsson pointed out the front window and

said, "Soon enough we'll be heading north-north-west. In a little while, the stars will be out. One of them is Polaris. It's the North Star. Actually, it's one degree off of the North Pole, but we'll let that go. When it comes out, it'll be 12 degrees to the port side before we swing due north, which will change because of the star's movement across the sky. Either the Staff Captain or Quartermaster or I will keep that in sight where it should be. We also have our lights on, which will help keep us from any collisions."

Larsson wasn't finished. "Notice that I released all officers to their quarters with the exception of these two. Why should they watch blank screens?"

Juan looked shocked. With experienced hands, he walked around to each of the dozen monitors, pushing buttons, appearing confused, spending long seconds working on the keyboards that were in front of both Wentworth and Evans. Wentworth stood and backed up to give Juan free reign to mess with his precious children.

While Juan played with the keyboards, Larsson added, "I forgot to tell you that help won't be coming. Did you take a close look at that helipad?"

Juan gave him a curious look.

The captain continued. "Obviously you didn't. There is a number 10 painted at the top of the circle. Sometimes the number is 15 or 20.

That refers to the gross weight of a helicopter that can land on it. The only one that fits in the category of 10 is a two-to-four seater at 8500 pounds and once we're underway we'll soon be out of range for it to make a return trip. We don't refuel choppers here. And they don't even know we're in trouble. Don't expect one anytime soon. The coast guard Jayhawk has the range for a round trip and can bring in troops and negotiators, but it weighs closer to the 15 category. Too much for our top deck to hold."

Jeff almost felt sorry for the man. Larsson had stuck giant sticks in his raft letting the air out. Nice term paper. Too many spelling errors. No passing grade. He did feel sorry for the passengers and crew with no way to contact home, no credit card processing for purchases for the second time—damn modern electronics—no notice that they had been captured.

Jeff reasoned it out. Maria already said, 'lose it all.' They had no guns or slingshots, and nobody was going to sacrifice a $2 billion cruise ship, its passengers and crew, to save a couple of lives, even if the lives did belong to top level personnel. McKenzie was the tool to get them to here so they could take control of the vessel. Okay, a no brainer. Would they kill the families? What leverage would they have then?

"If you're the brains of the outfit, you screwed the pooch, Juan," Jeff said, bluntly, watching Carmen look up from her endeavors.

"Your spotters identified the staff and provided your guys with the info to capture hostages. Unfortunately, you loaded the bus with a bunch of phony look-alikes and I had to alert John; sorry, Officer McKenzie, which made me suspicious enough to see you and him together and smelled a rat. Carmen was kind enough to stall you long enough for me to get here to warn the captain. So, what's the end of the story, Juan, your end game?"

For the first time, Juan's veneer cracked. Too many blows in succession. He sneered, "End game? We're going to sink this entire ship with everyone on it, unless we get what we want; oh, say, $100 billion. How's that for a real life end game?"

"Works for me," Jeff quipped, stupidly, as was his wont when under pressure. "I could use an extra $100 billion myself. You wouldn't believe the bills I have. "

Push their buttons, make them irrational, get them to say what they shouldn't, like a witness on a stand. He should have been a prosecuting attorney.

Juan walked around the room looking at the dark monitors, punching keys, trying to get them to light up, asking himself why he was goaded into giving his demands to some nameless guy rather than to anybody who counted.

He gave the appearance of one familiar with the devices, hitting shortcut keys and various key patterns. With nothing to fear, he walked back to the Control Room and did the same to no avail.

A long hour passed. Carmen continued to file her nails, blowing off the dust, waiting. Unconsciously, Maria, standing frozen in place looking out the giant curved window in front of her, checked her own and saw that they could use a little work.

At last, the ship gave two great and long blasts of the horn and, thrusters engaged, slowly pushed away from the dock under Larsson's experienced hands until he could start the propellers and unleash up to 80,000 horses. Automated systems only went so far. When it came to docking and undocking, human hands worked best. The big hotel slowly moved away from the dock and then came to a complete stop. In a moment, sediment caused by the turbulence from the props would rise from the harbor's bottom.

A pilot boat suddenly sped before them crisscrossing, far enough away not to create a heavy wake, a man waving, trying to communicate. The monster continued out of the harbor. A violation would be reported. Penalties would be incurred.

Unsure as to why the Princess Fairie had left port early and unable to make contact with her, the largest ship in the world, awaiting its turn to dock, backed off, giving the errant ship a wide berth.

"Where to?" Larsson asked.

"The open water," Maria said, looking at a glaring Carmen who was still casually working on her nails, a cat arching its back preparing for battle. To the men this meant nothing. She wanted to kill time to file her nails. To the two women, this meant everything, leaving killing in the equation.

Both Maria and Juan stood next to Larsson until the west coast of Mexico was out of sight. By dawn, they would travel past Cabo San Lucas at the tip of Baja California, about 300 miles distance.

Satisfied that his orders had been fulfilled, Juan declared abruptly, "We'll be back."

"You're coming with us," Carlos told McKenzie. In an instant, the three were gone, led by Juan. This time the four took the internal stairway. Somebody knew their way around.

About to say, "That was fun," Jeff bit his lip. Larsson would not think there would be any fun to find out his wife had been murdered or worse.

FIVE

Sven Larsson barely finished high school. In and out of trouble with the law, the day he graduated his father gave him an ultimatum: join the military or go to sea. The next day he found himself on a tramp steamer as a deck hand, washing, cleaning, loading, and unloading. The ship grossed but 10,000 tons. As a tramp, she sailed from port to port without scheduling, often carrying their own booms and cranes in case the port lacked the equipment.

He learned about work from hard able-bodied seamen who lacked patience for laziness and had an occasional talk with him below decks, convincing the lad that hard work is less painful than getting pummeled by fists. After that, he learned quickly and attracted the attention of the captain who schooled the young man in the art of working the heavy equipment and brought him to the bridge to educate him on the use of the tools at hand. He worked the tramp another two years then transferred to a 30,000 ton freighter and soon proved his skills in organizing and supervising the storage of goods and developing his people skills. Two years later he joined the Norwegian navy and after another 10 years joined the Norwegian cruise lines and worked himself up to Captain.

Through it all, he'd encountered armed pirates, ship fires, explosions, and collisions; onboard murders, typhoons, and ghost ships. Like any longtime seaman, Sven Larsson could tell a lot of stories.

Larsson said, "We're going full speed ahead. We're out of cell phone range now, but once these men realize they can call in their threat via cell, with me and John to substantiate their threats, they may want us to turn around."

At that moment a walkie talkie squawked. One terrorist was communicating with another for a check in. Larsson said, "We've got dozens of those among our crew. It seems the bad guys have some of them now."

"Are they all on the same frequency?" Jeff asked.

"No. Housekeeping is on one, security operates on another, so does medical, wait-staff supervisors another, and engineering still another," Larsson replied.

Before Jeff could comment, Carmen asked, "Why did they even need to leave Puerto Vallarta? Why didn't they lock down the ship and make their demands right where we were parked?"

"Because the international gods of hell would come down upon them," threw in Evans, who had remained quiet during the escapade, watching, assessing. "Whoever is behind this, if they blew up the ship, they'd also destroy the port. Other boats and their passengers might likely be harmed as well. Their entire families would be wiped from the map in nothing flat, and a lot more than that by an outraged world. Look at what happened in Beirut when a county's entire seaport, their major source of income, was destroyed because of hundreds of tons of fertilizer stored in a nearby warehouse exploded at once. In their case, authorities had received many warnings about its presence, but did nothing to remove it. It brought the country to its knees. Now imagine the same thing, if not worse, happening in Puerto Vallarta."

"I agree," said Jeff. "This smacks of long-term planning by someone. Typically Middle Eastern guys don't hire outsiders to do their dirty work and these three didn't look the part."

Jeff turned to Larsson. "Captain, who's in charge of cargo loading?"

"That would be Francisco. He's been with the line for years."

Jeff thought for a moment and said, "We can worry about Francisco later. I'm curious about how food supplies were loaded onto this ship in San Diego?"

Larsson shrugged, "Typically, 30 truckloads of provisions deliver a million dollars-worth of food on pallets and are ferried to 20 storage locations, depending on the items and their temperature requirements. On our ship, they are on 9 floors. We have aluminum-lined freezers and rooms for defrosting. We were fully stocked in San Diego, partially stocked in Vancouver, and minimally stocked in Puerto Vallarta. Plus we have storage for extra luggage, heavy furniture, and the like. All frozen fish and meats are spot checked, as are fruits and vegetables. A dog sniffs all pallets for contraband."

"Therefore, you couldn't slip in, say, as much high grade explosive as you wanted into some of these boxes or crates and set it off by a remote device."

"Correct," admitted Larson.

"Unlikely or not, I might suggest that, however they got in, explosives could be in one of the storage areas, so maybe it's time for somebody to go into those rooms to ensure their goods are safe. Hell, I'm just throwing it out there."

From his position looking out the window, Evans remarked, "I've worked alongside explosives people and there is a formula for computing the amount you need to do a certain amount of damage to a certain target. Sinking a superstructure like this would take a lot, but not as much as you'd think if placed in the right location. We're talking about sinking fast here, not a slow leak."

"Which begs a lot of questions," Jeff added. "Two of which are, how much and where is it?"

"I should think enough Semtex or C-4 in a confined space should do it," Evans offered. "Only 12 ounces of Semtex brought down the plane over Lockerbie, Scotland, not too many years ago."

"But luggage is all checked by x-ray, isn't it?" Carmen said.

"Correct," Evans said.

"And food supplies," she added.

"Correct."

"Even without the humans aboard, I'd hate to lose the Princess Fairie. It isn't as though she is destined for the bone yard, yet," Jeff stated.

"She's less than three years old," Larsson said. "There are several countries that build these. This one was actually built in South Korea at the Hyundai plant. It's one of three yards in the country and the largest in the world. I watched the final stages of construction. It's put together in sections with the cabins built at a location away from the shipyard."

Pondering the topic, Jeff found himself fascinated by the entire industry of shipping. For the moment, his sense of duty brought him back to reality. Changing the subject, he said, "Unfortunately we don't have fingerprints to send in. That might give us a clue as to what they are about."

"Honey, we do," Carmen replied, shaking her head at his non-sequitur, "They're on my phone." Then she repeated the conversation she'd had to delay the men and John's taking of her phone to look at it."

Jeff said, "I guess we'd need Sellotape for that. If so, it's probably in John's office."

Carmen thought that if she could play cat and mouse with Jerry Richards for days on end, she should be able to do this. She stood up and stated, "I'll get it. There's no reason for me to stay here. There are thousands of people out there enjoying themselves. I'm one more with only a few of us who know what's going on."

"Take the internal stairway back there. It'll

be faster." Evans suggested, Before Jeff could object, she swept out the door and was gone. She'd need either a key or would have to announce herself when she returned.

Larsson instructed, "Hunter, maintain your watch and let us know if anyone approaches."

Jeff had questions running through his mind. When were the captives taken? How will the captors know that they have completed negotiations? What if somebody comes over to a home where the captors are being held in the meantime? Who the hell are these people?

Larsson said, "Hunter, as soon as she returns, power up the systems so we can inform HQ of the developments."

Jeff added, "Sir, if it's all right, I'd also like to get those prints to my contact with the DC FBI and also apprise him of our situation."

An anxious ten minutes later, Carmen knocked at the door she left from, announced herself and appeared with a towel under one arm covering the roll of Sellotape. Evans punched in the passcode to provide power to the bridge ensuring the monitors were on, but the lights were off, and the men went to work.

Larsson said, "With McKenzie in tow, they'd have a key. We don't need to be surprised. Hunter, can we operate the cameras independent of the bridge power?"

"Not normally, sir. Now that the power is on, I can tie into either security or cruise director and that'll give us an independent screen. Are you thinking about keeping on eye on the stairwells?"

"Correct," Larsson replied.

The sun touched the western horizon. Soon the exterior lights of the great vessel would go on, which would add to those of the interior lights. Areas of the ship would illuminate in red, others in blue, and countless pinpoints of yellow-white light would cover her from stem to stern, like a giant 900 foot long Christmas tree lying on its side. The lone exception would be the unlighted bridge which would only give off a dim glow.

Within short minutes the work was done. HQ and the FBI had been updated and the cameras activated to provide a split screen view of the bottom of both exterior and interior stairwells leading to the bridge. Larsson contacted Barney, who was off-shift, and apprised him of developments.

Suddenly Evans announced, "Carlos is coming back. He's coming up the interior."

By the time Carlos unlocked the door, everyone was seated, including the captain with the power off again. Carlos took two steps in, then stopped. He looked around at everyone and everything. He walked forward and began touching monitors, fronts and backs. He concentrated on those nearest Wentworth and the ones across the aisle where Wentworth sat.

"These are warm, this one's hot. You've been using it. What is it?" Carlos asked, angrily.

Jeff sat next to Carmen only six feet from the man checking Carlos's unworked knuckles. No punching bag practice there, unless you wanted to count human bodies. Jeff computed that within a couple of seconds he could shatter the man's jaw and knock out half his teeth. It would take a little longer to drag him over to the rail and dump him into the ocean a good 100 feet down. Who, Carlos? He never showed up, they could say.

Jeff, calm down. Hopefully your time will come, he thought.

Wentworth wanted to tell Carlos they were speaking with authorities about him and his friends. Instead, he explained, "It should be hot. This is navigation and it's tied into 500 miles of wires and cables from the machinery below the water line to the rotating radar dish on the roof and the antennae. It's getting fed with juice from the engine room, but HQ shut down the power to the units."

Carlos stared at him a moment, turned, and walked out the door.

Larsson said, "I didn't know all that."

"I didn't either," Evans threw in.

"Neither did I until this moment," Wentworth grinned.

Everyone remained silent for a moment, until Jeff said, "LaMonde."

"What about him, honey? Are you getting hungry?" Carmen teased. Comedy relief in a tragedy.

Jeff scratched his head. "Yes, but that's not what I'm getting at. If a large quantity of explosives are present in the food lockers, maybe he can direct his people to look for them. What do you think, Hunter?"

Evans said, "Some of our food storage lockers are as big as a basketball court. They're insulated, aluminum lined, and with a steel flooring. Toward the lower level is the I-95 corridor, then below that is the crew's quarters, their restaurants, and exercise rooms. Below that is the engine room and the bottom of the ship, which is double-hulled. You'd make a hell of a mess if it went off in one of the lockers, but I don't think it would sink the ship, at least not in the way they might intend. I don't think they want a Titanic incident where people get to climb into lifeboats and wait for rescue—in this case, in relatively warm waters."

"Maybe they're only stored there," Jeff suggested. "Hell, I don't know," he finally admitted.

Evans held up a finger that he poked in the air to make his point. "If it was me, if and when it came down to negotiations, I'd need a show of strength, not some cell phone pictures—no offense, Captain. I'd need to blow up something first. Okay, then I might use one of the lockers, or the luggage storage area for something of limited quantity to pull out and show off. I think it's worth a try to conduct a search."

Larsson picked up a walkie talkie, adjusted the frequency dial, and was about to make a call when Jeff suddenly said, "Oh, shit."

All eyes turned to him. *What now?* Jeff stood and began to pace, then turned to the group like an actor on stage. "Plan B. Attract attention. How? Blow up something anytime they want. What's the best way not to get caught carrying enough explosive that will show up like a sore thumb? Have it already embedded, planted on the ship when it was constructed. What's the best way to blow off the bottom of the ship? Plant your explosives at the same time the ship is constructed back in Korea, maybe in the engine room. They like embedding people, maybe they like embedding explosives."

The others froze in place, digesting Jeff's words, exploring his theory, feeling it, tasting it. See if the shoe fit. The pieces of the puzzle came together, at least for the picture he was working on. No flaws could be found in the working theory.

"Captain, I'd like permission to meet Barney and his crew downstairs and see if we can find the mother lode," Evans requested.

"Permission granted, Hunter," Larsson said.

"Captain, I'd like to go with him," Jeff requested.

"Permission granted," Larsson repeated,

without hesitation, then he made the call to have all engineering officers meet in the lower deck. He also needed to call headquarters. Like Jeff said, they like embedding. Which meant they had their own people in Orlando and South Korea.

Larsson's sat phone rang. He answered and held up a hand for the others to wait. "Bill, get the com up again, and Carmen, if you don't mind, please, keep an eye out."

Listening to the FBI director's instructions, he turned off his sat phone and walked to the duplicate computer terminal in the Control Room, where Butler's face appeared. The face said, "I appreciate your need for brevity here, so I'll make it quick. Juan is Juan Fernando Cabrera, a Spaniard, international arms dealer and drug smuggler. He's a free-lancer and an absolute detail freak, worse than an engineer on steroids. He triples as a hostage negotiator, except that he's on the other end. People call him when they have hostages in order to get the best price paid for them. He gets a piece of the action, typically 20 percent. His family owns an entire hotel in Seville and has properties in Monaco, New York City, and Beverly Hills. He's a busy man.

"Carlos is Carlos Atondo Zatarain, a real nasty human, the product of a bad gene pool. We tied him directly to murders of 15 good Mexican police officers who wouldn't be bought and he probably owns a big part of the PV police department thanks to cartel money. Torture is one of his specialties. He enjoys strapping explosive devises onto children. A couple of cuts below your basic low life. By Darwinian standards, he should have been deselected at birth. We don't see people like him on these kinds of operations. That's what has us concerned. They're going for broke on this one, no bluffing involved.

"Zatarain lives in a large estate on the outskirts of the city, in all likelihood with his extended family including his wife, in-laws, four children and a minimum of two heavily armed security guards. He has an evil sister who ran around somewhere lost in the badlands until you sent us her picture from the bus. She tries to emulate him. In fact, she has done so on a number of occasions. We've been looking for a chance to nail the three of them when they're not protected. Now we have that chance.

"Using facial tech, we've been able to identify the couple you say are from Montana. She's Antoinette Gervais, a French woman who specializes in bomb making. Sometimes she goes by the first name of Marianne. People like her are a dime a dozen these days. In her case, her father owns a shipping line and she's got years of shipboard experience. The French say she does impeccable research before any job. These range from school buses to synagogues to entire office buildings. Even an embassy or two. We haven't gotten a fix on the purported husband yet. Another we've identified is, believe it or not, a South Korean, along with a German man.

Jeff actually blushed from a headrush of rage, listening to Butler's description of their foes. He took a quick look at Carmen to see her shake her head in disbelief, a look of horror crossing her face. She wondered how people got that rich. She had a cousin who wanted to substitute teach in California but couldn't get issued a license because the state told her there were so many fraudulent applications for the position of sub-stitute teacher that the board of education was considering phasing out the entire category and giving everybody a full teaching license and be done with the fraud. You can't make it up.

Jeff was the first to reply. "Sir, here's a thought. What's good for the goose is good for the gander."

Larsson's shift had ended along with that of his skeleton crew. Cruise lines were strict about timely shift changes. There was no rule that said he had to leave the bridge when the new shift ar-rived. When Compton did appear with her team, the spacious bridge became crowded. Larsson brought everyone up to date and tried to answer questions. He had no answer as to where the ex-plosives were hidden or if, indeed, they even ex-isted. Juan and Maria could have been bluffing. Calling their hand was not an option.

SIX

Muhammad Mohammad had reached the pinnacle of success. He was one of the most hunted persons in the world. It wasn't so much the money that kept him in fame. He had that. He simply enjoyed his line of work. As a master of disguises, Mohammad could speak several languages, had a passport to any country he wanted to have a passport to, and he had employees from China to Russia to Mexico and in between. Completely emotionless, the man was wanted for murder, extortion, embezzlement, genocide, terrorism, and crimes against humanity. And the perfect man for the job.

When tasked with the request by the New Generation Cartel to work up a plan to enrich them with an obscene amount of money, Mohammad began to think like a magician. Come up with an idea for an outlandish trick, then piece-by-piece, work out the way for the trick to be completed and then display it for all eyes to see. Through instinct and experience, like all good tricks, he had no doubt this one would require a lot of time, a lot of assistance, and, in this case, a lot of investment dollars.

A million dollars in $100 bills occupies 4.47 cubic feet of space, about the size of a large clothing trunk. A billion equals 4470 cubic feet of space, about four times the size of an average bedroom. But he didn't want hundred dollar bills. He wanted 10s, 20, 50s and 100s.

The money would have to be airlifted to several drop-off points around the world. Similar to what the Americans had airlifted to Iran in the middle of the night, over a billion dollars had been presented to the Persians to further their expansionist activities. Multiply this several fold.

Cash had its advantages. No electronic transfers to trace to their owners, or accounts to freeze, and easier to distribute for purchases and payoffs. His share would be in the billions, as would that of his negotiator, Juan. Not a bad payday for either of them.

Negotiations would take time. The hostages would be sequestered in previously designated locations away from their own homes once things dragged on beyond a day. Guaranteed. They would be missed and searched for. Fine. Comes with the territory. If he became impatient with the authorities dragging their feet while they attempted a rescue plan—another guarantee—he would order the ship's forest blown up. The fire would be large enough to be picked up by a satellite that will have been shifted to keep an eye on them. This would serve to emphasize his point as an accelerant to speed up the talks. And once video of their escapade reached the world, he had people in place to up the ante by bringing crew members and passengers into view while they got dismembered. Enter Carlos.

When he hadn't heard from his man aboard

ship that the call had been made to Orlando, to Washington, and to the Associated Press, he didn't have any true concerns. Delays can be expected. Small mishaps are the rule in a big operation. However, two hours after the appointed time, he attempted to reach his man aboard ship directly. The call failed to go through. He called his contact with the IMO based in London, but got no answer.

Another two hours passed until, at last, London called. The caller had been tasked with tracking the ship and he couldn't get away until now and "Yes," the SSAS had been activated and the ship opted to go dark. No communications in or out. It was a new tactic decided upon by the ship's captain. Worse, he was unreachable by sat phone. He had turned it off.

Mohammad sat back in his chair and now he thought, *Shit.*

Within minutes, a dozen senior officers and senior engineering staff casually sauntered into one of the doors leading to the three-level engine room that measured almost the length of the ship, located at levels B, C, and D. Near where they stood were trash compactors for recycling cans, glass, and cardboard, along with a paper and cardboard shredder, and a container for batteries and other hazardous materials. A sea water desalinization unit turned salt water to potable water.

On the next level down at the other end of the cavernous room, the noise of four 14-cylinder diesel-electric engines echoed throughout the chamber, each of the 56 huge pistons measuring 14" in diameter. Still, this was the quietest area to speak and hear. Rows and banks of machines, pipes, and tubes on all three tiers were everywhere. Workers wearing ear protectors took samples of liquids, checked gauges, and cleaned, while standing on areas of either solid steel sheeting or steel grating. The machines that provided data for air and lubricant flow and temperature, along with a dozen other parameters, sent signals to a data readout room down below and the Control Room above, like the vital signs of a person under constant observation.

The huge vessel once contained two million gallons of fuel. It now had somewhat less than that with fuel stored above the keel, the backbone of a ship that runs from stem to stern below where they stood.

"What are we looking for, sir?" Barney asked, above the clatter, loudly enough for all to hear.

Evans said, "It'll probably be off-white or red-orange and either tube-like or squared off. It's malleable, so it can be shaped. The catch is, it won't be visible. I don't think it'll be in a pipe because that would block the flow of whatever the pipe is carrying and we'd notice that. If it does go off, figure on a giant hole in the bottom or the entire bottom of the ship blowing off when the fuel tanks beneath us explode. We'd be lucky to save a single soul.

Jeff asked, "Can it be set off by remote control even if it is in a pipe?"

Evans answered, "Not by radio signals. Those won't transmit through steel. A UHF walkie talkie with a strong antenna will do it like the kind we use on this ship and most other ships. Those signals will go through or around wood or steel. Also, look for attachments to the explosive and don't touch anything. Call me as soon as you find anything."

After nearly an hour of searching, one of the engineers yelled from the bottom tier where a dozen pumps and lines of varying sizes ran up the walls and along the ceiling in an area primarily reserved for spare parts. "Sir, I think I might have found something."

The man led the group to a grating that he highlighted with a flashlight. A box appeared to be attached to the underside of the grating by steel mesh that blended perfectly with the color of the grating itself.

"Somebody get me a crowbar," Barney yelled over racket of two of the monster engines on the level immediately above their heads.

Barney cautiously pried up the grating. A heavy plastic box measuring some two-feet square and a foot in thickness came up with it. "Now get me some heavy shears," he directed.

Evans began taking pictures as the men proceeded with their activities.

"Let's pick up the entire grating and pull it over to the side so we can get a purchase on the box and shear off the attachments," Barney directed.

Several men muscled the heavy grating off its seat and slid it to the side. While two men held the box and others held the grate vertically, Barney cut its attachments. Returning the grate to its proper position, everyone stepped back to permit Evans access to the box resting on the floor. He found several clasps holding it closed. He unsnapped the clasps to find the box filled with 20 pounds of orange rectangular tubes. Probes led into each of them with a central device that appeared to be radio controlled.

Evans took the radio from his belt and walked a good 300 feet away so he could make a call to Larsson to ask the senior officers what they wanted to do with the Semtex.

Larsson and Compton thought of the options. They absolutely couldn't leave the explosives onboard, even if they were defused. If any remained, defused or not, both could be excoriated and their careers would likely come to an abrupt end. It could cause the death of the company, as well, if the public found out. But wouldn't they need evidence?

On the other hand, the terrorists had committed enough crimes to put them away forever, if they lived that long. Let HQ make the decision. Which is what they did. Compton chanced a sat phone call when a lookout informed them he saw nobody coming.

Within five long minutes, the reply came: "Take it to a loading door and dump whatever you find into the ocean."

A quarter-hour later, Larsson, his officers, Jeff and Carmen, retired for the evening counting it a partial success. Ortiz took over driving the blind ship.

Cabo San Lucas is a popular community at the southern tip of Baja California which belongs to Mexico. It is a popular vacation spot for tourists who enjoy water sports, quaint shops, good dining, and laying in the sun. No mountains or zip lines there. Lacking a marina, ships anchor off shore and tender passengers to the dock.

Generally, international waters start around 200 nautical miles from a country's shoreline and continue outward. To complicate it more, international waters are usually broken into sections, and different countries have various rights concerning these sections.

Ideally, Larsson wanted to reach international or American waters. With Cabo San Lucas as the next stop on the schedule, he knew they couldn't swing wide enough to make that happen. He would be destined to sail in Mexican waters, which would give Mexico priority over the terrorists. He needed to contact Bishop, who was unaware of the events, to make an announcement: "Due to minor engine problems, we regret to inform you that we will not be stopping at Cabo San Lucas and will continue onward toward San Diego. We apologize for any inconvenience and will be offering discount vouchers for those who wish to travel with us in the future."

Jeff and Carmen returned to the bridge in the morning, both restless and unable to sleep well or enjoy any shipboard activities awaiting any call from Butler at FBI.

At last, the sat phone rang. Larsson answered. Dawn had come and the ship sailed due north with the Gulf of California in the distance to their port side. Sunlight highlighted the water in front of the ship as it sped toward San Diego.

"You can turn your power on now, Captain." Butler instructed. "You'll need your screen for this."

All the power to the bridge returned and a score of monitors in two rooms lit up. Butler's face appeared on the monitor linked to satellite. He looked tired. His voice lacked energy. "This took some high level negotiations and string pulling with the end result that each country could do what it wanted and how it wanted as long as the end results were the same."

Scenes flashed on the screen in rotation, each

lasting some 20-30 seconds. Butler's voice over-rode the pictures and everyone crowded to see.

"First, this is the present situation facing Carlos's family." Dead bodyguards lay outside the compound. Within its walls, Mexican police were holding submachine guns pointed at children and family.

"This is the present situation facing Juan's family:" Juan's dead brother lay in a pool of blood. The remainder of his family in Seville faced guns held by Spanish militia.

Butler flashed another picture. "Captain, this is your wife." Kristine waved, smiling. In the background, police were leading a man away in handcuffs.

"This is McKenzie's family," Butler continued." Three children and their parents were at home in the company of FBI SWAT. Two bodies were being loaded into a coroner's wagon.

And so it went with Compton's family. All were free and safe.

Jeff mentioned the possible element of further explosives onboard, to which Butler replied, "We can't wait. They probably have others onboard who may be able to set them off."

Wentworth, Evans, and Carmen went to the CCTV screens and worked the restaurants first. With over 30 locations, it took several minutes to locate the two men and Maria lounging at a table eating and talking. Carlos was animated, gesticulating and pounding the fist of one hand into the palm of the other.

"I'd like the honors," Carmen said. "I'm certain they'll be pleased to hear that the captain wants to negotiate terms."

SEVEN

Six levels down, the small venue was nearly empty of diners at this early hour. Juan swallowed a piece of apple pie and washed it down with a sip of coffee. He said, "It's time to light it up."

"There probably won't be anybody up there, which is too bad," Carlos said. "If we can wait until 7:00 pm tomorrow night, they'll have their nightly show on deck with 2000 people attending. Anyway, afterward, I want to have a talk with that bald guy." He pounded his fist into his palm.

Juan looked at Carlos in disgust. It wasn't so much that he didn't care about so many people dying or getting them burned, it was about the fact that the man wanted to enact his fantasies rather than work for the good of the project. He had told Mohammad that Carlos was not a good man for the job because he was always too impetuous. Muhammad replied that he needed somebody on the team who was not—what's the word— squeamish?

"We're going to do it from topside before the fire and emergency personnel flood the place."

Juan said, exercising authority. "The crew practices a drill you don't know about. They do it weekly and make up possible problems they have to address. There are hidden passages and ladders they can utilize for speed. On this ship, a tragedy that occurs on the surface will bring them there soon enough and they are well trained and experienced. So we're getting up there before they do."

The three spent the next few minutes discussing the presentation of their terms before and after the forest and playground exploded.

About to stand and leave, Maria said, "Look who's coming. My favorite friend."

The others looked up to see Carmen entering the restaurant and approach.

"How did she know we were here?" Carlos asked.

"Beats me. Let's see what she wants," Juan replied.

Carmen walked to their table grim faced and said, "The captain wants to negotiate terms."

Juan sat back and pondered her statement, his slick hair reflecting the light of the restaurant. He asked, "If there is no communication, how is anybody going to know what agreement we come to?"

Carmen said, "He told me to tell you that corporate turned on all their power and they're ready to talk. That's all I know."

"Who the hell are you?" Maria demanded.

"A messenger girl like you," Carmen said.

"Let it go, Maria. You'll get your chance," Juan said. "Right now, it's show time." The three looked at one another, cautiously expectant and followed Carmen out the door.

A few minutes later, the four returned to the bridge via the outside stairway with smug looks on the faces of three of them. Carmen's lips were set tight, determined. Once they entered, Carmen closed the door. Larsson stood tall and proud, relaxed like a swimmer on a starting block ready to take his mark. The monitors were on as were the bridge lights. The skeleton crews of both captains were present with Compton's actively on duty. Everyone looked tired. Hell Week compressed into a few hours. The spacious glass-enclosed room looked crowded and busy.

Larsson announced, "We found your explosives in the engine room and dumped them in the ocean."

The terrorists looked doubtful. Larsson directed, "Look at the monitor in front of Mr. Wentworth. By the way, we're linked to home base and the IMO."

The three moved forward as one, like three yoyos being pulled by a single string.

Butler's face wasn't there, only his voice. The crew members, Jeff, and Carmen stood to the rear, behind them. They had already seen this show. The voice on the screen described the scenes of the captured or dead captors and the freed captives.

"Do you have anything to say to us?" Compton asked.

No answer.

"How about to these pictures?" Butler voice asked. In the next scenes, he displayed the videos of the terrorists' families held at gunpoint.

"You lost the game," said Jeff, from behind them. "Everything you worked for is gone. Your lives are gone. You'll always be looking behind yourselves to see who is going to shiv you in prison or who is going to be your next lover."

What's good for the goose is good for the gander.

This time Larsson spoke to the screen. "Sir, we believe we have more explosives onboard. If you don't mind, we'll get back with you."

"Acknowledged," replied the voice. The screen went dark.

Jeff said, "Good, he didn't have to watch anyway. He might not like what he's about to see."

"Watch what?" Evans asked.

Jeff, fully aware that what he was about to do, could cause him serious legal problems later on an international scale, grabbed Juan by the right shoulder. He pulled him back and around so they faced each other, then slammed him in the balls with a rock hard fist. The man bent over and Jeff rammed a second fist into his midsection. The man's mouth opened from air escaping from his lungs and he instantly vomited his meal before dropping to the floor.

Three seconds had passed.

Jeff said, "Juan, that's disgusting."

Another two seconds.

Jeff was clearly out of control. Turning to the others, he said, "The bastard puked on my slacks. Now I'm really pissed."

Time slowed for Jeff. He turned toward Carlos. He thought that a bad judge might let them all go free if they promised to be good from now on. He thought that he could face severe penalties for what he was doing. He only knew that their millions and billions of dollars wouldn't spare them from the pain that other humans felt. He so desperately wanted them to remember the humiliation of this day whether they lived or died. They were ready to kill thousands on their way to killing millions with their drugs, a work in progress.

Carlos stood close by to the right, surprised at Jeff's moves, his fallen leader with his expensive clothing, now in need of a good dry-cleaning. Jeff had always tried to use his intellect to channel his anger. Not this time. Letting it all go, he quickly took a step back and launched a horrific kick to the side of Carlos's left thigh, pushing his hip into it. Under normal circumstance, even a light blow to the area separating the thigh muscle from the hamstring can be extremely painful. In this instance, the kick fractured Carlos's femur. The man screamed in pain and went down.

Goose and gander.

Three more seconds.

The others cleared away as though a bomb had gone off. Jeff fell with all his weight on the broken leg causing the bone to separate further and grabbed the stricken man by the mouth, squeezing so hard the man's eyes bulged out. Holding him in place, Jeff took several seconds to whisper in his ear, then let him go.

Twenty seconds all together.

With the exception of the captain, the watchers stood as though paralyzed, never having witnessed such mayhem, at least not in the command center. Larsson would take this any day compared with armed men boarding his ship and shooting virtually everyone they saw. He wanted this to go on, but there were too many observers. He stepped in and grabbed Jeff by the arm, pulling him off of Carlos. Incensed, Jeff pulled his arm free, tried to stand, appeared to stumble, and, with his knee, landed squarely on Carlos's hand and wrist, breaking several bones in each. Inwardly smiling, he thought, *That one is for men you never knew who came after my wife and for the babies you hurt.*

Moans and cries of pain echoed throughout the enclosed space of the bridge. It reminded Larsson of the early days when he was on the receiving end. He took a step forward in order to separate the parties like a referee calling a halt to a one-sided fight. He pulled Jeff off again and said, "Enough." This Shenero character might be smart in some ways, but he had some anger issues. Perhaps he did as well.

Two down one to go. The herd had thinned. With Larsson distracted, Carmen saw her opportunity. She said to Maria, "Hey, it's your turn."

The street-savvy woman glared at Carmen, fury in her eyes, tightened the muscles in her body, clenched her fists, pulled back her right arm several inches, and replied, "Bring it on, bitch. I am so looking forward to . . . "

Maria never finished her sentence. Carmen raked the nails of her left hand deeply down the side of Maria's face. When Maria yelled and grabbed at her face with her right hand, Carmen threw a vicious right cross hitting her in the nose and upper lip like a heat-seeking missile flying toward a homing beacon. Throwing her hips into the punch, as Jeff had taught her, she hit the nose on an angle with her knuckles, snapping it far to the right, splitting the upper lip wide open in a vertical gash. A geyser of blood exploded from it like a volcano erupting. Maria threw both hands to her face and several front teeth fell to the ground. The woman dropped to her knees, blood running down her tan shirt. Carmen stood over the fallen woman and shouted, "More beauty marks for you. What's that? I didn't hear you.

You're going to do what?"

Less than 30 seconds had passed from start to finish of the affair.

Larsson had the thought that both the Sheneros could use counseling. He finally let go of Jeff and pulled Carmen aside, saying, "Why don't you two get some fresh air," nodding at the door. He added, abruptly, "Wait, hang on a second. It looks like Juan might be the first to recover. When he does, we'll ask him about any remaining explosives."

This time Compton wanted in. She knelt next to Juan and politely asked for the location of the explosives on deck along with the names and locations of the rest of his team, explaining that if he didn't talk, the Spanish militia were authorized to murder this family.

Juan hesitated. He looked over at Carlos writhing on the ground trying to find a way to ease the excruciating pain in his leg and trying to cradle his fractured wrist at the same time. The femur break looked ugly. From his own position on the ground he could see the inside of the pant leg pushed outward by the splintered bone. Should Carlos survive this ordeal, he would never walk right again, or use his right hand without pain. He saw Maria, her face broken.

Juan looked at the woman who had done the damage. She stood proudly over Maria like a knight who had slain a dragon. Who the hell were these two? They didn't look or act or dress like security personnel. Why hadn't he been informed of their presence? The bald guy was smiling, nodding at him, glancing at Carlos, a glance that promised he would be next. Juan weighed the options. His people wouldn't kill him for following directives. They would kill him for revealing information. And his own people would kill his family. Or perhaps the Mexicans or Americans would order it. He hadn't signed on for this. He signed on to murder 8000 people and go down with the ship, perhaps to become a martyr, not to get beaten by a mad man and watch his own family die—well, one of his families.

To make matters worse, after the Americans got finished with him, he would be turned over to the Mexicans and then to the Spanish. He could count on getting tortured mentally and physically several times over to reveal what he didn't know; the identity of the man at the top who had hired him, having had contact with his representative two and three times removed. Nobody was going to believe him when he screamed that he didn't know who had hired him. They would take him for a hard case and work him over even more, but keep him alive. Based on his experience, he didn't have the slightest doubt that the same thing would happen to the other two, injuries or not.

Caught with his pants down, for the first time in his life, the always suave and debonair Juan felt great fear. His assets would be confiscated. First one there gets there first. There was no way out. Unless he negotiated.

"Who's got the trigger?" she demanded.

"She does. The dummy phone's in the pouch," Juan said, nodding his head back toward Maria. "Do you think I'd let her have the real thing? Come on. Set my family free and maybe I'll tell you who does know where they're hidden."

"How does she fit into this and is she his sister?" Compton asked.

Juan replied, trying unsuccessfully to stand straight, terrible pain shooting through the core of his body. He needed to pee, but couldn't, even if he had the chance. His entire groin had swollen. "Yes, she is. She wasn't part of the original plan. Carlos brought her along, insisting she needed the experience so he let her come."

"He's willing to let her die?" Compton inquired.

"Yes. I wouldn't mind seeing it either. She wanted to be part of the project and play the biggest role."

There. He had compromised. He was dicking with them at the same time. He had told them she had a fake trigger, but not where the explosives were located. The fact is he didn't know where they were hidden just like the batch they said they dumped into the ocean. They could be anywhere and everywhere. That information was above his pay grade. Once onboard, all they had to do was to show dirty pictures on their phones, make demands, blow things up and maybe torture and kill a few innocents.

"A role? You mean such as dialing the numbers that would murder all these innocent people?" Compton asked. She turned her head back to where Maria lay on the ground in a growing pool of blood, next to her brother, who coiled and uncoiled like a snake that couldn't make up its mind, wishing she had been the one who had hit her, even if it meant the loss of her career.

Juan said, "Again, we knew there were explosives so we could make our demands. Nobody told us where they are. Our divisions are separate from one another."

"Good. Thanks. I feel so much better now," Compton replied, sarcastically.

Larsson listened to the exchange, amazed at Compton's poise through all. He had never seen this side of her. If only a bomb or drug-sniffing dog were available. He considered that if this were the middle ages, each of them would be tied to a stretching device, broken bones or not. In fact, in those days, people were tortured first so that suspected criminals would be reluctant to commit a crime later.

Compton pulled the pouch from Maria's neck and looked inside to pull out a cell phone. "Is this it?" she asked Juan.

Jeff said, "Never mind him. I think I know

who might have it. Does anybody have a passenger manifest?"

EIGHT

Negotiations were off. Juan looked at this
guy who just kept hitting him like whack-a-mole
till he struck at the heart of the problem. And
how was your day?

"I do right here," replied one of Compton's
officers, pulling up a slate and accessing the
ship's records. He handed it over to Jeff, trying
not to step in the blood.

By maritime law, the manifest contains the
names of guests and crew members and their
rooms for each voyage. In modern times, the list
is maintained in the cloud for a limited period of
time for reference purposes.

Behind Larson, Evans said, "I'll get John out
of lockup. We'll get his team together to find
the explosives and take these guys to share cells
with their friends. I don't think I've ever worked
a ship with this many locked up at once."

Larsson addressed no person in particular
in the crowded space when he said, "Search all
three of them for weapons, top to bottom, inside and outside, before taking them out. I don't
want any suicides or killings, if possible. And no
house arrests. I want them jailed. Take Juan and
this Maria and a couple of men with you when
you go. Take them down the back elevators out

of sight. As for Carlos, we'll have security haul him off on a stretcher."

Hoping the matter had concluded, Larsson's trained mind shifted toward what might happen at landfall. First, a host of agents would surreptitiously board the vessel, position themselves accordingly, await the departure of some 6000 guests and finally, escort their captives to, at this point in time, unknown destinations. Once the passengers were cleared, 30 truckloads of foodstuffs would brought aboard and cleaners would begin the endless task of polishing, changing sheets, and washing dishes, along with the addition of another two million gallons of fuel. Within short hours, in the morning, a new voyage would begin with another 6000 passengers.

Marianne should have picked a more common first name like Sue or Peggy or Patty. There were only two women named Marianne listed among the guests. One was 82 years old, the other 45. This was confirmed by her appearance when she opened the door at the knock.

Marianne would spend the rest of her life in prison. Which country and which prison remained to be seen and likely make a big difference in her survival chances. She only had to trade information about her partners, where the explosives were hidden, how she managed the job in South Korea, all her contacts, and who headed the operation. She and Maria could be sent to the women's prison of Ciudad Juarez, a nasty place in the city of Juarez across the border from El Paso, Texas. Known as El Cereso (Centro de Re-adaptacion Social), it is housed with women, 80 percent of whom are there for narcotics related crimes, ostensibly because of their husbands' activities. Or not. Alternatively, she could be sent to maximum security Riker's Island in New York, where domestic and foreign terrorists are housed. The men faced similar circumstances, depending on who got them last.

Larsson ordered, "Search these three for weapons, inside and out."

Ready volunteers leapt to the task. To no one's surprise, short minutes later, Compton found a razor sharp short ceramic knife with a finger hole for easy purchase beneath Maria's belt. Carlos expressed his extreme displeasure at the weapons search on his person lead by Jeff. No others were found.

Addressing Wentworth, Larson, now full Captain and Master again, directed, "Bill, compute our speed and adjust downward. We're a half day ahead of schedule by not stopping at Cabo San Lucas. We have a boat full of people who made arrangements for flights or to get picked up. We're well over two days out of San Diego. Tell Bishop's crew to make the appropriate announcements. Let's get us there at the expected arrival time. Oh, and call housekeeping while you're at it.

"Yes, sir," Wentworth assented, and began the calculations, programming them into the nav.

Jeff said, "Captain, if you don't mind, Carmen and I will be out of your hair." He took Carmen's hand and prepared to leave.

Larsson grinned, thinking about what he wanted to say, and then said it, "If you're not too busy, I'll see you at my table for our last dinner on this cruise."

"It'll be an honor, sir," Jeff replied.

Walking out in the cool breeze of the early morning, holding hands, Carmen asked, "Honey, I'm curious. What did you say to Carlos when you had him down?"

Somewhat reluctant to tell her, he recalled what she had done to Maria's face and determined that she had the strength to handle it. He said, "I told him that the pictures he had been shown were old and that every single member of his family had been killed, including his parents, his cousins, and his children, and his house had been burned to the ground."

Shocked at his words, Carmen asked, "Dear Lord. What? I mean how do you know they . . . "

Jeff answered, somberly, "I made it up. I wanted to give the piece of shit son of a bitch something to think about while he rots in pain in the brig on the way to the States. I also told him we didn't have any pain killers onboard, but I'll get him an aspirin tablet if he begs nicely."

Carmen listened to her husband's words and wished she had thought of something like that to say to Maria. She did say, "Better get two aspirin tablets. My girl is going to be a mouth-breather for a long time. Maybe one of her friends knows how to fix noses. It should hurt a lot."

Jeff had overheard Evans remark that he was going to let John oversee the welfare of the prisoners once he got out of the brig and after they found the explosives. It made him want to say, "Can I watch?"

"These aren't a few members of the gang that couldn't shoot straight," Jeff added. "If you think about it, this operation has far reaching tentacles and took years to plan. They missed a couple of details that's all. The good news for them is that their little prison is meant for drunks, not for a gang of terrorists. It has a shower, a cot, and a toilet. What else do they need? Five to a room. It's Luxury City."

"I'm hoping we got most of the ship's gang including Jose, Carlos, Maria, Marianne and her boyfriend, along with those that Butler's group identified. Hopefully, one of them will talk more," Carmen said.

"Scratch and sniff. The real stink is where the guy is who planned this," Jeff mumbled. "Let's go downstairs. They're going to clear this area of passengers in a minute for the search."

Carmen checked her watch and said, "We'd better hurry or we'll be late for breakfast. After that, I would mind a little sleep."

Jeff saw her shake her right arm and asked, "You okay?"

"Sprained by wrist. I think I bumped my hand on something. Not only that, but I broke a nail. Wish I knew how that happened. Damn, I tried to be careful."

"Same here," Jeff reported. "The first time I hit Juan, I hit him so hard my fist collided with his pelvic bone."

"Oh, sweetheart, I'm sorry you're in pain. Seriously, though, I've never seen you act like that before."

"Back at you."

"Don't get defensive with me, Jeff. Where did all that come from. For all the time we've been together, I've seen you angry a lot of times. I've never seen you physically hurt someone, not like that."

Jeff sighed. "Babe, It was always there, truth be told. Respect for the law always kept me in check. When Butler told me what that beast had done to mothers and babies . . . I guess something snapped. If we'd been alone, I would have kept going."

"And then what?"

"I'm not sure. I've never been there before. I might regret it later. Right now I regret not having done more to him."

"Well, it sure rubbed off on me and it damn sure felt good. We're in this together. Isn't what marriage is all about?" Carmen conceded, desperately trying to reason out her own emotions.

Jeff stopped and put his arms around her and kissed her.

Pushing the button for the elevator to go down, she said, "Honey, I'm trying to understand this. Passengers like Marianne were the spotters, right?"

"Right. They probably had a good idea beforehand who was going to be the Captain and Staff Captain, and the Control Officer. For this operation to be successful, a good idea is not good enough. Early on they needed confirmation of personnel and the only way to do that was to get on the cruise and personally ID these key people, then quickly get the info to their superiors for the kidnappings to occur and the time plan to be executed, all within a couple of weeks."

"Why did they leave Bishop alone? After all, he is the Cruise Director."

"Same reason they left Pierre alone. There was no reason to. In Bishop's case, it's pretty hard to be Mr. Happiness when somebody you love is having their life threatened. Sure, if the tension affected his job, his staff could take over. There would be no real advantage to it. That's too many variables. Keep it simple. Besides, this operation was clandestine. Not a single passenger would need to find out. Do you have any idea how many law enforcement guests and wannabe heroes are on the average cruise ship? Probably a lot; you and me for starters.

"As I see it, Juan wasn't the brains of the project, he was the onboard head of operations and the negotiator. I'll bet that guy has laundered so much money he must have a dry-cleaning business somewhere. He probably had the final say. Fortunately, we never got to see his talents."

The couple rode the elevator to the main promenade deck to find a quiet spot by the window, enjoying a light breakfast. A few hours of sleep would bring to mid-afternoon. The all-you-can-eat buffets would still be open. They always were.

Within the hour, Marianne led McKenzie and his team to find a half-dozen three-ounce charges of Semtex hidden in the playground area within the plastic seat of a swing set and in close proximity to the highest density of plastics for maximum smoke production, and in the forested areas near the largest concentrations of burnable wood.

The following day after receiving a number of phone calls from Orlando, Korea, and London, Mohammad also had a thought: *Not a good trial run. At least from this point we'll be better prepared for next time.*

In the waning hours of sunlight the following day, Jeff found Carmen by the outdoor pool examining her ring in the fading sunlight.

"Nice ring, there, Mrs. Shenero."

Carmen held it up to show him. "You think so?"

"I told you, I could have gotten you a bigger one," he teased.

"And I told you it's not size that counts," she teased, in turn. "What matters is the loving intent."

"How does it feel to be invited to travel on a big cruise ship anywhere in the world anytime you want for the rest of your life for free?" Jeff asked.

"You tell me. Anyway, I don't know, yet. I'm trying to get over the last of this vacation," Carmen replied, somewhat facetiously. "Also, it depends on who I go with, and, did you note the caveat?"

Jeff said, not understanding, "Caveat?"

Carmen laughed and said, "This tour will be out. From now on it has to be the Caribbean or a world tour."

Jeff Joked, "With Larsson's luck he'll be the Captain with us as guests. I don't want to think about a full month on the ocean."

After a moment of silence, with only pool sounds as background, Carmen said, "I'm a little concerned about what you did to Carlos. There were a lot of witnesses and you can't claim self-defense. Nobody is going to lie about it. It's not exactly a matter of he-said she-said. In a word, you decided to be the judge, jury, and executioner," Carmen summarized.

Jeff said, "None of the above. You heard Butler. He's already been adjudged and found guilty. As for the latter, I don't want him executed. I want him to live a long, miserable life. Oh, let's not forget what you did to Maria."

"I'll testify that I didn't like her vibes or the way she looked at me. I didn't even like her makeup," Carmen quipped.

"Typical female response," Jeff quipped in return. "You'd probably get away with it, if you can get more women than men on the jury."

Another moment of silence. Then Jeff said, "Speaking of Butler, he did call me a while ago."

"And?"

"Remember way back when you had your affair with Richards, what, a few days ago? The hacker's name is Alexandr Vasiliev, a Russian, and he's not Marina's husband. The agency is thinking about hiring them both for purposes of counter-espionage, they're that good. You know, use them to track down other hackers. It's either take them in the fold or turn them over to Interpol where they'll spend the rest of their lives in prison."

"Like the counterfeiter who was so good they hired him to spot bad currency?" she asked.

Jeff said, "Exactly. Why waste the talent. Apparently, Jerry Richards was the brains behind the scheme. He got the relatives involved—although some wanted nothing to do with it—in order to raise money to pay for Marina and Vasiliev. Richards has a lot of relatives in jail now trying to post bond until their court date on a long list of charges. Each of them will have to repay what they received from their scheme, including having to sell their homes in some cases to pay back the cruise lines, who, by the way, have endless lawyers at their disposal."

Carmen chuckled and took a sip of wine. A glass of water stood in the second cup holder. "So the really bad international criminals who have stolen and continued to try and steal hundreds of millions get a cushy job with the feds in a gold mine and the little guy gets the shaft."

Jeff corrected her. "I wouldn't call fraud at the level this family was engaged in little guy games, especially considering their scheme to rip off the cruise line corporation. This particular line is owned by a country, not by individuals, so they committed crimes against the state with a dozen felony charges against every one of them. No small potatoes."

Carmen said, "I guess the only positive thing going for Jerry is at least he stopped coughing."

After they stopped laughing, both were silent for some time. Carmen asked, "What are you going to do about the business?"

"I don't know, I don't know," he mumbled, rubbing his hands over his face and his pate, very concerned.

A wash of guilt overcame Carmen. She had given him a hard time when she called him in India to pull him home. She didn't trust his instincts when the poisonous products came to their house in her name and wouldn't speak to him for days about it. She badgered him into taking the cruise and had maneuvered him into marriage and doubted that the ship was under attack from within.

Now, supposedly safe and sound, he faced a conundrum, like a long string with the ends tied together all balled up. No matter where he began, he would go round and round to end up where he started from. Like a Mobius band. He had disgruntled employees who had signed on for serious research on the verge of leaving, despite their high rate of pay. Less qualified people could do the same work his select staff were doing. Worse, Emily, a graduate student, who had been conducting the only hot research, had left after graduation.

Jeff felt the same way they did. He couldn't return the money to the government. That's a no no. If he did, the word would be out and he could lose future grant monies. He might as well shut the doors. If he did accept grant money, he had to be careful not to co-mingle funds. Lawyers get disbarred for co-mingling. Scientists might face criminal charges, professors fired.

He needed to calm the troops, buy time, stay out of the limelight, and talk it over with some personal friends, although doing so went against one of his most basic tenets: Whatever you need to do, you can do it yourself. There had to be a solution.

Sharing these thoughts with his wife, she responded by contributing, "Honey, I know you never finished what you wanted to do in India. How about if we both go this time. You can explore all you want and I'll even go in the jungle with you. Believe it or not, it'll make me feel at home. We'll take it easy and not get into any trouble. The employees can stand to be without you for another couple of weeks and it'll give you, us, a chance to concentrate on working out problems with your business from a distance without too many distractions. What do you say?"

Jeff looked directly into her dark eyes for a long time. He grunted softly. "You're right. We'll keep it nice and simple."

"Good. You can call it pleasure, or you can call it business. Now, how are you going to explain to our employees that you're going away again?" Carmen asked, deeply concerned. She had a stake in her husband and the future of his business.

Jeff replied, flippantly, "I'll tell them we're leaving for personal reasons and when we come back we'll bring them good news."

Carmen raised her eyebrows and inquired, "You've got me curious. What might that be?"

"I haven't the slightest idea," Jeff responded, truthfully.

NINE

Sadly, Carmen knew he spoke from his heart. Deciding to change the subject, she attempted to lighten the mood and asked, "While we ruminate about that, how about if we make a promise to go on a strict diet for the next month to make up for our gluttony on this trip."

"Deal," agreed Jeff, and shook hands with his wife.

At last, the Princess Fairie made contact with the Port of San Diego. At that moment, Bishop gave one final announcement, thanking the passengers for their visit and invited everyone back again. He concluded by saying, "We have been informed that an unusually large storm has hit the Chicago area and has affected all flights coming from and going to O'Hare. This ripple effect will be noticed by anyone planning to leave from San Diego International Airport over the next day or so. Be prepared for a lengthy delay. Please see your airline ticket agent for more details."

There are worse places in the world to get stranded than in San Diego for a day, with its museums, eateries, mild weather, parks, beaches, and tourist shops. It's also an excellent place to break a diet not yet started and to make plans for a well-earned relaxing trip to India, this time for both of them.

Chapter 5

RETURN TO INDIA

Typically, it takes two week of relaxation to recover from two weeks of vacation. Hoping for a quiet return to business as usual, the couple found themselves immersed in a massive number of bills, complaints, phone calls and left-field nuances that affected life in general. Energy was in the air. Carmen's newly hired assistant, efficient as she was, could not keep up with it all.

Dwelling on unfinished business and what Carmen had said about going to India, Jeff set a final date, one month hence, for a return to that country. Surely, no complication could arise from a simple trip overseas. This time no ships would be involved. First Class all the way. At least the discovery of the toxin had temporarily defused the crisis at work, but unless more toxin was found, or he came up with a solution, he could face a mass exodus of employees.

One month later, to the day, the couple arrived in Visak. Only a single day was lost in transit, which put them a day behind schedule.

After Jeff had accepted his offer for another visit, Steven had contacted Raj to set up the gathering. Everyone expressed enthusiastic joy in learning Carmen would be coming with him.

Grace, Steven, and Henry met them at the airport and took the couple to see the sights of the city, such as they were, then returned them to their hotel to rest before the evening activities. As the current president of the Visak Rotary Club, Steven ensured the hotel was properly prepared to receive the foreign dignitaries.

Accustomed to late evening activities, at 8:00 pm, Raj escorted the couple downstairs. Having been forewarned, and with great trepidation, Jeff and Carmen entered the meeting room to find it already packed with a portion of the front row reserved. They had spent the previous two hours at the finer Western stores shopping for appropriate attire for the event. Hoping to arrive the day before, this day had already been long.

More than a hundred invited guests occupied the seats, several of whom belonged to Raj's immediate family. Others included dignitaries, movie stars, and many members of the upper crust of Indian society selected by Raj, or rather his father, after learning that the Sheneros would be coming to India.

Steven presented a lavish introduction of

the couple, after which Jeff, thoroughly embarrassed, stood to begin the tale of his shipboard adventures. He and Carmen had earlier decided to completely omit the story about the terrorists for a number of reasons. He and the cruise line didn't want the world to know what had happened because it might reflect poorly on the industry in general and their lives, in particular, and, God knows, he didn't need any more publicity, or to be looked upon as a hero again. It had to stop sometime, didn't it? Only Steven, Grace, and Henry would hear the complete tale, with the promise they would never tell another soul.

Although a high percentage of the listeners were there to see Jeff, just as many were there to see Carmen, with her Bollywood looks. Many thought her dark complexion, large black eyes, black hair, trace of Aztecan nose, and enticing figure, would have looked better in a sari rather than in a skirt, or preferably, with nothing on at all—a sight reserved for Jeffrey Shenero alone, the bastard.

India had always been a marvelous blend of humanity, from the best to the worst, like any nation. Like most other nations, it possessed a multitude of languages, dialects, and religions, coupled with hard-core communists, terrorists, and fanatics, amidst a country filled with good folks.

Unlike most other nations, all billion plus

were packed into a tight land mass with arguably the largest population density of any country on earth. Technology butted heads with ancient superstitions and the struggle to succeed butted heads with remnants of a caste system. Traveling across India was like traveling from New York to New Jersey, to Virginia and throughout the entire country. Cross a state line, speak another language. Yet, somehow, it worked.

Most of those present had either read or heard about the couple's adventures aboard ship. If they hadn't, the Chatfields ensured they were teased with anecdotes about the coughing epidemic and the onboard drug ring, which never made the press, anecdotes the couple would share with them this evening.

After Steven made the introductions, Jeff began their tale by presenting a quick review of events, beginning with his chance saving of the little girl to his and his wife's meeting with LaMonde to relating what happened after the Richards and the two hackers had been caught with their hands in the cookie jar.

He told the tale to an audience whose lives were enwrapped in soap operas, whether they were real life or on-screen. Steven had warned Jeff that listeners expected to hear every little nuance so they could put themselves in his place. The more cringe-worthy they could make the story, the better. From her medical standpoint, Carmen made everyone cringe as she shared their deepest concerns about what possible unknown diseases might be lurking in the shadows.

At the end Jeff asked for questions.

Several hands raised. He allowed Grace Chatfield the honor of asking the first question. She sat next to Steven and Henry in the front row. "How did Richards know the top floor had its own air conditioning and why did he do it at all?"

Jeff said, "To answer the first question, the company advertised it in their literature in order to fill the expensive suites. Even if they hadn't, a man of Richards' skill could have easily found it out online, just like he found out the location of the A/C unit that served it by dredging up the blueprints for the vessel.

"The second part is something he's not talking about. We think it's because Carmen said she had a suite there and he strongly believed she wanted him to admit to a crime such as false claims about a disease. So he teased her with the truth, without there being any evidence. By the time he got searched for the pepper, he had already loaded it onto the filter. To him, it seemed like a harmless prank. It wasn't like he added poison gas to the air. Unfortunately, that act alone will probably add 20 years to his sentence. Richards was not a violent man, but he did have a sense of vengeance. It's fair to say he's sworn off women since then. Actually, he has no choice."

The audience laughed again.

Jeff added, "In my experience, Richards could have done some serious damage, if he had a mind to. I once encountered a similar circumstance where a terrorist added fungal toxin to an A/C unit in a sports arena. He also poisoned the filters on passenger planes. That memory gave me the idea of the air handlers being involved.

"Any other questions?"

One person asked, "If he thought Carmen was trying to trap him, why did Richards tell her about the plot to hack the cruise lines account?"

Jeff answered, "Great question. That one never came up during the interrogation. The authorities were laser focused on gathering evidence for the crime itself to put these people away and to stop the ring of hackers. However, Carmen and I think that, despite his suspicions, he did feel her allure. He never said the hackers were onboard, he only told her he needed money for their hire. It became a he-said, she-said argument with no proof. Even if she reported what he said—which she did—he had a clean record and might simply be a person given to telling tales of fantasy. I think we have all met someone who can exaggerate a story with little truth to it. Perhaps we all have at one time or another.

"From what I'm told, he and Marina had been texting each other. He offered her the car, but she and Alexandr only dealt with cash, so he offered it to Carmen. Even after the job was completed, Jerry needed to pay them the balance out of his portion of the theft, that's how hard core they were."

Jeff called on another person who said, "This question is for Carmen."

Carmen stood and came to the microphone. The man identified himself as a reporter for the *Times of India,* a world traveler himself, who asked, "Mrs. Shenero, what did you think when you and your husband got the same symptoms Richards had?"

She answered, "I thought: This is identical to the other symptoms even though I haven't been putting pepper up my nose. We began to wonder what made the penthouse level unique. Jeff put it all together."

Following their presentation, numerous guests crowded around Carmen for several minutes before the call came to begin the grand feast in the ballroom, a normal event for the hotel.

Jeff didn't see himself in the same light as observers here saw him, detractors notwithstanding. He didn't bask in the light; in fact, he shunned it. He yearned to fully express himself verbally and professionally, yet withdraw into himself when it felt comfortable to do so. Unfortunately, fate dictated otherwise. He was destined to solve problems, many of which were of great magnitude. He sought not fame and glory, things just worked out that way. Honored at home, he found himself a celebrated guest at sea and now in another country, while doing his best to wall it off.

During the walk to the ballroom, Carmen at first refused lucrative movie offers from producers and wealthy businessmen who yearned to let her advertise for them. At first reluctant, she replied she might do so, if proceeds could be channeled to charities of her choice.

The guests of honor and their friends sat at the end of a long table. At one point during the meal, Jeff leaned over to her and said, "A word of advice. Watch out for the curry. It's crazy hot," to which Carmen replied, "I already had some. You call that hot? What a wimp."

Later, while Jeff chatted, Carmen fell asleep in the back seat on the way to Raj's house on the outskirts of the city. They would remain his guests for three days before moving in with the Chatfields in Bimli, some 20 miles to the south. The wayfarers would need a lot of sleep. Tomorrow, Raj and his driver would take them deep into the jungle of Srikukulam.

Chapter 6

THE SRIKUKULAM JUNGLE

The Indus Valley brags one of the three oldest civilizations on the planet, along with Egypt and Mesopotamia. Evidence pointed to its settlement during the Bronze Age, some 5000 years in the past and some 3000 years before the Chinese established their strongholds. Humans migrated downward into the sub-continent and many found their way to this locale, with the Bay of Bengal only two miles to the east, which was subject to occasional typhoons.

The Srikululam district of the state of Andhra Pradesh is renowned for its brassware products and cashews, along with a variety of other artistic goods. The pendulum swings the other way when one considers extremely primitive jungle dwellers who live among crawling creatures. Jeff failed to mention these incidental factoids to Carmen. He did ensure that Raj carry a supply of anti-venin and other first-aid equipment. For himself, Jeff had his permits, instant ice-freeze packets, pocket microscope, an all-purpose utility tool on his belt, and a pistol loaded with buckshot rounds Raj had given both him and Carmen.

Entering the dense thicket of the jungle covering the northern coast of the state, the Jeep's driver, Padeep Murty, carefully negotiated a small rutted road leading them beneath the canopy and out of the sunlight. Occasionally, Raj would make a comment such as. "Watch out or snakes crossing the road," or "Last month a sloth bear walked through one of the villages we're going to visit," or "I hope you put on plenty of insect repellent."

Finally, Carmen laughed. "If you're trying to test me, Raj, don't try. For years, my father took me to visit old archaeological sites buried deep in the jungles of Mexico, especially the one near where we lived in Guadalajara. He was an archaeologist."

Jeff sat up straight and said, "You never told me any of that."

Carmen replied, simply, "Honey, you never asked," which caused Raj to laugh in turn.

Jeff felt foolish. He wondered why children didn't ask their parents about their earlier lives, or, in his case, details about their spouse's ancestry unless it's offered.

At one point the Jeep approached a small stream. Jeff said, "Hold on. This area looks ripe for picking." Murty stopped the vehicle and Jeff got out to look more closely at the various life forms growing on softened woody debris in the slow moving water. "We'll stop here in the way back," he announced.

Raj said, "We crossed a lot of streams, Jeff, how are you going to know this one?"

Jeff held up a finger in the universal language meaning "Wait a minute," and from his backpack, pulled out a roll of yellow tape. He began to string it from one tree to another. The tape read in black lettering: CRIME SCENE POLICE LINE DO NOT CROSS. On second thought, he re-rolled the tape, then took several minutes to carefully collect his samples, while the others watched his exactitude. When he returned to the vehicle, he said, "Changed my mind. I figured I'd better to get them while I'm here in case it's dark when we get back."

Once underway again, Jeff asked Raj, "Is this first village the one you told us about yesterday where everybody has the skin disease?"

"Yes, the same one," Raj replied.

"Did you manage to find the chemicals we requested?" Carmen asked.

"Yes, the container is either in the back or on the roof with the other supplies," Raj answered.

On a slow approach to the village, Murty blew the horn several times to inform those working in nearby rice paddies of their arrival. The small community appeared to be comprised of some 30 huts. All were set six inches off the ground. Several of the men began to unload specified items from the car, including a side of pork that Raj had obtained from somewhere. Although many of the natives held religious beliefs against eating meat or even pork, survival reigned as the God Almighty and trumped other beliefs, which could be temporarily discarded in light of a pending celebration.

On the outskirts of the collection of huts, Jeff saw a light pole with a shaded light and power wires he hadn't noticed on their drive. The country was making a great effort to electrify outlying villages. Whether the lights came on or not might be a different story, thanks to power shortages, especially during storms and overuse of fans and A/C units during the hot season.

From what the visitors could see, these people weren't exactly making bronze statuettes to sell to tourists. The place resembled an outpost. Most small communities and villages in the country had light switches on the walls and a good percentage of the public at large had television. This place had snakes, bears, and a three-inch very nasty red scorpion, along with mold reportedly growing on their skin—definitely not a hotbed for tourists. No cruise ships would be unloading passengers who wanted to brave the drive to this village.

Women arriving from the paddies had their saris hiked up to expose their upper thighs. One of them approached this strange woman who accompanied the district supervisor and the bald man. The visitor wore a baseball cap, white Tee-shirt already sweat-stained, blue jeans, and work boots Raj had scrounged up from somewhere. According to Raj, Murty didn't like to use the air conditioning in the jeep because it used up too much gas.

The woman handed Carmen the lit cigar from her own mouth. Carmen graciously put it in her mouth, took a drag, coughed, and handed it back, to the great amusement of the others. She had been initiated. Jeff thought about telling them his wife was a movie star, although he doubted any of them had ever been to the cinema. Their idea of personal hygiene differed from that of regular movie goers and in all likelihood, they wouldn't have been admitted into the theater.

Jeff quickly identified the fungal disease afflicting the natives as Tinea Versicolor, a yeast infection demarked by discolored patches of the skin. The patches had sharp margins and caused occasional itching due to continually moist skin providing an environment suitable for the yeast to grow.

With Carmen treating the women in one hut and Jeff treating the men in another, they applied a solution of copper sulfate with cotton balls onto the various areas of concern. In their language of Telugu, Raj told the natives to expect another application in the evening, which should finish the treatment, although it could take weeks for the skin to return to its normal appearance.

In addition to the meat, the chief gained two one-pound cans of ground coffee, iodine, bandages, a basket of fruit, another of nuts, and two large jugs of whiskey. There would be a feast tonight, something these people seemed to relish like a dog gobbling up good food before other competitors could get to it. Tomorrow would take care of itself. For better or worse, it always did.

At the completion of the first round of skin treatments, the foursome bid the chief farewell promising to return in the evening for the celebration, after dropping off supplies to other villages.

By the time darkness had fallen, Jeff had collected a number of other mold samples, while Carmen had sutured a gashed leg. In the third village, she found herself called upon to deliver twins in one of the huts. The natives slept in cots inches off the floor of the hut to further lessen the attack by ground-based insects, such as scorpions. Carmen found that bending this low for purposes of delivering a child had other challenges when a King Cobra slithered inside the hut. The relatives immediately departed.

Although the King Cobra rarely attacks humans, Carmen's mind wasn't on statistics at the moment. Jeff had schooled her on the venomous snakes they might encounter and this one was not at the top of the list. It quickly took top honors. The snake and Carmen saw each other at the same time. The cobra raised its head, flaring its hood in an attempt to scare its opponent, tongue snaking in and out, smelling, sensing. Carmen found herself having to draw her pistol to shoot, while wearing slippery surgical gloves. The woman on the cot did not seem to be as concerned as was her attending physician. Three missed shots later, the snake got the idea that odds were not in its favor and slithered outside, while Carmen returned to her duties.

When the jeep returned to the first village, the single electric light on the pole cast eerie stretched-out shadows over the compound. With the fire blazing, the party goers feasted and sang among the beasts and insects of the jungle, as their ancestors had done many years in the past. A cook pot hung over the fire set on a heavy branch that was set into two Y-shaped branches well anchored in the ground.

It wasn't Amazonia, but you'd never know the difference. Jeff loved this simple life in the land that time forgot, at least for a one night stand. Gatherings such as these highlighted the superficialities brought about by wealth and always gave him cause to appreciate the basic goodness of human nature when people were free from governmental overreach without reliance on material goods. It made him appreciate what he had and more, appreciate what he didn't need. Except for the clothing, the drums and dancing might be similar to that of their ancestors. Once again, he'd been thrown back in time. In one sense, he felt comfort in knowing that some things never change.

To the chief's great delight, Jeff awarded him the roll of colorful police tape for his personal usage. What he might do with the gift was irrelevant.

The ride home proved to be adventurous. A torrential downpour had begun and a singing Murty merrily sped the jeep through muddy ruts, slipping and sliding, yet somehow managing to remain on the path without crashing into the brush or overturning the vehicle. Only Raj remained relaxed while Carmen held onto Jeff with one hand and the built-in hand grip with another.

Murty had served as Raj's personal driver and servant for years. He lived in the Raj family compound in a separate building with his own family. As such, Raj felt compelled to include the man in these festivities, including the drink. At least no police car would pull them over.

"Is this what you meant when I first called you here and you slurred saying you were coming back from a 'get-together'?" Carmen asked, her teeth chattering as the vehicle hit a series of ruts.

"Sweetheart, how could you imply such a thing?" Jeff retorted, looking abashed.

"That's what I thought. You answered my question." She didn't laugh, recalling the painful reason why she had called him in the first place.

The joyful Murty attempted to slow in order to avoid a series of deep ruts. The right front tire went deep into one, bounced out, and an instant later, the rear tire found the same hole. The vehicle came to an abrupt stop. The tire spun in deeper the more Murty tried to get them out until Jeff said, "Stop."

"Carmen, get behind the wheel and set the brake. We're going to find some rocks. Raj, where's the jack to this car?" Jeff inquired, taking command.

While two men used flashlights to find rocks suitable to fill the rut, Jeff had a difficult time setting the jack because the frame of the car touched the ground at the front of the rear axle. He looked at the rear of the car, still slightly above the sodden earth and managed to find purchase for the jack in a deep rut beneath a portion of the bumper. He raised the vehicle enough to clear the right rear tire a few inches, hoping the car would not slip off the jack. He directed the others to place the rocks beneath and in front of the tire. When that work had been completed, he lowered the jack enough so that at least three tires were on the ground, but not so low that he couldn't grab the bumper from beneath. He found a rut he could put one foot into for leverage then said, "Stand clear of the rear tire in case it throws up any rocks," he directed.

Jeff did what had always worked for him in these situations. He didn't want to take a chance of lowering the jack and trust to the rocks alone for the tire to gain a grip, so he directed Carmen to ensure the car was in four-wheel drive and await his command to release the brake, then drive forward slowly. Turning his back to the car, he squatted down to reach beneath the bumper for purchase, directing the other men to push, one on each side of him.

Jeff shouted "One! Two, Three!" Carmen released the brake, touched the gas lightly, Jeff lifted, the others tried to push, but Murty, wearing flip-flops, was next to useless. He slipped and fell face down. An instant later the vehicle fell off the jack, hit the rocks and rolled free.

Carmen, still completely dry, slid over to the front passenger seat, while Murty, coated in mud, stood in the rain with his face upward for several minutes letting the water wash the mud from him. Since he was the one who would have to clean the car's interior the next day, he might as well lessen the effort with a thorough shower. Eventually, soaked through and through, he resumed his role as driver. Jeff and Raj had already slid into the back seat. Only Carmen remained dry. If a film maker had been present, he might have included the entire episode as another chapter in the life of the Keystone Cops or The Three Stooges.

Once safely home, Raj called a couple of servants to get them robes and to dry their clothes. Once comfortable, he offered to put Jeff's samples on dry ice and have his people air-freight them back to Jeff's lab.

The couple spent the next several days as house guests, being waited on, eating fine meals, and relaxing for the first time in a long time.

Saying their goodbyes three days later, the couple moved in with the Chatfields, where they relaxed, read, and walked on the beach at night. No city lights could wash out the stars of the galaxy shown edge-on in the cleared skies. Nothing could possibly disturb this well-earned vacation from here on out.

On their second day, Jeff could contain himself no longer. After dinner, and in the presence of Henry and Steven—Grace had collared Carmen to show off her shell collection—Jeff opened up about his problems with his employees at work and the excessive amount of government money he received each month, not generally something people complained about. Henry suggested, "Why don't you build an add-on to your own facility and hire who you need? This will allow you and your people to get back to doing the research you love and give you a tax write-off."

Steven offered, "That's not a bad idea. Or, you can sub out the work to one of our numerous affiliates. The closest one to you would be in Kansas City, Missouri. It's close enough for you to keep a watchful eye on it from your place in Oklahoma. Since you're under the aegis of the Consumer Product Safety Commission, the head of whom I helped get appointed, you should get approval for the shift and not have to spend time constructing an add-on. The FDA won't be involved because you're not dealing with food or drugs.

"I'm thinking the approval and the shift could take place within three months, maybe two. It's not complicated. These things go on all the time and it's legit."

The next day would see their departure, not for home, but to begin an episode in their lives which should go smoothly. On the other hand, from Carmen's point of view, with Jeff around, one could never know what dangers might circle in dark waters. If some people found themselves in harm's way, Jeff would find his way into harm's maw.

Chapter 7

PHOTO SHOOT

During the great banquet following their presentation in Visak, both Carmen and Jeff gave in to badgering and made commitments to do magazine cover shoots. Steven had advised them to expect a few complications. Photography wasn't his area of expertise. Legal pitfalls were. He set up the couple with a law firm accustomed to working with movie stars and other personages in exactly this manner, protecting their integrity and ensuring they received the best money possible. In her case, the money would go to their designated charities.

One thing she could be certain of, whatever made the press in India would make the press in the States simply because the rights to pictures can be sold or transferred to sister periodicals owned by the same corporations. These sister periodicals also had affiliates in Europe and

Asia. Agreeing to this would bring everyone more money, including the orphanages.

Both had buyer's remorse. Carmen had dredged up the same sense of reluctance that had overcome her aboard ship heading for an unwanted meeting with Richards. Except that now she had become the fish to be caught and she knew the identity of the sharks chasing her, perhaps with other swimmers lurking nearby waiting to feast on any remains.

Jeff felt worse. To the good, given their shipboard adventures, they had not gained in public notoriety. Perhaps they did in the eyes of men like Butler and Larsson and the agencies they represented, but no press had resulted from their activities. And they had spoken before a Rotary club in India. Big deal. This magazine business, however, could be a worst case scenario. Like rock stars, their pictures and names would be plastered on magazine covers and interiors to reach continents far and wide.

He had done it for her because it all came to down one thing: She wanted children and he didn't and now they were doing this big orphanage thing. Not only that, but the fallout could be disastrous and probably wouldn't give them a moment's peace.

Thinking ahead, with a solid physical exam, Jeff wanted to make an attempt to get on the next shuttle flight to the moon because the Earth was too close to home.

Once known as Bombay, Mumbai is India's largest city with busy shipping traffic. It brags a population of some 22 million in its greater metropolitan area, ten times that of Visak. Beggars became wealthy by learning a dozen languages in order to barter with shippies from every corner of the world. It is the country's financial center and the heart of the Bollywood film industry, arguably the largest producer of movies of any country in the world. In addition, newly minted Vogue and GQ were headquartered there. They became so popular a read that a full one-third of their monthlies were filled with advertisements, a true indication of success.

Because the cover of Vogue displayed both sexes, the magazine became interested in the married couple, each worthy of display individually or together. GQ expressed more interest in Jeff than Carmen, having retrieved from somewhere an earlier picture of him in Speedos, shirtless, and cut like a gymnast. Between his shaved head, oriental eyes and prominent scar, not to mention his overall square fame, he became ripe fodder. The legal firm engaged by Steven put their staff to work on it. Money was no problem for anyone, but a loss of personal integrity could make it all meaningless for the couple if a single misstep should occur.

"Honey, we can always back out," Jeff offered. "Children's charities will always exist, with or without us. We can up the donations we already make without having to do this."

Despite her lack of total commitment to go through with upcoming events, once again, Carmen felt a certain thrill of diving into danger. She wasn't so naïve as to ask herself "What could go wrong?" Simply believing that to be a valid question could be a forerunner to lengthy hate-yourself episodes. These would be similar to those that ravaged her when she had a chance to finish her medical degree. She chose to stick with Jeff, instead. All right, it worked out for the best, although it took a long time for the regrets to go away. Unfortunately, all the regrets of choosing the wrong crossroad were resurfacing, as they did on occasion during the dark hours of the night when the mind dwells on things done wrong.

If she were to believe her superstitious husband, one should not believe the words: "See, you expected bad things to happen, yet everything turned out all right." To him, having no expectations cleared the mind and minimized the chance of failure. When you think about protesting before the challenge, you lose the gold medal. Get the gold medal first, then file your complaint.

Vogue insisted they be picked up by helicopter on the first morning for reasons of publicity, wanting the media to film the new celebrities arriving on the rooftop of the building. It didn't matter they could walk there from their hotel.

At 6:45 am, the couple sat in the hotel lobby, waiting. At 7:00 am sharp, a low noise became louder as a helicopter landed in the courtyard, causing the building to shake and windows to vibrate. Guests rushed to look out, thinking the world might be coming to an end.

Jeff smiled sheepishly at the hotel clerk. "That's for us," he said. A man came out a side door of the chopper to lead them to the aircraft. Holding her hand, Jeff followed the man who led them to the noisy machine, not often seen on the hotel grounds, while Carmen hunkered down to protect her hair from the whirlwind. The man opened a side door for them and helped them to enter, take their seats, and buckle in. He provided them with noise-cancellation headsets to communicate with the pilot. Then he climbed into the passenger side next to the pilot. Jeff had the flagrant thought that the four-seater had the capability of landing on a cruise ship with the number 10 painted at the top of the circle.

The pilot tested the headsets and Jeff acknowledged by replying, "There's some place I'd like to go to first, if you can."

"Sir, I'll have to call it in for permission," replied the pilot. "Where is it you want to go?"

Jeff told him. The pilot called it in and received the okay. A moment later, he lifted off, headed straight west about 100 yards then made a sharp turn northward up the coast only a few miles. Shortly, the airship flew slowly over the largest ship graveyard in the world. Scores of ships lined the beachfronts two and three deep with piles of metal on the beach reminding Jeff of pictures he had seen of remote islands that displayed millions of tons of plastics washed up on their shores. Here, everything was com-partmentalized: furniture, glass, larger pieces of metal, machinery, smaller metal objects as far as the eye could see, with thousands of work-ers weaving in and out of the scrap, cutting, torching, and carrying pieces to waiting trucks. No derricks and cranes here, as in Turkey and elsewhere. The gravity method on these shores meant that heavier objects were usually hand or machine-pushed off upper decks into the al-ready outrageously contaminated water. The big money came from the recycled steel. No money could be made from the dead fish that could be found miles out to sea.

"Down there is where I grew up," said the pilot.

"How's so?" Carmen asked, flabbergasted at the sight, staring out the window at thousands of human-like ants crawling over and around piec-es of metal or climbing onto higher structures of the ships.

"I worked there every day for three years, seven days a weeks in my early teens," replied the pilot. "Summer, winter, monsoons, it didn't matter. "He held up his right arm where an an-gry burn mark remained. "Backed into a red hot piece of metal for part of my pay."

"Did you get medical?" Carmen asked, without thinking.

"Sure did. Wrapped it up and went back to work the next day," laughed the pilot. "Went back to my five brothers and sisters and tried to study. Kept seeing these planes flying overhead and wanted to be like them some day."

"And here you are," said Jeff.

"Yes, sir," agreed the pilot.

Reaching the end of the graveyard, the pilot was about to bank left for the turn-around when Jeff said, "Wait, what's up ahead?"

"It's the city dump," answered the copilot.

"It's huge," Jeff remarked.

"Yes, sir," the man agreed. "The mountain of trash in the middle is a good 120 feet tall. You're looking at some 300 acres of city garbage collected over a hundred years."

Flying over the dump, again human worker-ants could be seen crawling over the countless items, picking scraps where they could for personal use or for sale. The co-pilot contributed, "You people have landfills. This is how we dispose of our waste. There are some 3000 places like these in our country, some large, some small. Although, there is talk about building a recycling plant here."

"How would that work?" Jeff inquired. "You'd have to hand-separate out the plastics and the smaller metal objects. You've got to have lead and cadmium in there. You couldn't burn those elements or the plastic unless you wanted to kill off half the population."

"Sorry," concluded the pilot, in a tone suggesting he didn't want to think about the problem. "Not my area of expertise."

An instant later, he said, "Hang on, we're going back." He banked hard left and returned past the ship graveyard, this time a little farther out to sea.

The copilot picked up the story. "I used to fly freight in the Middle East. You get out to Turkey and you might see a number of modern cruise ships getting trashed, big ones, too. Some 800 ships a year get decommissioned. Companies lost billions during Covid with nobody wanting to sail anymore. Ships got sold at auction to end up at unregulated places like this and sold for millions in scrap. Figure it takes at least a year to dismantle each ship. Steel is worth a lot. Here in India, asbestos isn't considered hazardous, neither is lead. It's recycled into building materials."

"Beauty and the beast," Carmen laughed, not out of humor, but out of irony. "We recently sailed on one of those monsters. Is there nothing permanent anymore?"

"How sad," Jeff lamented, unsuccessfully trying to grasp the disparate concepts of nothing permanent anymore vs. some things never change. He gave up.

He felt as she did, recently having been integrated with a living breathing sea-going giant creature that, at any moment, could be stripped down to its bones on dead shores somewhere, if not taken down by an explosive charge to litter the sea floor where underwater life would populate the debris. He tried to put a finger on his feelings. Perhaps it was the ignoble end to man's genius that disturbed him so much, from the countless billions of tons of plastics created to make life easier that ended up floating or sinking in the seas of the world, or washed up onto shores to enter the food chain of all living creatures, to the broken ships that began to serve his pleasures, to the throw-away trash in general, never mind what couldn't be seen.

No, more than that, nothing could or would be done about it. Perhaps one day the Earth itself might shake off the surface detritus like a dog shaking-off water or dirt, in an effort to get itself reorganized.

"Prepare for landing," declared the pilot. The visitors looked out to see the helicopter approach and drop to a large X on the roof of the Vogue/GQ building after only 20 minutes off schedule. Numerous reporters and cameras of every ilk awaited them.

The Vogue building was located on the first floor of a large complex of buildings in the financial district of Mumbai. Gentlemen's Quarterly occupied the second floor of the Condé

Nast Indian magazine empire and situated only a mile to the north of the famous Taj Majal Palace Hotel. Reportedly, the hotel had the reputation of having been built backwards with the arms of the U-shaped structure and the inner courtyard reaching out toward a back alley, rather than toward the bay itself with the Salvation Army Hostel visible to the north west of the eastern arm. Because of this, many superstitious Indians believed the hotel bought bad luck and shied away from booking a room there—the same hotel where the Sheneros were staying.

The first day at Vogue, a Friday, began with the signing of documents which had to do with rights and privileges and financial considerations, all of which had been prearranged. Following legal proceedings, Jeff was introduced to a middle-aged extremely handsome Indian who had retired from acting full time to take up an executive position with the magazine, while a guide introduced Carmen to his female counterpart.

A tour of the facilities followed the legal aspects to include their respective make-up rooms, editorial areas, photography, break room, and managerial offices. The actual printing occurred at another location, which received copy via electronic transmission to create the slick magazines bringing in many millions of dollars annually.

The day had been extremely long. At the end

of the paper signings and finalization of contracts, Jeff remarked: "There's a day gone in our lives we'll never get back again. We need some good news," to which one of the Vogue representatives replied, "If you want something to look forward to, I'm delighted to say we're going to shoot you both tomorrow."

By 8:00 pm, the couple left the building. Their driver awaited them at the door with the car parked just outside. A large crowd began to form to start the celebration of a holiday. The driver aggressively pushed people aside in order to open the back door of the car. "It's Diwali," he announced.

The festival of lights, Jeff had read, was the biggest celebration of the year celebrated by Hindus, Sikhs and Jains, with gift giving, the lighting of candles, and displays of fireworks. The event celebrated light over darkness, good over evil, spiritual awakening, human betterment over bad intent, five days that interrupted businesses accustomed to such interruptions.

The following day, Saturday, began at 7:00 am with an hour of make-up for Jeff and over three hours for Carmen, after which the couple went through various poses and clothing changes. Jeff had an early panic attack, slamming himself for getting involved in this business in the first place. He had no problem with those who accidentally fell into an opportunity and took advantage of it. However, he openly loathed those who took advantage of their celebrity to flaunt themselves simply for financial gain.

Yet, here he was doing exactly the same thing, wasn't he? He had to tell himself, No, Jeff. You're doing this because you want to give it all to children's orphanages here in India and back home, to find better foster parents for them, to get them good medical attention. And you'll do whatever it takes to make that happen. Once he reminded himself of his purpose, the perceived problem dissipated.

The work day finished at 8:00 pm. The driver nervously waited inside the front door standing beside a security guard. Outside, a slowly moving current of people flowed from south to north, jammed more tightly than the laws of physics should allow. The guard unlocked the door to the building, the trio exited, and the guard locked the door behind them to disappear into the building in order to make his rounds. Holding Carmen's hand, Jeff walked a few steps to the curb where the sedan stood, the river of humans flowing around the vehicle like flotsam stuck in a slow moving current. When the driver tried to open the door, he got swept away in the current, followed by Carmen, and then Jeff.

Jeff tried to see her black hair among a populace of a billion black-haired people, all of whom appeared to be at this one location, moving together, cheering, waving lighted signs, dressed in every color imaginable.

It reminded him of the time he went to the Oklahoma-Texas football game down in Dallas back in the old days, when the river flowed in one direction, making a long circuit as direct-ed by law enforcement, occasionally passing a liquor store. He would purchase a six-pack at three times the going rate, and drink it along the circuit until the next pass. Was this flow going in a circuit? If it were, it might sweep him around to his hotel a mile in the other direction.

He came back to the original problem. He had lost his wife. Although she had her cell with her, he had left his phone back in the hotel on pur-pose. Why would one want to bring a phone to a photo shoot? He was proud of himself for man-ning up by leaving it without having the feeling of nakedness one normally gets when it is acci-dentally left behind. He wouldn't need to make calls or take pictures. At the moment, however, he believed he might have been in error.

For Carmen's part, she started out the day tired. Now she was tired and hungry. Except for a brief respite for lunch in the building cafete-ria, she'd been on her feet all day. She was so looking forward to a Kobe steak and a relaxing drink of tea, comparing notes with her husband, laughing about the various poses they'd gone through.

Pushed by the mass of humanity, her life seemed to her to be no different than a single bird in a great murmur, swaying to and fro, pushing forward, until it hit a log jam, which would soon break free, only to surge forward again, with no particular destination in mind. Countless people carried lighted pole flags and banners waving like wheat in a breeze. Nowhere could she see vehicular traffic of any kind. She thought about working her way to the edge and finding a store in which to find shelter and soon saw every business closed. Why didn't anybody tell them about this holiday? Would this be an all-nighter?

She had grown up with large celebrations in Mexico, such Dia de los Muertos, and had been to Mardi Gras with Jeff; however, this was other worldly, appearing like an over-populated happy riot, like a towering cruise ship compared with a tramp freighter.

Wait, she could still make a call. But to whom? 911? She tried to forget about her problems when she realized her husband probably had the same issues, trying to get to their hotel, any hotel, all behind them. Suddenly, firecrackers went off, causing the great beast to pulsate. She made an effort to get to the very edge of the crowd to escape her condition of being completely surrounded to minimize the chances of being crushed.

After what seemed like an hour of being buffeted like a ping pong ball in a closed space, the road split into three. Trying to work her way over, somebody in front of her dropped a flag pole and the dominoes fell. When Carmen hit the ground with both hands, the right hand took the brunt. Already sprained from her fight with Maria, the wrist shot flames of pain up her arm. Flinging both elbows around her to clear the bodies falling into her and not caring if she made contact with somebody's head at this point, she managed to stand.

Hugging the near edge of the crowd, she flowed with it along the left branch and within a short time, saw a large bearded policeman armed only with a baton. He did not like loitering in the thinning crowd, encouraging people to move along, but probably wouldn't mind five $20 dollar bills in his pocket. She had long since discarded her small clutch, placing her cell in her pocket along with her hotel key card. She needed both hands for this fight.

Approaching the policeman, she put both palms together in a namasthe gesture and asked, "Can you help me?"

She did not know Marathi, the language of the state of Maharastra; however, she had learned a few words of Hindi, not exactly the official language of the country, but close enough, because of the number of people who spoke it. For God's sake, this was the financial district of the country, the man might even speak English.

The policemen took in this disheveled creature with hair like a soggy mop and the last person one would expect to see on the cover of Vogue. Clearly, she did not belong to the crowd. He replied, in a sing song rhythm, "Just I am helping you."

The man spoke English. Carmen explained, simply, "I am American. I am lost. I am staying at the Taj Mahal Royal Hotel. Can you find me a ride there? I will pay." She pulled out the money she had folded into a small rectangle and handed it to the man. He took the proferred gift, looked at it, smiled, and said, "Come."

She followed him around a corner onto a dark lonely street, concerned she might have gone from the frying pan into the fire. She had the sudden urge to run back into the crowd if necessary, mentally reviewing the self-defense moves Jeff had taught her, until she saw the man lead her toward a small scooter chained to a tree. He unlocked it, tucked the chain into a small box on the rear, and patted the tiny seat behind his own.

Carmen took the seat, precariously balancing on the end. She found a set of foot pegs and held on for dear life, while her personal driver sped through the back streets of Mumbai weaving in and out of traffic. Carmen wrapped her arms tightly around the big man in front of her, keeping her head down, her wrist hurting all the while.

Heavy traffic flowed along the side streets, the main thoroughfare blocked by revelers. For an instant she had a humorous thought: Who's going to try and stop a scooter driven by a policeman racing through traffic with a hot sweaty woman on the back with her arms wrapped around him? There's something to be said for alternative lifestyles. She almost giggled at the image of a new hot Vogue cover. And here's what Carmen Shenero is up to on her days off!"

In the major and minor cities of the country, literally hundreds of thousands slept on sidewalks and in the street itself, near their small stall or store. Not so in this section of Mumbai with its glitter of glass and tall buildings, with no small stalls to be found.

Only short minutes later, the policeman pulled in front of the brightly lit hotel. Carmen dismounted, kissed her savior on the cheek to leave a big red lipstick mark, and said, "Thank you," once again. Let him tell that story back at the police station, she mused, smiling at the broad grin on the man's face. She wondered what the final version of the story would be.

Her hair a mess, Carmen took the elevator to their suite and called the dining room to place her order. She undressed and threw her clothes into a pile to be laundered. After a cool shower and a quick hair-dry, she thought about buying an elastic bandage for her wrist at the hotel pharmacy, but decided to eat first. After a little hair brushing and untangling, and a change of clothes, she prepared to go downstairs to eat, thinking, *Jeff can take care of himself. I'll bet he's probably trapped somewhere with no way out, just the way he likes it.*

Nothing so complicated. A quarter hour behind Carmen, Jeff found the same side street she had. At least he didn't have to worry about rapists or thieves, especially if he ran.

Time is relative depending on perception. An hour in a crowd moving at half-a mile per hour can seem like a ten-mile-long trek. He began an easy jog, taking in a brightly lit billboard promoting birth control: LOOP BEFORE YOU LEAP.

Just as Carmen closed her room door to go down to dinner, Jeff appeared. "What a coincidence," he declared, sweat running from every pore from the heat, humidity and exertion. "You never know who you'll run into when you travel. Don't you look nice and refreshed? Did you have a good time?"

Overjoyed to see him safe, Carmen had learned to joke about a bad situation. "There's no justice. I can't even run away from my husband." She gave him a quick kiss on the lips, the second man she'd kissed in the past half-hour. "I'll go down and order for you," she concluded.

After his own cold shower, Jeff changed and met his wife for a satisfying dinner and conversations about their day's adventures. Tomorrow would be an off-day, with more make-up sessions and poses looming ahead early next week.

Tonight and tomorrow belonged to them.

In another week, the couple would call it quits in India and fly home, hopefully to some peace and quiet and obscurity.

Chapter 8

THE AGENT ORANGE EPIDEMIC

ONE

Flies are attracted to raw meat. The Sheneros fit into this category. As the raw meat. Short weeks after their return, and after addressing an exuberant staff regarding upcoming changes to their routine, as per Steven Chatfield, a magazine representative called to inform them that the next American and British additions of Vogue and GQ would soon run their stories along with photos different from those used in India.

This information upset the couple. Jeff called it ripples from a big rock tossed in the still pond, or leftover tendrils from a major event. Carmen called it bullshit they didn't need, and, not for the first time, she deeply regretted her decision to become an object of attention. Deep down, painful as it might be, she had done it to hurt Jeff. He loved children, he just didn't want anything to take time away from research, his first love. She felt comfortable in counting herself as his second love. Beyond that their personal lives had become a quandary, a perplexity, and a work in progress.

The next event occurred when Jeff received a video call on his private computer office/lab line. The image of Emily Kaufman appeared on screen.

"Good morning, Emily," he said cheerily. "Do you have another discovery so soon on the heels of the last one?"

Emily didn't laugh. "Yes, doctor"—she insisted on using formalities rather than calling him by his first name—"It's more an observation than a discovery. You know how *Jeffrus shenerii* needs oil to produce spores and to proliferate? Well, there are oils and there are oils."

"Let me pass your knowledge along to the staff," Jeff said, in his most sarcastic manner. Emily knew he liked to tease. Basically, he meant. "Get to the point."

"It grows on anything with oil," she threw out, teasing back, testing him.

"Like bacon or salad dressing or motor oil?" Jeff guessed.

"Yes, and like human skin, doctor. We have a small epidemic here in the building,"

"You mean everybody is turning orange?" Jeff laughed.

"Yes."

"Shit."

"That's what Arnold said. I'm sending you some pictures."

Jeff turned to his computer and opened her email message, then made a quick call to Carmen to join him. He split the screen with Emily's picture on one half and the pictures she sent on the other half. A chill ran up his spine, as though he were staring at photos of bears standing on their heads with the caption: *What's wrong with this picture?*

The pictures depicted arms and heads of men and women. Each had orange to orange-red splotches tending to run together with normal appearing skin between them. He could see Emily patiently watching him examine the picture when Carmen came in. He motioned for her to take a seat, quickly summarizing the circumstances. Her eyes widened when he did so.

Leaning into the computer for a closer look she said, "Emily, let's hope this doesn't get loose into the public at large?"

"I don't want to think about it," Emily admitted, with a sense of dread in her voice.

TWO

Each mold has its preferences. The black mold *Stachybotrys* is most happy when it can grow on high carbon low nitrogen substances such as drywall or glue-down mastic; *Cladospo-*

rium loves fallen leaves, paint, wood chips, rubber; and sheetrock; the ringworm fungi prefer the keratin in the skin and nails; and this new mold, previously buried in permafrost, prefers oil.

Jeff summarized, "It wouldn't produce spores on the tar paper when I first found it, but once it got fed hydrocarbons, it became infectious. Is that correct?"

"Correct," Emily replied. "It can be transferred from person to person. We think it may also become infectious via airborne spores. We don't know for certain. It could be either or both."

"What are you doing to contain it?" he inquired, in a *déjà vu* moment, returning him to a conversation he'd had onboard ship regarding a supposed respiratory virus that made people cough.

"Everything we can," Emily replied. "Each microbiological lab here has independent surgical room filtration, so there's no air mixing from one to another, but we have people getting the infection who are not even associated with the labs. Maybe it gets transferred from person to person in the break room. We're limiting its growth by wiping ourselves down with rubbing alcohol to remove the surface oils, but we can't use alcohol forever. I'm sending you another group of pictures. These represent the 'after'. You just looked at the 'before'."

She continued, "So far, only six of us have it, including Arnold and me. Nobody's going anywhere."

More photos appeared on-screen with the same arms and heads with a notable orange cast. Emily gave the couple time to examine the new group of pictures, then said, "We think the spores are embedded, but it's way too early to know much more. Arnold wanted me to bring you into the loop, doctor. Several of us are working on this. More help would be nice."

Jeff actually laughed, his trademark response to pressure. He announced, "Glad you called, since the damn thing is named after me." *Laugh in the face of danger. There's plenty of time to cry later.*

"Have you checked your animal facilities?" Carmen asked.

Emily answered, "Yes, and we're not seeing anything beneath the fur. They, too, are on an independent air purifying system. We check every day."

Carmen said, "As I recall, sebaceous glands are most numerous on the face and scalp, especially the nose. Human sebum is a mixture of triglycerides, fatty acids, waxes, cholesterol, and related oils. Our friend has plenty to choose from."

"Which is no help at all except to give us more avenues to explore," Emily summarized. "Arnold wanted me to call you before his supervisor called the CDC. I'm worried, Jeff," she concluded, in a rare use of his first name.

Emily began punching the keyboard. In an instant, new images appeared. The couple stared at the screen, with heads almost touching, as they looked at pictures of threads interwoven among square-off bodies. Neither said a word. The photos depicted skin scrapings of threads of mycelium in and around the larger cuboidal skin cells. Mold spores were giving rise to germ tubes like Bermuda grass seeds sprouting and spreading runners both beneath and on top of the earth, except that the threads in the pictures were also penetrating the cell membranes of the skin cells.

"Phospholipids and sterols," Carmen said, referring to the composition of cell membranes. She didn't need to elaborate. In addition to using the sebum, the mold sought the lipid components of membranes to feed itself. In a word, it was digesting skin and possibly other tissues, such as muscular and nervous, all of which had oils it required.

After a moment, Emily said, "Symptoms are insane itching, which, of course, will drive the spores and mycelium in deeper when we scratch. This is coupled with paranoia, because nobody knows what the outcome will be. You're looking at my arm. The alcohol temporarily eases the itching, but it's way too early to see if there are any systemic reactions.

"Every exposed person gets a daily blood test. Arnold's super wants to shift another dozen people onto the project. Unfortunately, nobody wants the assignment unless we go to Bio-Containment Level 4, which is what we're doing. Things are moving pretty fast around here."

Emily looked off to nowhere, gathered herself, and returned her attention to the screen. She seemed to be at a loss of words. Tears came to her eyes and she shook her head back and forth a couple of times, obviously loathe to what she had to say until she said it, "We're in big trouble."

To Jeff, the word "we" had a lot of implications. It could mean those working on the project or it could mean the entire human race, if it got loose. He said, "It's not my decision to make, and obviously, I'd leave the CDC out of it for the time being. First, it's an in-house lab occurrence—you can't even call it an accident. It doesn't affect the public at large. The last thing you need is for the feds to stick their noses into it."

A noise could be heard behind Emily. She turned to see Arnold take a seat next to her. The presence of orange tinges on his nose, temples, cheeks, and forehead confirmed the previously infected areas.

"Arnold, how nice to see you," Jeff quipped.

"Very funny," Arnold had to laugh, knowing what he looked like. "A small bit of information:

The wife of one of our infected men just called to say their two children have the disease. In a word, it got away from us."

"There's a Mongolian Cluster Fuck, if I ever saw one," Jeff said, fully aware that any hackers tuning in on this conversation, who claimed Mongolian ancestry, might take offense at the statement and report him for racism. "Now, you have no choice but to call the feds. At least, over at Chatfield, you're better equipped to investigate this problem than I am."

Jeff fell compelled to help any way he could. Emily was desperate. They all were. He offered, "If you'll tell me what you've found out so far and send me your new data, I'll do what I can to help from here. Everyone is going to have to work fast because it appears this new contagion waits for no one."

THREE

Ringworm is a term reserved for three genera of soil fungi that attack the keratin in hair, skin, and nails of humans and other mammals. The disease forms ring-like patterns as the mold grows outward from a central point. It can be transferred from one person to another via contact, or from one part of the body to another when scratching is involved.

Jeff contemplated this strangely colored skin-related mold that grew in patches, not in ring-like patterns—more like the skin yeast he found attacking the tribe in India. He felt sorry for his friends in Boston who couldn't devote the time required to continue their investigations into the positive aspects of the mold. Instead, they had become consumed with trying to keep it from attacking them, like a dog snapping at a kind master.

Both Jeff and Carmen knew what the feds would do. They had no option. They would quarantine the residences of the three men and one woman who were infected, and quarantine the Kaufman home. And rightly so. A hazmat team would post a big radioactive sign on the door with yellow tape and QUARANTINED DO NOT ENTER signs all over the place. Their families would be trapped for an indefinite period of time. Their neighbors would go ballistic, the press would go nuclear.

Furthermore, the six affected employees of the company would remain in isolation and not be permitted to leave the building. Cots would have to be brought up to them with sleeping bags along with their meals. Their activities would be limited. A warm touchy-feely research expedition just became a nightmare, and not reporting its presence would be unthinkable. This thing could spread faster than a California wildfire unless it got contained immediately. Fortunately, although several scientists at big pharma were infected, they had access to top-of-the-line research equipment. At the moment, they lacked direction.

As off-putting as these events might seem, the picture became more complex. The infected housewife had left work early to visit her hair salon and then visited the supermarket before going home to celebrate her son's birthday with friends; one of the three men had gone to his usual bar after work; another had stopped at a hardware store; and the third man had waited in a line to fill a prescription.

When the press in Boston ran the story of the outbreak, a full 50 people claimed to be infected with demonstrable rashes and another 150 who only made the claims. An astute reporter covering the science beat saw Jeff's name out of the information dump, a name shining like a spotlight in a dark room. *Jeffrus Shenerii,* sounded an awful lot like Jeffrey Shenero.

FOUR

AP

The CDC announced the presence of a new skin infection. It appears to have its origin in the Boston area. Authorities believe it may have escaped from a laboratory where experimental work was being conducted with the agent, but denounces its similarity to the Covid-19 virus that escaped the Wuhan, China, viral research laboratory. Any mention of a pandemic caused by this new disease is unwarranted.

According to experts, scientist Jeffrey Shenero first discovered the agent while visiting India and brought it back to Boston for further study at Chatfield laboratories, well-known for the manufacture of numerous widely used pharmaceuticals.

Dr. Shenero, who owns and operates his own research facility in Norman, Oklahoma, is widely known for his unraveling of various criminal plots. Sources say he is assisting Chatfield Pharmaceuticals with their efforts to find a cure for the strange orange-colored disease dubbed Agent Orange--a throwback to a toxic chemical used during the Vietnam era.

He says it is similar to ringworm, a worldwide skin infection caused by mold. Both can present extreme itching and discomfort on the parts of the body with the most oil glands. (The outline of a face and body appeared with arrows pointing to the primary areas of infection.) *Both are spread by contact. Dr. Shenero says that, unlike ringworm, many confirmed cases of the new disease appear to cure spontaneously. Investigators are at a loss as to the cause of this.*

Like Jeff, the first thought of conspiracy theorists would point to the government's denial of Agent Orange's similarity to Covid-19's escape from Wuhan absolutely proved the two were identical in that manner. Therefore, the government is lying. What else is new?

Jeff stayed up late pouring over the data initially submitted by Emily and Arnold when she first contacted him aboard ship. He hand-plotted sets of numbers on a simple x and y axis, numbers appearing to be random at first, and saw a downward slope. The growth rate of the mold decreased when the pH increased. It refused to grow at an alkaline pH above 8.0. He looked up the pH of human sebum, the term used for human skin oil, and found it to be 5.6-5.8. Could the solution to the problem be as simple as this?

The next morning he called Boston with Carmen seated next to him. Emily appeared on-screen. When Jeff explained what he had in mind, Arnold's orange face appeared. "That's crazy, man." he said.

"I frequently tell him that," Carmen agreed.

"Let's find out," Emily said, and broke the connection, until she called again a moment later to say, "Forgot to mention it, but congratulations on making the covers of the magazines. Everybody is talking about them. I'm supposed to send you copies for your autographs."

AP

The Shenero Institute for Medical Research, Chatfield Laboratories, and the CDC is recommending the following for elimination of the new disease-causing agent dubbed Agent Orange:

Wash your face and body with normal bar

soap (pH of 9-10).

For those interested in more traditional treatments, a list of medications and treatments is listed below:

Jeff rubbed his forehead, wishing he could live in a remote village somewhere, herding goats, fishing, or planting rice, anything but this. He wasn't meant to live in a civilized nation during modern times. If he could go back to, say, 20,000 B.C., he would only need a sturdy club to conk things with and a good woman. Maybe he could start a brewery. That way everybody would protect him and love him at the same time, like a medic in the Marine Corps.

His cell phone dinged with an incoming message. *What now?*

Jeff, old boy: I see you made the news again. Thank you for helping us come out on top. Your instant cure saved us from having to chase our tails forever and spending a fortune. With the CDC on your side, the quarantines were lifted and my people were able to get back to their normal lives. As always, stop by when you're in the neighborhood. P.S. Grace has your picture from the cover of GQ Magazine posted on her wall. I'm not sure I'm too happy about it. In retaliation, I posted a picture of Carmen from Vogue. Regards from Henry.

Steven Chatfield

P.S. Thank you for accepting my offer to shift

your project to Kansas City. My man in Washington tells me he'll take care of the paperwork.

Long months of worry had come to an end with this missive from Steven. He could finally call a general staff meeting to inform the troops that everyone could soon return to hard research full time.

What he personally needed was a simple mold job, nothing fancy, just something to get him back on track.

Chapter 9

CULTURE DISH – THE HOUSE CALL FROM HELL

(Adapted from *The Incubator*, by Mark R. Sneller, in Strange Adventures,
Ghost River Images, Publ. 2021)

With rare exceptions, Jeff had given up making house calls, although an occasional caller might entice him to do so as a favor. He didn't need more angst after his recent adventures. Money had nothing to do with it. At least his short-lived project coordinating with Chatfield Pharma on the orange mold gave him a chance to stretch him mind. He thought something as basic as a house call would be a refreshing change, like going home to see mama.

He certainly didn't need what happened next, when he went on the house call from hell.

I refuse to die with freaking black bread mold growing on my skin and inside me in a humidity chamber, as if I were a loaf of bread in a sealed package.

Four of us were holed up in a home on the outskirts of Lawton, Oklahoma, about an hour's drive from Oklahoma City, southwest along U.S. Highway 44, and slightly less if you're coming from the University of Oklahoma in Norman. Let's keep it simple: A very unpleasant death appeared to be the singular option because of its utter grossness.

We were entombed in a life-sized culture dish, or, death-sized, if you will, solidly trapped in a warm room with mold growing at our feet which began to grow on and in our bodies. Only one uncertainty remained: the manner of our death: Would it be a slow respiratory strangulation or would it occur by some unknown and probably hitherto undescribed affliction?

A cloudless sky greeted me in the cool morning air as I left Norman and drove to Lawton. I had received directions from the insurance company on how to find the new neighborhood because it would not yet be listed to make my GPS functional. I took in the upscale residences in the neighborhood and the quality of the late model vehicles parked in the drives. No cars up on blocks around here. A number of lots were vacant and several had houses under various stages of construction. The housing business appeared to be good shape in north Lawton.

The Thomas' residence stood at the end of a cul-de-sac in a quiet neighborhood on a rise with a view of a small lake to the south. A similar style home stood next to it to the west. Vacant lots occupied the remaining portion of the immediate area with dogwood and elm trees predominating the local vegetation. An occasional towering pine made its point.

Pulling into the large drive with my SUV, I parked behind one of two pickup trucks already in the drive, one of them a clean white Ford 150. Lettering on the door read: "Ted's A/C and Heating, Lawton OK," with a phone number beneath the lettering. I looked upward and saw two men on the roof working on the air conditioning units. Presumably the units belonged to the upper and the lower portions of the home. Music blared from a small radio near where the men worked.

I parked behind the second truck, a beat-up old Toyota with some dents on the driver's side. The rear bumper had been displaced. On the door were, the words "Ken's Restorations--We serve all of Oklahoma," painted in red. Smaller letters presented a phone number.

I moaned. From riches to rags. From cheery sunlight to darkness in a flash. Please, not Ken. *Jeff, bail out or enter the twilight zone.*

Indeed, to reinforce my bad decision to see what could go wrong, to ensure Murphy's Law had not vacated the premises, my old nemesis, Mister Crew Cut Ken Bradley, stepped out of his truck to greet me. Apparently, the insurance company had made a terrible mistake and hired Ken's Restorations to conduct the repairs. Notice I didn't say, "Complete the repairs."

"Junk people drive junk cars," somebody had once told me. While that didn't apply to most professional people with whom I associated, in Ken's case, it couldn't be a truer statement, although the word 'professional' might be stretch.

Nose-and-Tongue Ring Ronnie, his six-month-pregnant well-tattooed bimbo assistant stepped out of the passenger side wearing cut-offs and sneakers. Her pink butch haircut added a perk to her dress ensemble.

I suspected Ken had already trained Ronnie in other matters. No doubt his former wives would agree. Word had it he was three times divorced and made child support payments for five children. The expenses were killing him. After the first two, he swore off women and got married again with the understanding there would be no babies. His latest divorcee assured him she was fixed and there was no way she would have any children. She had triplets. Couldn't have happened to a more upstanding citizen. Now Ronnie had entered the picture.

She was not without her own issues. She'd moved from company to company because of a modest background in her father's construction business. Ronnie got fired each time for various violations related to "consorting issues." Obviously, Ken's Restoration found that she possessed the necessary skills to be an important adjunct to his business. This suggested she'd worked for him several months, given the state of her pregnancy.

When the call came to my office, the insurance company told Carmen that the homeowners, Thomas by name, would be gone for the day. Both wife and husband were attorneys. She worked in Lawton. He worked in Oklahoma City. Carmen told me to get the key from the man next door to the south. We scheduled the time that I would inspect the area of the area that had the problem. Nobody told me Mister Wonderful would be there.

In this particular case, a water supply line to the upstairs bath had broken thanks to city pressure testing. A retired neighbor who watched homes for the neighborhood had discovered the water loss soon after it occurred and had called a plumber to prevent further damage after checking with one of the Thomas's. The city wasn't talking about when the pressure testing occurred. It never does.

I can formulate a number of reasons why we do things against our better judgment. These reasons might include desire to please, desire for a better outcome than the first or second time, bucking heads with fate because you were in the mood to do so, a poor perspective on the problem at hand, and so forth.

Therefore, despite my better judgment based on hard lessons, common sense, and a screaming voice in my head to run away, I agreed to permit both Ken and Ronnie to accompany me, and thusly, had permitted bad luck to be my partner for the job.

Neither of us even thought about shaking hands when we met that day. Our shared experiences go back years when somebody had to fix his messes. My feeble mind could not fathom why he remained in business.

As if he had been called by name, the neighbor came out of his house with the key and introduced himself as Walter Fitzgerald. Walter appeared to be somewhere in his seventies with most of his faculties. Everybody in the neighborhood relied on him to look after their home in their absence, according to him. Walter shook hands with Ken and said, "Say, we met a few days ago. Right? You too," he said to Ronnie.

"She was here with you?" I asked Ken.

"She needs the experience," he replied.

The top two buttons of Walter's shirt were undone and I could see a lengthy well-healed scar beginning from the top of the breast bone and dropping down beyond sight; a sure indication of open heart surgery.

Walter led us to the front door, inserted the key and bade us enter the domicile. "Can I see what you've done so far?" he asked to nobody in particular.

"Sorry, Walter, we don't like non-work personnel to enter a contained area."

"Oh, it isn't contained," responded Ken. "We didn't need to."

"Then I can go in," Walter said, enthusiastically.

"Sure," responded Ken.

"No, you can't," I stated flatly. "It's against regulations and common sense."

Walter looked at Ken who just shrugged. If that was an emotion from Ken, it might be the first one ever observed. Walter waited an instant and saw that I remained resolute, so he returned to his house. The three of us entered through the unlocked front door and Ken led us up about fifteen steps to a balcony area with a railing that overlooked the great room. The homeowners had good taste in artwork and furnishings.

Ken led us down the hall to the bathroom at the end of the hall on the right. The door was only partially closed, nor contained in heavy-gauge plastic, and wasn't taped shut. An air return register was set in the ceiling outside the bathroom.

Before the bath we passed one bedroom and across the hall lay two more. Ken told me his company had removed the upper layer of flooring from the water damage and needed an inspection and clearance test to check for the presence of mold. I was reluctant to permit a pregnant woman to be on-site under conditions where the unknown prevailed, but Ken assured me we would be in and out of the bad area within only a few short minutes. Also, he wanted her to gain more experience.

Ken pushed on the swollen oak door and it refused to be moved. He placed his right shoulder against the door and pushed. The door opened, albeit reluctantly. "Tell you what," he said, proudly, "What's inside sure stays inside."

I entered the room and hauled along a collapsible tripod, a cosmetic case containing air pump, collection cassettes, and other accouterments necessary for air and surface testing. Ronnie and Ken followed me. As I opened my mouth to caution him, Ken leaned his hulking shoulder against the door and slammed it shut.

Once inside, I flipped on the light switch and five one-hundred watt bulbs were reflected off the vanity mirror. The simple bathroom held a single-sink vanity and a step-in shower; no tub. I could see the shower surround consisted of a single piece of wrap-around plastic. A small window above the window brought sunlight into the room. *Pretty cheap for a custom built home,* I thought. At the same time I saw that the floor was completely black. Taking it for glue-down mastic, I asked Ken about it because the place reeked terribly with eye and throat-burning pungency. "There is no mastic. This is just the layer between the upper and lower portion of the sub-flooring. We cut the floor in a jiffy and that was that," he retorted matter-of-factually.

Wrong. My mental alarm bells went off and I immediately took out a quick sticky tape surface sampler and touched it to the black floor we were standing on. My portable microscope didn't lie and neither did my nose. This could only bespeak of formaldehyde, octanol, along with a score of petrochemicals produced by actively growing mold.

Looking up from the microscope, I provided the male portion of my audience with the bad news trying to hide the quaver in my voice, yet smiling all the while. Trust me, the smile was born out of great fear. "Did the thought ever cross your mind that whatever you do, you do it wrong? We are standing on what looks like a pure culture of *Aspergillus niger.* This mold loves to grow on damp structural materials. To the human, it is invasive and does very nicely in persons with a lowered immune response, such as guys like you."

Ronnie looked frightened. Holding her belly, she asked, "Is that as bad as the black mold?"

"It is black," interjected the gym rat, proudly exhibiting his vast knowledge about colors. "That makes it black mold."

It's worse than that, folks. My armpits were beginning to sweat. I said, "No, actually this is the same kind that grows inside your bag of bread." This particular species produced ten thousand times the number of spores than did the reputed famous black mold known as *Stachybotrys*. "Just about any microbe can be harmful under the right circumstances. We have the perfect circumstances right here. You locked the three of us in a trap, Ken. If it grows on wood and petroleum-based glue-downs and bread, and fruit and dust, and soil, why the hell shouldn't it grow on a person's flimsy body?"

I hadn't meant to be so gruff, but Ken is one of those people who knows how to push your buttons. Under these circumstances, as the expert in the room, I had no reason to skirt the issue. Everybody needed to know the facts. "Why do you think your eyes are burning?" I threw in as a closer.

"My eyes aren't burning," Ken responded.

"Those must be tears of joy," I commented. "I estimate that the level of toxic gases is a good hundred times the normal indoor concentration. Face it, if the spores don't get you, the poisons in the air will."

"Then we need to get out of here," Ronnie screeched.

"Exactly," I commented.

"Okay, let's go," shrugged Ken, as easily as if he were pumping another set of barbells—dumbbells in his case—and probably wondering what all the fuss was about. He made a move to grab the door handle.

I knew he would try that and said, "In case you didn't notice, the upstairs air return register is located in the hallway just outside this bathroom, in the 'OFF' cycle when we came in. Now it's 'ON', and if we open the door, the register will suck in spores from this room and send them into every room. Then the home will have to be cleaned."

"The filter will take care of that," contributed Ken, smartly, digging deep into his vast warehouse of memorized facts. I wanted to slap him. "And don't talk to me what to do or what to notice," he concluded.

"Somebody has to since your mother isn't here." I tried to push the bastard to the limit, adding, "Were you born stupid or did you take advanced classes?"

My mouth owned me, not the other way around. "First, why didn't you get this vanity out of here? The commode, as well. You damn well know the mold is going to grow on the particle board of the counter and grow beneath the unit.

"Number two: The filters that are here will not handle spores this small. Basically, whatever is harmful goes in one side of the filter and goes out the other side."

"You're just full of knowledge, doctor. It must be nice to have a career where you get to run people down." We were both seated and were facing eye-to-eye.

"That wasn't the bad news, bubba. That was

the good news. The bad shit will come later," I whispered, such that only he could hear it. "You know, when the mold begins to grow out of every opening in your body. You made it all happen. Lucky us."

Which probably won't happen until after we were all dead, but I didn't feel like telling him that part. Let the prick think about it.

"I have to pee," whined Ronnie.

"Tie it in a knot," sneered Ken.

I so dearly wanted to throw down with the guy. The kid might be promiscuous, but she had to deal with her pregnancy while stuck in this bathroom with the two of us at each other's throats.

The man stood six-two and weighed two-thirty. He carried too much belly fat, although one couldn't deny he possessed a lot of arm and shoulder strength. He'd been a bully all his life. The time had come for the bullying and life as he knew it to come to an end. As things stood, it could also apply to all of us. (Thankfully, Walter had not been trapped in this room with us when Ken had slammed the door shut. The nightmare could have been a screaming death for all of us.)

In contrast, I stood five-eleven, weighed fifty pounds less and ran a lot. My old college years as a water polo player and karate guy gave me endless memories of the old days. Today, my temperament and drive remain to motivate me every single day.

Ken and I were both in our early forties. I could hit as hard as ever whenever the seductive temptress of opportunity smiled my way. This temptress was giving me a side-wise, yet encouraging glance, which bespoke the words: "Just a straight shot to the point of the chin." I shoved out further thoughts best left unspoken.

Instead, I put my actions into words. If you can't strike while the iron is hot, use a different hot iron. A good fighting philosophy is this: If you defeat your opponent physically, he can come back to hurt you. If you defeat him in spirit, the victory is permanent. If you defeat him physically and in spirit, it's a fair guess you won the battle.

"Shut up, Ken. You're the one who didn't fix this place properly. You didn't set up a proper dehumidifier; you didn't set up proper protection outside this room. And what were you thinking when you removed the top flooring? You knew there would be water retention between the layers of particle board. Boy, are you a royal screw up."

I began to disturb myself. I had become unscientific and too pissed off. Okay, it felt good to become belligerent with this monkey, although that didn't help the cause of self-preservation, especially because the path down the future road frightened the hell out of me. Literally rotting away in a jail cell for hurting this guy held no attraction to me. Neither did trading my life for his. I'd rather rot away in the comfort of my own home with watching a football game than be comfortably ensconced in a jail cell.

My immediate problem had become Ken, as if he were an object, an end goal. Habitually, I face a problem head-on, not avoid it. For some reason, I feel secure doing that. Let the shrinks work that out. I found myself out of character, deflecting, not trying to solve the problem of escape. Instead, I made Ken into the problem, which made absolutely no sense, unless my thinking process was becoming warped. I could think of only a single reason for that to occur.

Ken knew I had hurt him when I brought up his job performance, but the humanoid said nothing. No great surprise, because one of his many nicknames is "Ken—my dick is bigger than your dick—Bradley." Normally he would have a retort whenever somebody espoused real knowledge. Then he'd try to modify your knowledge based on the narrow range of his own life experiences.

I couldn't stop my mouth. If my previous comments didn't hit him in the BBs, maybe the next salvo would do it. My thoughts carried me to the extreme. I teetered between rage and professional behavior, legal versus wanton destruction of another human, yet not concentrating on finding a way out of this mess. My throat was getting sore from the chemicals in the air and from talking so much in this alien environment.

I almost shouted, "Not only that, Ken, but you screwed up the big hospital job last month. You allowed the containment barrier to fall down and you exposed the cancer patients to a high concentration of mold spores that killed two people. Oh, I'm sorry, didn't you follow the cases? I had access to the autopsy reports."

"Hey, don't tell me how to do my job. I've been doing this stuff since I turned fifteen," Ken puffed himself up. "How long have you been lording it everybody you meet? I mean, when the word got out you would be on this job, I just tingled with excitement."

"Oh, you got me there, Ken. My parents made me go to school so I could learn to read and write and add and maybe gain a few social skills. So you've been unprofessional a lot longer than I've been professional. Don't you even care that the same mold spores I identified were the same ones that killed three people?"

"Bullshit, Shenero. They were dying anyway. And nobody can prove your mold killed them."

My mold? "Wrong again, Bradley. Watch for the coroner's report and make plans for another life. It's called either second or third degree murder. Probably second because your negligence caused the deaths."

Ronnie jumped on the band wagon. "Yeah, Bradley. You're a screw up. That's all you ever do, isn't it? Screw things, up!" Her hands flew to her belly. Another rumor had it that Ronnie always called men by their last name, even in bed.

"Hey," Ken responded defensively, almost flippantly, as the great ape postured. "I hired a bad worker. It can happen to anyone."

"No matter what, you're responsible and you're the bad worker," inserted Ronnie. "I was there. Remember? You told me a whole different story from what the doc here says and I believe him. So, you think this is bad, wait until we get into court. We'll see what I can get for child support. You lied to me, Bradley."

Gee, Ronnie, why beat around the bush? And what did he lie to her about? Did he say he loved her or perhaps make her a partner or he would give her money or take care of the baby? Knowing Ken, my guess is that he dug himself a hole in which he is presently standing and is proceeding to pull in the dirt behind himself.

The man stared at me as though he had been watching TV for twelve hours straight. But the sub-human refused to give up the fight. From nowhere he brought forth a bellow: "Sure, Ronnie, you've got two others you're collecting free money on. What's one more?"

"Back at you," she volleyed, spittle flying from her lips.

Ronnie began to rub her temples. I felt the same way. It wasn't like smelling a little musty dirt. Here, the odors would soon go away, an indication the chemicals were deadening the sense of smell—a defense mechanism. It could happen with perfume and it could happen with poison. Our brains would want for oxygen thanks to bad chemicals dissolved in the blood. Our thinking would cloud and things could go south fast after that. Correction: Our thinking is already clouded.

True as all this might be for the sake of science, we were trapped in a damned bathroom with no obvious way out. "All right, guys. How about we hop onto the vanity so we don't disturb the spores on the floor," I said, doing an about face from my thoughts and deflecting the conversation back to the problem at hand, a good deflection from endless accusation. Generally I use people like Ken as a measuring stick. If one does exactly the opposite of what they suggest, you're bound to be right almost all the time. If the idea had come from him I might have thought there would be something wrong with it and would be tempted to stay put.

Parts of the floor puffed up with spores as we moved. Other parts were so wet and slimy that we chanced slipping and falling, if we weren't careful. I knew we were already covered with the tiny life forms and once on the skin or on clothing, each of the millions and billions of tiny three micron-size spores would be sending forth a germ tube, just like a bean projecting a sprout in order to begin growth into an adult. They will quickly mature into another plant with countless seeds of its own. With one major difference: Beans didn't digest fabric, flesh, lungs or brain tissue. If you get enough bad guys overrunning the stockade, your defenses won't matter anymore.

My progressively worsening thought sequences drove me to cold sweats. Dying didn't bother me. Dying under these circumstances along with these two scared the hell out of me. What would we do when the end came? Would we hold hands and sing or forgive each his own trespasses?

I gently hopped onto the vanity, with Big Ken next to the door, me sitting in the middle and Ronnie sitting on the far edge with her feet resting on the commode and her back to me. The shower was directly in front of her. Where I sat, the faucet poked me in the back. I had about three inches on the edge to work with.

"What other complaints do you have," Ken sniped with considerable venom. His day-to-day mood swings were well known, but today under pressure, the man appeared to be on the fringe of being out of control. We all were.

Ronnie attacked, pivoting around so she faced the same direction as we were and looked sharply to her left so she could eye Ken. "Complaints, Ken? How about the fact that you should be cleaning toilets for a living, you'd probably screw that up too. Here's the drama. Yes, the baby is yours and I'll prove it when the time comes. That'll be when I file a lawsuit against you for this mess right here."

Unless I miss my guess, Ronnie had decided she didn't like her latest employer. The woman was sharp and must have had some kind of education. I liked the part about the lawsuit. That meant I would get to testify in detail about Ken's incompetence. If I lived through this.

If Ken felt dejected, he didn't show it. Instead, he wouldn't let it go. "What's the matter, Ronnie? Don't you love me anymore? You sure loved me once."

"Does drunk and nearly asleep your definition of love? Do you remember when I said, 'No'?"

Ken laughed. "You saying 'no'? That's a laugh." The man ran a hand through his crew cut—a nervous reaction.

"Okay, little man. You give your version to the judge, and the baby and I will give ours," she sneered.

Good point, Ronnie.

Ken shrugged. Nothing affected this guy.

Suddenly, the power went off. In true Einsteinian fashion, a physicist might say there occurred a folding back of the space-time continuum where two disparate crises meet at the same time and in the same place. Others like me might say, "Oh, shit, what now?"

The power outage had undoubtedly occurred because the workmen were servicing the air handlers on the roof. We weren't in total blackness because a small window above the shower permitted a little of the early morning light to enter the room, albeit the window faced the north.

"This is good," said Ken. "There is no suction outside from the air return to spread the spores through the house so we can get out of here."

"You mean like you probably did the first time you worked on this room? Go for it," I suggested, knowing what would happen; actually awaiting the outcome of his antics in a diabolical manner, expecting comedy relief.

From his seated position on the vanity next to the door, Ken pulled on the door handle, silently at first, then followed by entertaining noises. The brute grunted and stained as hard as he could. The door had swollen into place, as if had been welded to the door frame, thanks to Ken's initial shove against the entire door to slam it shut. His meager efforts were a cheap comedy show, with only our lives on the line.

Ronnie and I did an eyeball exchange which triggered a laughing attack that only stopped when we both began to cough and gag from the spores and the stink in our lungs. Every time either of us began to talk the laughter began anew. Finally, with a hoarse and raspy voice, I managed to utter, "Uh, Ronnie, I wonder how the door got closed so tightly."

Through her own tears, Ronnie directed her attention to her former bed partner. "Now what, big shot?"

The employee had just fired the employer. The woman did have her little peccadilloes, like having unprotected sex and not learning from her mistakes. Like everybody, she had her own hornet's nest to deal with. She had a wit and might have turned out all right in another life. Who knows, she might, yet. Before Ken could give a rejoinder, she added with a plaintiff cry, "I really have to pee."

"Go ahead and use the shower drain, if you need to," I said. "We won't watch." At least Ronnie had a door to close to cover her actions.

If Ken had spoken a single word during these moments, my right fist would have spoken for me, but we didn't need a writhing bleeding body on the ground to cause the release of more spores. Hopefully, my time with Ken would come, just him and me—no witnesses.

Shifting from my uncomfortable position, I stretched out my legs. I felt as though I sat on one of those old fashioned stocks to sit in public for days on a wooden board with a thin ledge going across your ass with your arms bound onto some other device. The only thing missing here was people throwing stones or rotten fruit at you.

So far, we had accomplished nothing. The jerk continued being a jerk; he and I were coming to blows, Ronnie had to pee, and there nobody had any creative thinking. So be it. Would it be necessary to tell them what will happen if we don't get out? It's coming to that.

What were the spores doing on my skin? That was the first thing I had to know, like a bubble forming way beneath the surface to finally rise atop the muck.

My work equipment lay in the bag at my feet, so I hooked one of the straps on my nylon tote bag with my foot and pulled up the bag to where I could reach inside. In the dim light, I pulled the portable microscope from its small case that measured about five inches on each side. I retrieved a microscope slide from the bag and scraped my exposed arm skin with one edge and along my face with another edge, followed this with the placement of a cover slip over the cells that I had scraped off. I placed the slide beneath the self-lighting scope to witness a quite spectacular view.

Countless small black spherical spores were sending down tiny germ tubes into my skin. These would soon become threads of mycelium. The cold sweat of fear ran from my forehead down the back of my spine and mingled with the stench of the petrochemicals in the humid air. I repacked the instrument and set the bag back down on the floor.

Her own task completed, Ronnie returned to her perch and offered, "An idea," she held up one finger. "How about if we all fit into the shower. Can't we wash this stuff off of us?"

"Theoretically . . ." I began to explain the

pluses and minuses of her suggestion, until Ken chimed in.

"It won't work," he said. "Before we cut out the sub-floor, I turned off the water to both floors at the manifold in the utility room."

Ronnie began to cough and scratch her neck.

Somebody once thanked me for giving them moral support for their project. In Ken's case it would be safe to call it immoral support. I don't know how it works. All I know is that whatever some people touch or try to do turns out wrong almost all the time. Is it tied to the thinking process or something below that; some, as yet, undefined truth to the universe?

This bastard needed a "real larnin'," as country folk like to say. If we survive this, I'll take care of Ken, trust me on that. I'm like a dog latched on to a pants cuff. Except for one minor addition: I go for the jugular. This guy had a bad reputation. He paid off plumbers to obtain referral on water-damaged buildings, strictly against industry policy. He gouged the homeowners whenever he or his small staff of employees did the work. Since the insurance industry paid him directly, Ken felt he could charge whatever he wanted. So far, he'd gotten away with it. However, if I should survive this day, Ken will become my new pet project. He had no business in this business. How many times I didn't know about had he endangered the lives of others? How many people had actually gotten ill or died as a result of his incompetence?

Why was I so flagrantly hostile to this man? Incompetent people are a dime a dozen. Is it because of the many lives he has negatively affected? Maybe because people like him give the industry a bad name? No, that's too thin. Perhaps there existed some underlying factor where I saw myself in him, in some regards? There must be a psychiatrist somewhere who would be willing to put the blame on me because of my intense distrust and dislike of another person. The shrink might say, "What the hell's the manner with you, Shenero? How dare you dislike a man who tries so hard to make an honest dollar and raise a family? Or two? Or three?

No. Ken exuded the quality of dislike from the first day we'd met years before. If he had any positive qualities they were well hidden. You could look into his eyes and they were always the same: stone cold, humorless, emotionless—a shell filled with a cluster of mistakes and bad luck events waiting to happen. The bells were ringing to toll our deaths together. Hopefully, it would be in mortal combat. Guaranteed it would not be in loving embrace.

I shook my head. The chemicals were taking over. The violence could start with me.

Ronnie sat next to the role of toilet paper, so I asked her to tear off several squares for us to hold over our mouths and noses to breathe through. I didn't want to give one to Ken. I wanted him to breathe in the spores and become a case study for the medical literature.

At least the paper would keep out the spores and minimize the smell of chemicals. The bathroom stunk like a toxic waste dump. In fact, by the EPA's definition, this room actually did qualify as an undesignated storage facility for toxic and hazardous substances. Certainly, the formaldehyde produced by the mold was at least equal to the amount found in any new manufactured home. At least builders are required to post a warning about the issue. How many homes provided to the New Orleans' victims were unsuitable for habitation just because of one problem alone? Tears ran from my burning eyes. I tried not to look at the floor; black in its entirety.

"Doctor Shenero, maybe you could bang on the ceiling with your tripod and somebody could hear us," Ronnie offered, with limited enthusiasm.

Ken scoffed at the idea, but I tried it for several minutes to no avail. Apparently the pounding did not overcome the music coming from a radio on the roof.

"Here's another idea," I said, and pulled out my cell. "Ken, we're going to call your company and instruct them as to how to set up a critical containment barrier outside this room with a change of clothing for all of us including themselves and for them to force the door open with whatever means so we can get out."

Four people's lives were at stake here including the baby and all were in the hands of Ken. Scary thought. His motto should be: *If you can't do it wrong, then don't do it at all.* For years, I'd taught this stuff at the university and now I was here; hopefully not making history.

"It'll take them two hours to get here to do all that," Ken said, his voice objective.

"You on a schedule?" I queried, noting that Ken stood a good chance of being the most likely to be the first to be infected thanks to his poor immune response, in turn thanks to his steroid usage. I got Ken's office number from him since it is not part of my Contact's list, hit SPEAKER, and punched in the number. NO SERVICE appeared on the screen.

"Let's try yours," I demanded, rather than suggested.

Resignedly, he gave it to me and I got the same response. "I could have told you there isn't any service out here," Ken contributed, smugly. I should have guessed. A nasty storm came through here the previous week and had probably taken out the cell phone towers.

I gently lowered myself from the counter and stepped into the shower stall. I tried the same number with each of the phones with the same non response. I tried 911 to no avail.

My mind's eye could picture the spores beginning to grow in our lungs and black fuzzy mold covering all of our bodies while being poisoned by the mold's chemical byproducts. I saw newspaper headlines: *Trio found dead in bathroom covered with black masses of mold. Workers gag and several hospitalized. Experts fear the contagion may spread. Lawton Health Department calls CDC to investigate.*

I began to scratch and cough. The itching that Ronnie exhibited had become real for both me and Ken. We also scratched various exposed places on our body and coughed. I desperately wanted to relate to him in lurid detail about how we were lower on the food chain than the spores which were utilizing our bodies as substrates for their survival and, concomitantly, for our demise. If Ronnie had been absent, no problem.

How long would it take for someone to figure out we were here? They couldn't reach us and we couldn't reach them.

"So what's going to happen to us?" Ronnie stared at me almost pleadingly, coughing as she spoke.

"We're all going to need medical attention. We're going to need to watch for symptoms of persistent coughing after we leave here and tell our doctor what happened. He might want to follow our lung function and run some blood tests."

Clinically speaking, of course. The last thing she needed to hear was the truth about mold growing inside her body and on her skin. Ken tried to give the appearance that he cared less about any of it. Hey, when you're a man, you're a man. Right Ken?

Ronnie declared. "Screw this and screw you both. I'm calling for help." She jumped down from the vanity to go for the window and hit a slick spot on the floor. She fell hard onto her back with one leg crumpled beneath her striking the vanity with her head. A dark cloud of mold spores billowed up from the floor as though someone had taken a fan to a quantity of gunpowder. The spores quickly melded with the rest of the air space and settled onto our bodies.

Ken looked on as if it were a TV commercial or a boring game show as I gently stepped down and slowly straightened her leg. Only semi-conscious, Ronnie cried out in anguish. I reached into my tote kit and pulled out a couple of small packets of alcohol wipes which I tore open and applied to an oozing area of blood on the back of her head.

Coughing, almost without control, I seated her onto the commode while she held her head in both hands. I said, "Look, how about if we just kick out a section of sheetrock between this room and the next. There's space between the commode and the vanity we can use. We'll tear out enough drywall to kick out the wall in the next room. Ronnie is the smallest one of us and can escape through the hole and go for help or make a call for help."

Seated on the vanity we faced the exterior wall and there would be no chance of escape through the shower. The door to the hallway was firmly swollen shut which left only one option.

"You better check for studs first," Ken advised.

I knocked on the wall between the commode and the vanity, a space of only fourteen inches. I hit a solid sound in the middle and hollow sounds on either side of that.

We all heard the vibrations and echoes and knew what they meant. I had hit a solid two-by-four wooden stud right in the middle. No escape there. Or could there be. Those studs are only attached at either end with nails. A few good kicks may do the trick to loosen at least one of them to aid in its removal. That was one plan. Were there any others?

"Okay, guys," I said, digging deep to sound confident. I felt as if we were on the right track. "Let's deal with the area above the commode. I can get up onto . . . "

"Forget it," contributed Ken. "That is, unless your pocket knife can cut through water pipes."

"No, but we can bang on them. I have a lot of metal objects in my kit. Even my knife will make noise."

"Not much. These are all plastic pipes," contributed Mister Positive.

I refused to die like a loaf of bread in a sealed package. What would the headlines read after we were found and would my students say that Dr. Shenero died in the must perfect way for him.

My thoughts about my classroom took me to the stories I told about archaeologists who had found various tombs where mold grew on the mummies and who subsequently died because of the "curse of the mummy." They, too, had inhaled countless spores in a short period of time. Was this room to be our mummy's tomb?

"What's inside sure stays inside," Ken had said.

I muttered some curse words and began to cut out the sheetrock in the wall above and behind Ronnie, who sat bent over to make room for me, massaging her head with one hand and scratching various areas of her body with the other. She reminded me of a monkey.

The power came back on and our senses were blasted with a thousand watts of brightness just as our eyes were dark-adapting. Footsteps could be heard on the roof. The workmen were leaving. It also meant one man was already on the ground and had thrown the breaker switch and a moment later a work truck started up.

"Ken, get to the window and yell for help," I demanded.

"Why me?" he asked.

"Because you're the dumbest one here and you're also the tallest and have the best chance of yelling through the window. That's why."

"What am I supposed to say?" asked Ken, in

full denial of the present circumstances that had befallen us.

"Hey, tell them you want to order a large pizza," Ronnie contributed, sarcastically.

The window faced the wrong direction anyway. There wasn't much chance for the men to hear anybody yell. They didn't. The truck drove off back to Lawton.

I had another idea. "Okay, big shot, let's see some of that steroid strength of yours. Grab the commode and rip it off the bolts holding it to the floor."

Ken saw I was serious when I took Ronnie by the arm led her into the shower to give him room to work. As if he does this sort of thing before breakfast every morning, the beast wrapped one arm around the tank and one around the base of the commode he began to yank and pull and rock it. Within sixty seconds the toilet lay on the floor and we had a good three-foot by five-foot hunk of drywall to work with. Ken and I started kicking. When we made holes, we grabbed the sheetrock and pulled it loose. We kicked out a couple of vertical studs and kicked out the adjoining wall in the adjacent bedroom. All three of us made it through the opening to freedom.

The entire home would not be expected to be contaminated because we had avoided opening the door to the bath and didn't have to expose the air return to the spores. A professional might request an entire air testing of the home for a variety of reason related to this event. That professional would be me.

I took my work equipment with me to the car sucking in deep breaths to try and clear my lungs. I went to the trunk and grabbed my gym bag and walked back to utility room. I found the water control valves, turned on the one for the downstairs, left the one off for the upstairs, and took a long soapy shower in the master bath, coughing and blowing up as much muck as possible. I changed into my gym clothes, packed my khaki slacks, work shirt and shoes in the bag and returned it to the car. The other two were stood next to the truck a few feet away arguing heatedly. I checked my watch. It read almost eight thirty. Less than a half-hour had elapsed for the entire episode. So much for Ronnie's five minute exposure time.

I must have cut a great figure; a big yellow flower, standing there in sneakers, yellow jogging shorts and yellow Tee-shirt for visibility during street running. When I motioned for Ken to come over, he grinned and followed my beckoning wave like an obedient little doggie. I led him around the rear of the house, away from the prying eyes of Walter, as well as from Ronnie's view, should anybody ask her later about the incident.

A few moments later, I returned alone, gave Ronnie a slight wave, to which she gave me a

Texas' Hook 'em Horns sign with her fingers. Then this bedraggled scientist climbed into his SUV and headed back to Norman.

Ken was going to have to deal with the insurance company that hired him along with their bills for damages he incurred regarding his negligence on this job, my formal report, lawsuits, various doctor's bills from my physician and Ronnie's, and his own. He'd have to deal with the state health department and possibly the Feds for the hospital incident, an assortment of lawyers including the homeowners' claims for damages, major dental surgery, and Ronnie. Of course, one could always count on the unexpected.

I congratulated myself on making up the story about the deaths in the hospital. It might have happened, if the air currents hadn't carried the spores in the other direction. I figured the jerk would sweat plenty thinking about murder charges until it was time to sweat reality. I only hoped the reality wouldn't include illness or worse to Ronnie or me.

As it turned out, Ronnie and the baby were fine. It took her a couple of weeks for the cough to go away, but I have every faith she'll be healthy. I heard she moved in with her parents.

Not so, Ken. His cough got worse by the day. He didn't develop what we call Farmer's Lung from breathing in a lot of spores from mold growing on hay or grain. He developed a classic case of disseminated aspergillosis, in other words, with no immune system to control the little beasties, the spores spread throughout his entire body and his brain. He died a month later.

Sometimes mold spores do what they want. That the part will continue to bother me the rest of my life.

To the best of my recollection, that's how my dear husband told me the story, after which I massaged his neck and suggested to him he might want to go on a relaxing ocean cruise, this time to the Caribbean. It's not polite to tell you what he suggested to me. I'm sure he didn't mean it.

About the Author

Mark Sneller, PhD, is a former professor of microbiology and medical mycology. He lives in Tucson, Arizona, where he operates Aero Allergen Research, a company specializing in indoor air quality and the identification of mold in contaminated buildings. He is the author of several health-related books, as well as the Jeffrey Shenero series of adventure novels.